Praise for John H

"Harvey's series about Charlie Resnick, the jazz-loving, melancholy cop in provincial Nottingham, England, has long been one of the finest police procedural series around."   —*Publishers Weekly*

"The characters in John Harvey's urban crime novels are so defiantly alive and unruly that they put these British police procedurals on a shelf by themselves."
                                    —Marilyn Stasio, *The New York Times Book Review*

"Without doubt the best cop on the Britcrime beat. Harvey has set a benchmark which the genre must now measure up to."
                                    —*Literary Review*

"One of the masters of British crime fiction."
                                    —*Sunday Telegraph (London)*

"Harvey reminds me of Graham Greene, a stylist who tells you everything you need to know while keeping the prose clean and simple. It's a very realistic style that draws you into the story without the writer getting in the way."   —Elmore Leonard

"Much like Elmore Leonard and James Lee Burke, John Harvey has far transcended his genre."   —Jim Harrison

"Charlie Resnick is one of the most fully realized characters in modern crime fiction ... Lifts the police procedural into the realm of the mainstream novel."   —Sue Grafton

"Harvey's Resnick novels are far and away the finest British police procedurals yet written."   —*GQ*

"Nobody writes police procedurals better than John Harvey. Nobody."   —*Booklist*

Enjoy the complete Resnick series from Bloody Brits Press

LAST RITES

JOHN HARVEY

BLOODY BRITS PRESS

Ann Arbor and Alnmouth

2008

Bloody Brits Press
PO Box 3671
Ann Arbor MI 48106-3671

BLOODY BRITS PRESS FIRST EDITION
First Printing October 2008

First published in Great Britain in 1998 by William Heinemann

Printed in the United States of America on acid-free paper

Cover designer: Bonnie Liss (Phoenix Graphics)

Bloody Brits Press is an imprint of Bywater Books

ISBN 978-1-932859-61-4

Mixed Sources
Product group from well-managed
forests and other controlled sources
www.fsc.org Cert no. SW-COC-002283
FSC © 1996 Forest Stewardship Council

For Marian Wood

One

It was twelve years since she'd seen him. Not that she hadn't wanted to, hadn't written to him often enough, in the early days at least, asking him to change his mind. Featherstone, Haverigg, Wandsworth, the Scrubs. Begging him, near enough. He'll get over it with time, she'd thought, feeling the way he does.

At first she had gone anyway, long journeys, sometimes by car, more usually by train. Not to contravene his word, only to be there, be near him, share something of the same atmosphere, the same air. From a distance she would watch the visitors at the gate: wives, lovers, got up in their best, hair specially done and makeup refreshed; others burdened, encumbered, dragging kids who skulked and slouched and scuffed their shoes. Coming out, she would mingle with them if she could, snatch bits and pieces of their conversations for her own. Then, abruptly, she stopped going; she wrote to him instead, regularly, the first of every month. Her ritual. Family gossip, bits and pieces about the kids. She persuaded herself it didn't matter that he never replied.

Some evenings when she stood upstairs alone, gazing out across the roofs of the other houses, noticing the way the light caught their edges immediately before it fell, she would try to remember the way he used to look at her, something bright flaring for a moment in the slate-gray of his eyes.

Life. After all that waiting, it had been out of the judge's mouth almost before she had heard or properly understood. That word: life.

She could still see her mother's face, the soft sigh of pain as if the air had been released from within, the pale skin puckering, sinking in. She could feel again her own panic rising in her veins. Life, was that what he had said? As though he were giving and not taking away. A term of no less than twenty-five years. She had wanted to shout out then, turn it all back, the short days of the trial, the photographic evidence, exhibit A, exhibit B, the summing-up. Begin again. No: farther, farther back than that.

For a moment, as she leaned against the heavy wooden railing of the gallery, he had turned his head toward her, tilted up. And she had read it there on his face, the apportioning of blame. Just that moment and then the officers on either side had moved him on and down. Anger, even guilt—what she had felt most from him was shame. Not for himself, or what he'd done, but for her.

Two

Resnick had woken at a quarter to six, blinked at the light already filtering promisingly through the curtains, and decided to allow himself another fifteen minutes. Entwined near the foot of the bed, impossible to tell where one ended and the other began, the middle pair of his four cats, Miles and Pepper, breathed as one. Bud, the skinniest of the oddly adopted litter, lay with his head not quite touching Resnick's pillow, one paw covering his eyes, snoring lightly. Dizzy, scornful of the comforts of home life, would be out patrolling the neighbors' gardens, stalking the hedgerows for voles, field-mice, birds, occasionally a slow-moving rat, once a young squirrel, more than once a rabbit. Trophies that he would drag through the cat flap and lay with due ceremony at Resnick's feet, bright-eyed, arching his back with pride.

This morning, though, when Resnick finally shuffled his way, barefoot, from bedroom to shower, shower to bedroom, down the wide stairs to the hallway and on into the kitchen, there were no bodies waiting to ambush him, dead or dying.

An electrician friend of Resnick's, a man he knew from the Polish Club, had rigged up a second set of speakers in the kitchen and, after filling the kettle and setting it on the gas, Resnick wandered into the front room and pulled an old album from the shelf, scratchy vinyl, the cover with its reproduction of a painting by Henri Rousseau, *The Repast of the Lion*—not quite Dizzy, perhaps, this large cat devouring its prey among giant flowers, but close enough that Resnick could see the family resemblance.

The record was *Thelonious Monk Plays Duke Ellington*, one of the first pieces of modern jazz he had ever heard or owned; that

3

strange piano sound, so familiar now, insistent yet fragmentary, Monk stalking Duke's tunes with eloquent uncertainty.

Back in the kitchen, he opened a tin of Choosy, chicken-flavored, and emptied it into the four colored bowls. Coffee beans he varied from time to time, his present favorite being a mixture of French Roast and Mocha bought at The White House on Parliament Terrace. He tipped a handful of the shiny beans into his hand, savoring the strong smell before tipping them into the elegant Krups grinder Hannah had bought him for Christmas.

Hannah; oh, Hannah.

A trilling little four-note pattern repeated four times, a shuffle of Kenny Clarke's brushes on the snare, and Monk sailed jauntily into "I Let a Song Go Out of My Heart."

What had happened with Hannah? To Hannah and himself? When had he last felt the urge to pick up the telephone and dial the number he still knew by heart? One of the cats nudged against his leg and began to purr; someone happy at least that Resnick's nights away from home were less frequent, that his presence in the early mornings was more and more assured.

He sliced some dark rye bread and placed it under the grill. Damson jam or marmalade? He thought damson jam. There was a book he'd started to read—reread in parts at least—*Talking Jazz: an Oral History*. Jackie Ferris, a sergeant with the Yard's Arts and Antiques Squad, had sent it as a gift at the conclusion of a case they'd been working jointly. Segments of recorded conversation, it was ideal for the ten minutes he allowed himself in the easy chair before setting off for work.

The patch Resnick was charged with policing sat nicely on the edge of the inner city, perched as it was on the front line between the poorer, largely working-class area of Radford and the more affluent and middle-class former private estate of The Park. To the east of the Alfreton Road were the student flats of Lenton and to the west was the city itself, with its burgeoning clubs and pubs, and ever-present hordes in search of the ultimate good time.

The CID room was on the first floor, Resnick's office partitioned off in the farthest corner, the squad's desks crammed with telephones, scraps of paper, stained mugs, directories, chewed-up ballpoints, printed forms, keyboards, VDUs.

Kevin Naylor, one of the four detective constables in the team, phone wedged between chin and shoulder, was doing his best to calm an elderly woman who had come down that morning to find her front door wide open and her TV set, camera, microwave, and the hundred and fifty pounds she kept in an old Huntley and Palmer biscuit tin all missing. "Yes," Naylor said, and "Yes, of course," and "Yes," and "Yes, I understand," using an HB pencil alternately to scribble notes on a lined pad and stir his tea.

Sharon Garnett fidgeted absentmindedly with a loose curl of hair, as she scrolled through a list of known offenders, searching for a possible match between an address in Radford and a name she had half heard in a crowded bar. Close to the side wall, Carl Vincent, cuffs turned back neatly against his wrists, was cross-checking the details of last night's stolen vehicles with one of the information officers at Central station.

All there was to show of Ben Fowles was a half-eaten bacon cob in the middle of his desk. Resnick pushed the temptation to the back of his mind.

Graham Millington, his sergeant for longer than either of them cared to remember, hovered close to the door to Resnick's office, chest puffed out, mustache bristling. A stoat, Resnick thought, hankering to be after the rabbit.

"Morning, Graham."

Millington grunted.

"Lot of activity."

"Aye."

"Normal night, then?"

"Was it, buggery!"

Resnick sat behind his desk, eased back in his chair. "Best let me in on it, then."

"You know that club, used to belong to Jimmy Peters ..."

"The Golden something-or-other."

"That was last month. Tarted itself up with purple paint and a few blow-up pictures of that Jennifer Allbran off the telly, legs akimbo, calls itself the Hot Spot. Not far off the mark last night, any road."

5

"Trouble?"

"Ambulances screaming down the Alfreton Road like it were World War Three."

"And?"

"Half a dozen carted off to Queen's, bleeding all over the A and E. One serious, stab wounds to the face and neck, touch and go in Intensive Care. Up to a dozen more treated by paramedics on the spot. So to speak. Jimmy Peters wailing and gnashing his teeth over a thousand quid's worth of damaged upholstery and broken glass."

"Likely double that off the insurance."

"And the rest."

"Anyway, what happened to his security? Jimmy'd not open his doors without a brace of muscle in shiny jackets and combat boots."

"In the thick of it. Pigs in muck."

Resnick drew a breath and exhaled slowly. Why was it, whenever they succeeded in clamping the lid on some things, it blew off somewhere else? "Okay," he said, "any idea what got it started?"

Millington snorted. "Take your pick. Only thing most folk seem to agree on, this bunch of lads came in around two, several sheets to the wind already. One of 'em took a fancy to someone else's bit of tally. You can guess the rest."

Resnick shook his head. "These lads, Graham, black or white?"

"As the driven snow."

"And the girl?"

"Girl was white, too. Not them she was with."

On his feet, Resnick walked toward the window and stared down through smeared glass. Growing up in the city, he'd been haunted by the race riots which had dogged his childhood. Made him frightened, ashamed.

"Color," Millington said, "that's what you're thinking? Racial, what's back of it."

"Am I wrong?"

"Maybe not. Not entirely. Only I think somehow there's more to it than that."

"Go on."

Millington shook his head. "I'm not sure. Can't put me finger on

6

it. But the way they were answering questions, them as was most involved ..."

"Shifty?"

"More the opposite. Couldn't wait to spill how it'd happened, started, chapter and bloody verse. Everything save who did the actual stabbing. Couple of 'em down in the cells now, cooling their heels. Mark Ellis and Billy Scalthorpe. Not that there'll be much point holding them. Waste of time and money."

"No weapon, then?"

"Not by the time we were on the scene. Magically disappeared." Millington flicked something stray away from one side of his mustache. "I've got Ben Fowles down there now, taking statements from Peters and his bar staff, couple of the security guards. See if he can come up with something fresh."

"And the laddie in Intensive Care?"

"Wayne. Wayne Feraday. I'm off out there myself now."

Resnick grinned. "It'll be late breakfast at Parker's, then?"

"Happen."

"Bring us back a sandwich, Graham, egg and sausage, heavy on the brown sauce."

As Resnick sat back down at his desk, he could hear Millington's cheery whistle making a fresh assault on the Petula Clark Songbook.

Three

Convinced she'd be unable to sleep, Lorraine had gone off almost the moment her head had touched the pillow. She'd not woken till Derek brushed her shoulder with his fingers, so that when she blinked her eyes, there he was, standing over her, smiling down.

"Hello, sleepy head."

"Whatever time is it?"

"Quarter past eight."

"What? It's never." Throwing back the bedclothes, she sat up. "I've overlaid, what happened to the alarm? Why ever didn't you wake me?"

"Thought a lay-in would do you good."

Lorraine pushed past him, reaching for the dressing gown that hung behind the door.

"You don't have to rush. There's bags of time." He followed her along the landing, only stopping when she turned at the bathroom door.

"Well?" Lorraine said.

"Well what?"

"D'you think I could have some privacy or what?"

Derek stepped back and she closed the door and slid the bolt, sat on the toilet with her head toward her knees. She was being unfair to him, she knew.

These last weeks, he had been wonderful. Looking after the children, fetching and carrying, fixing meals, shopping, Lorraine at the hospital all hours while her mother had lingered on. And then, suddenly, when it was over and Lorraine, despite all warnings, went numb, he had stepped in to handle the arrangements for the funeral, the crematorium, flowers, everything.

She stood up and looked at herself in the mirror, not liking what she saw. There was a packet of Neurofen in the cabinet and she took two, swallowing them down with water. She could hear the children's voices from downstairs, then Derek's, warning them to be quiet.

They were anxious, she knew: Sandra, who was eleven, fretful about sitting in the car on the way to the chapel with everyone staring, worrying over what she had to do during the service, what she would wear; Sean, nine, wanted to know why his best friend couldn't come with him, what there would be to eat afterward, what happened to his nan's body when the coffin rolled back along the platform and into the flames. That's what happens, isn't it, Mum? Nan gets burned in the flames.

Derek had driven them to his sister's yesterday, to help take their mind off things. Which meant, of course, that Maureen would spoil them as usual.

Maureen was nice enough, Lorraine thought, if a little over fond of herself; a little, well, overflashy. She was several years older than Lorraine and with no kids of her own; she earned a good living, managing her own place selling second-hand designer clothing, enough to afford a cleaning lady three times a week, wax and manicure once a month, and, of course, a mobile phone. Sometimes, Lorraine caught herself wondering if she were jealous of Maureen's money, her apparent freedom, before deciding that no, she was not.

When Lorraine appeared in the kitchen some thirty minutes later, she was wearing the black suit she'd bought at Richards for the opening of Maureen's shop, black tights, shoes with a low heel. She went straight to the stove and lifted the kettle, tested the weight of it for water, and carried it over to the sink.

"I'll do that," Derek said, half out of his seat.

"No need."

"Toast?"

"No, thanks." She caught herself, the angry snap in her tone, and smiled, relenting. "I'm sorry. I don't know what's the matter with me. Yes, I'd love some toast, that'd be great."

9

Sean came running in from the other room, Sandra chasing him, the pair of them skidding to an untidy halt just this side of the kitchen table.

"Now then, you two," Derek said, "behave."

"It's Sandra, she was punching me."

"I was not."

"Just because I wouldn't let her ..."

"Hey!" Derek said. "Hey! Settle down now. I don't want to hear it. That's enough."

"Is that for us, Dad?" Sean said, looking at where Derek was starting to butter the toast.

"Mum," Sandra said. "Will Uncle Michael be there? At the funeral?"

A glance, quick and awkward, passed between Derek and Lorraine.

"I'm not sure, lovey," Lorraine said. "I expect so. I hope so. Now why don't you both run along?"

"Yes, go on, the pair of you." Derek waved the knife in the direction of the door. "Get yourselves back in the other room and let us have a bit of peace."

"Oh, Dad ..."

"And see you're careful with those clothes. You don't want to be getting in a mess now, we'll be leaving soon."

"Mum ..." Sandra said, eyes widening. "This top, is it okay?"

Lorraine had been looking at her daughter, not so far off twelve now and springing up, starting to fill out. Sandra had put on her bottle-green skirt, wearing it for a change with the waistband not rolled up, her almost new shiny blue sandals, the light-gray CK sweatshirt she'd bought in the market with her own pocket money. Sean was wearing black jeans, trainers, a clean white Umbro T-shirt with a blue band around the collar and along the sleeves. He looked as though he'd borrowed some of his sister's gel before combing his hair.

"Perfect," Lorraine said. "You look really perfect. I'm proud of you."

Sean tried to pinch his sister's arm as they squeezed back through the door and Sandra settled him with a quick kick to the shins.

"Remember what I said now," Derek called after them and turned toward Lorraine with the plate of buttered toast, Lorraine standing there with tears rolling down her face.

Derek touched her arm lightly on his way to the sink. "I'm still not sure, you know. How good an idea it is. Michael."

Lorraine dabbed at her eyes. "She was his mother."

"Yes," Derek said. "Like your dad was his father, I suppose?"

The motorway traffic was slow, slower than usual Evan thought, even allowing for the fact they were scarcely out of London. In truth, they were barely a mile from the North Circular Road. "Will you look at that?" he said, angling his head round toward Wesley, who was sitting, indifferent, cuffed to their prisoner in the back seat.

Wesley grunted something, not really paying attention. He was busy working out his money, how much he could realistically say was left after seeing to his bills each month, making calculations in his head. Just the other night in the pub, Jane had been getting on to him again, how paying out two different lots of rent for two separate flats, each the size of a postage stamp, didn't make sense. Not any more. What with him sleeping over at her place three or four nights a week and Jane staying with him weekends when he wasn't pulling duty at the prison. But even pooling all their income, Wesley worried, getting the kind of place Jane was talking about wasn't going to be easy; a maisonette, maybe, something in one of those old houses that had been divided up round Camberwell, Coldharbour Lane, Brixton Hill.

"See what I mean?" Evan said again.

"What?"

"All those cars, nose to tail. See how many just got one person in. Not a single passenger. One car, one driver. You imagine doing that, in and out every day, morning and evening. Crazy. A nightmare."

"Yes," said Wesley. "Right." Hoping that was enough to shut Evan up; not a bad bloke, he supposed, but Jesus, wasn't he one to rattle on? Even if they could find somewhere to rent, Wesley thought, that wasn't really what Jane was after. In reality, her reality, he knew that she was thinking five per cent down payment, she was thinking mortgage, she was thinking the whole ninety minutes plus penalties after extra time.

"How about you, Preston?" Evan asked, nodding his head backward in the direction of the prisoner. "Traffic—you got any thoughts on that?"

From the way Preston continued to sit, staring blankly through the car window, one arm folded across his lap, the other, the one that was attached to Wesley, resting by his side, Evan supposed he had not.

Twelve years into the man's sentence, Wesley was thinking, at least another twelve to go, he didn't see the overall transport situation as being high on the list of the man's concerns.

Evan Donaghy, at twenty-seven, three years in the Prison Service only, and Wesley Wilson, two years his senior, but with one year's less experience, the pair of them detailed to escort Michael Preston, convicted of first-degree murder for the killing of his father, Matthew, in 1986 and currently serving a life sentence, to the funeral of his mother, Deirdre, there and back in the day, the prison governor grudgingly agreeing to the visit on compassionate grounds.

Four

Ben Fowles was the most recent recruit to Resnick's squad. A local lad-made-good from Kirkby-in-Ashfield, Fowles had been brought in when Mark Divine, victim of a life-shattering assault, had been forced to take early retirement on grounds of ill health.

Fowles was twenty-six and just inside the height requirement for the force at five foot eight. An open-faced young man with an outlook to match, ambitious, the hobbies section on his application form had read rock climbing, music, and soccer. When he wasn't inching his way at weekends, handhold by handhold, up some slab of sheer granite in the Peak District, Fowles's energies were divided evenly between playing in a band called Splitzoid, and harrying his opponents' ankles in the busy and aggressive midfield mode pioneered by Nobby Stiles and kept to the fore more recently by the likes of David Batty and Paul Ince. After the heady days of trials for Chesterfield, Mansfield, and Notts County, Ben now practiced this particular brand of artistry for Heanor Town reserves.

"Splitzoid," Graham Millington had asked, "whatever kind of a band is that?"

"Ah, well," Fowles explained, "we used to be thrash metal with a trace of dub, right, but now we're getting more into trip-hop and garage with a touch of techno on the side. Maybe we ought to change the name to match the new image, Serge, what d'you think?"

Millington's reply went unrecorded.

Fowles gave him free passes to an upcoming gig in a pub on the Derby ring road and Millington promised to check with the wife, see what Madeleine had on her calendar. He had an idea it might be rehearsals for *Carousel*; if it wasn't her University open access night—currently engaged in a survey of Magic Realism and the Mid-Century Novel, if Millington wasn't very much mistaken.

Jimmy Peters was an entrepreneur of the old school, a failed rock-'n'roller with angina and a face like crumpled paper. He'd gone into management when a touring American singer—a minor celebrity with two top-fifty hits—had seized Peters's guitar during a late-night session at the Boat Club and hurled it into the Trent. Jimmy Peters could take a hint. Within six months, he was managing more bands than he had fingers to count and poised to take over the license of his first premises. Take away the ballooning and the beard, and a low-rent Richard Branson was born.

"So, Jimmy," Ben Fowles said, not for the first time, "from where you were standing, you couldn't see exactly how the fight started?"

Peters scowled and rolled his eyes.

"But it was this lot as come in late ..." From force of habit, Fowles checked his notebook. "... Ellis and his mates, they were the ones that started it?"

"If I've told you once ..."

"And you knew them? They were what? Regulars?"

Peters lit a fresh Silk Cut from the nub of the old. Ash shone like glitter from the velvet lapels of his jacket. "They might've been here once or twice, it's difficult to keep track." He glanced round at the interior, shabby and stained in the daylight. Over by the entrance to the toilets, a cleaning woman was swabbing away listlessly with a mop and listening to local radio on a small receiver propped against the bucket. "Most nights it's busy," he said hopefully, "folk come and go."

"But members, Jimmy?"

"Hmm?"

"All members. Condition of your license, bound to be, drinks served to members only, outside the normal hours."

Peters smiled. "Members and their guests."

"Duly signed in."

"Not Ellis."

"A minor slip-up. Small irregularity. Heat of the moment, it can happen. Well, you'll understand." Peters wafted smoke away from his face. "I've had words with the people concerned; it'll not happen again."

Fowles had had words with the door staff himself—a walking ad for Wonderbra in a black peek-a-boo dress and silver wedge sandals and a shaven-headed bouncer with an apparent steroid habit from Gold Standard Security. Neither had been exactly forthcoming. As opposed to those who'd faced up to one another when the fracas had started: they were all reading from the same script and well-rehearsed. Too much drink. Heat of the moment. No hard feelings. Handshakes all round.

Well, not exactly that. Not with one of the home team taking up coveted space in a high-tech hospital bed, a few thousand pounds of equipment monitoring his every cough.

"This bloke who was stabbed ..."

"Wayne."

"Yes, Wayne. He's a regular, a member, right?"

Peters nodded.

"No reason, far as you know, why anybody might have it in for him?"

Peters pretended to give it some thought. The cleaner had switched stations and was listening to *Woman's Hour*, a lively discussion about the benefits of folic acid in the early stages of pregnancy. "No," Peters finally said. "Nothing that comes to mind."

"He wouldn't have got involved in something a bit chancy? Stepped out of line?"

Smoke drifted across Peters's eyes. "Not his scene. Student, I believe. You know, mature. Clarendon College. Media Studies. Brought his mum in once, some kind of anniversary."

Fowles had had enough. "If you do think of anything, you or any of the staff ..." Out on the street, he breathed in deeply before setting off back to the station. There were dark patches close against the curb, where the blood had dried and not been washed away.

"He'll live," Millington announced, back from the hospital and pushing his head round the door to Resnick's office. "Not look so

15

pretty, mind. Seen better stitching on them cardigans the wife's mother knocks out of a Christmas."

"What's he got to say about it?"

"Wayne? Not a great deal. Same yarn as everyone else, give or take. No idea who it was used the blade on him."

"And you still don't believe it?"

"How it happened, yes. Just something else won't sit right, giving me indigestion. I mean, why him? Wayne. If it's just a free-for-all, nothing more, how come he bears the brunt of it? Oh, and here ..." Despite being wrapped inside two paper bags, the egg and sausage sandwich was copiously leaking grease as he passed it into Resnick's hand, "... you'll be wanting this. I'll mash if you like? Mug of tea to wash it down."

"Right, Graham."

But when Resnick wandered out into the squad room some minutes later, he found Millington bending over his VDU screen rather than the kettle.

"Here, take a look at this by way of a CV."

Resnick focused on the lines of slightly broken text. Wayne Feraday had graduated from unlawfully and maliciously throwing half-bricks at a moving train with intent to endanger the safety of its passengers, through the more normal taking of vehicles without consent, on to two charges relating to the illegal possession and sale of a controlled drug.

"Both charges dropped," Millington said. "Insufficient evidence. Now why does that ring a bell?"

"But you think that accounts for what happened? Something drug-related?"

"Maybe Wayne's short-changed someone on his supply. Got behind on his payments. Crossed over on to someone else's turf. It'd not be the first time."

Resnick's face turned sour. "I just hope you're not right. 'Cause if you are, it'll not be the last."

Not so much more than an hour later, Mark Ellis was standing on line with two of his mates in Burger King, wearing his new leather jacket and fresh plasters down one side of his face and across the knuckles of his right hand. Stupid fucking coppers! What did they know? He was feeling spruce enough to laugh at one of Billy Scalthorpe's jokes, even though he'd heard it twice before.

At the counter, he joked with the ginger-haired lass who was serving, ordered a Whopper with cheese and a double portion of fries, onion rings, apple pie, and a large Coke. He was halfway back to the doors, Scalthorpe still haggling over his order, when the two black youths fell into step either side of him.

"Hungry," said the one to his left, Redskins baseball cap reversed.

"Huh?"

"Hungry, yeh?"

"What the fuck's it to you?"

"Here," said the youth to the other side, reaching inside his silver zip-up jacket. "Eat this."

And he pushed the barrel end of an automatic pistol hard against Ellis's cheek and squeezed the trigger.

Five

Lorraine stood on the paved area between the rose garden and the entrance to the crematorium chapel, while around her, small clusters of men and women, somberly dressed, engaged in desultory conversation. She didn't even know who they all were.

She took a tissue from her bag and blew her nose softly, pulled at an imaginary thread by the seam of Sandra's sweatshirt, and shook her head at Sean to stop him kicking at the pale gravel of the forecourt. Then there was Derek's sister Maureen approaching, a broad smile more suited to a wedding than a funeral.

"How you doing, then? All right?" She left a smudge of coral lipstick on Lorraine's cheek as she gave her a hug. "Nice outfit, understated, just right for the occasion. I like that. Though you could have come to me, of course. I'd've found something for you, special. And a good price, too." She hugged her again. "Family." Maureen herself was wearing a black dress with a scoop neck, mid-length, with a deep split in the skirt, front and back.

Derek and Maureen went off into a little huddle and several people came up to Lorraine to tell her what a grand lady her mother had been and shake her hand. A man with purple veins etched across his face and a runny eye bent to kiss her on the cheek and squeeze her arm. "She did well, Deirdre," he said, his voice low, as if this was something between the pair of them, special and caring. "Hanging on the way she did. Coping. After what that bastard—s'cuse my language—did to your father. He was a wonderful man, your dad, God rest his soul. A gentleman—but I don't need to tell you that."

"Here's the vicar," Derek said, as a slight figure, prematurely balding, bounced brightly toward them, hand outstretched, smiling.

18

But Lorraine's eyes were fixed solemnly now on the middle distance, the pair of iron gates, open, through which the vehicle bringing her brother would enter.

Evan was never sure how he'd come to take a wrong turning. But somewhere between Wesley's map reading and his own instincts, they had ended up on the wrong side of the Trent and heading east. He could feel Michael Preston's unexpressed anger burning into the back of his head as he swung the car into a U-turn. Stay calm, that's what his father would have said, stay calm and do your best. "It's okay," he said over his shoulder, "ten minutes now, fifteen at most."

In the mirror, Preston's eyes were flat and staring. Sweat gathered at the base of Evan's neck.

"We'll get you there, don't fret."

"Come on, love ..." Derek's voice patient and understanding.

"No, wait ..." Lorraine shrugged his hand from her shoulder, a quick shake of her head. "Tell them they'll have to wait until he's here."

Derek's glance went from the direction in which his wife was looking toward the open chapel doors, through which the clumsy sounds of the organ could already be heard. "It's too late. They're starting."

"Then tell them ... explain ..."

He gripped her more tightly, one arm along her back, edging her forward. "He's got held up somewhere, traffic, you know what it's like. Roadworks, most probably. He'll be here, you see. Now, d'you want to borrow my hankie? No? Okay, stiff upper lip then, here we go."

Derek, serious-faced as he led her into the chapel and down toward the empty spaces reserved for them in the front row beside Sean and Sandra; the vicar standing at the center waiting, smiling now his careful smile of welcome, and everyone else leaning forward, not wanting to be seen staring but concerned, inquisitive, staring all the same. And with each step he took beside her, proud at her bravery, Derek thinking if there was any such thing as justice then Michael would not be serving life nor anything like it, Michael

19

would have been taken from that place and hung by the neck until dead, dead as his father before him. "Okay, now?" he whispered as Lorraine stood beside him. "Okay, sweetheart?" And squeezed her hand.

The crematorium car park was full to the gills and they had to pull over against the grass verge, temporarily blocking the way. When Evan switched off the engine, the sound of singing could be heard, muffled, from behind the chapel doors.

"You take him," Evan said, sitting round in his seat. "I'll deal with the car. Go on. Before it's too late."

Preston leaned forward. "The cuffs," he said. "I don't want to go in there wearing no cuffs."

Evan hesitated.

Alongside Preston, Wesley shook his head.

"Do it," Evan said decisively. "Uncuff him."

Disbelief in Wesley's eyes.

"We're wasting time."

Out of the car, Evan moved in quickly on Preston, stopping close enough that their bodies were almost touching. "I'm trusting you," he said. "Don't let me down. When it's over, you stay inside, wherever you are, let everyone else leave. That's when the cuffs go back on. Agreed?"

Preston held his gaze for a moment, then nodded once, Evan hesitating, waiting perhaps for thanks that didn't come. "Okay," Evan said, stepping back.

Wesley walked with Preston toward the chapel doors, keeping approximately half a pace behind, Evan standing his ground until they had stepped inside and the doors had closed again behind them. Then, without looking either to left or right, he got back into the car and drove it slowly up toward the road.

If this goes wrong, he was thinking ... And then, if this were my dad, here in my shoes, this situation, what would he have done?

It was Derek who noticed Michael first, glancing round at the sound of the heavy doors squeaking to a close. Michael standing quite still for a moment, blinking at the change of light before starting to walk

20

slowly forward down the center aisle; the black man—his guard, Derek supposed—who had come in with him, remaining where he was. The congregation was singing a psalm about passing into the golden yonder.

Lorraine sensed Michael's presence before she saw him, recognizing, perhaps, the weight of his footsteps, clear along the cold tiles. Like a slow wave, voices broke around her and she, almost alone, continued singing, unable to turn her head for fear she was wrong.

"Hi, Lo." He repeated their old joke greeting close into her ear and something clutched and swept through her stomach, and then it was his hand steadying the small blue hymnal that shook between her fingers. "Budge up."

To Lorraine's left, Derek moved along to make room, edging the children closer to the wall; Lorraine standing there with Michael's shoulder touching hers, his elbow hard against her upper arm. The warmth of him. Lorraine terrified she might cry out, faint.

The last sounds of the organ echoed to a halt and the vicar stepped forward, head raised, waiting for silence before beginning to speak.

"We are here to celebrate the life of a remarkable woman; one to whom life presented a more than usually difficult path. A path which many of us would have found too arduous or too long, yet one which Deirdre traveled with great fortitude and grace." The voice was oddly high and clear, somehow both old and young. "She was a valued member of the community, a willing worker, and, as the presence of so many of you here today testifies, a loyal and much-loved friend. Perhaps above all, though, we will remember her as a devoted mother, the loving and strong center of her family, a rock of consolation and forgiveness which held firm in the face of adversity of a singular and most terrible kind."

Lorraine sensed Michael tense beside her, heard his breathing change, a low clearing of his throat. Behind them, the chapel was silent, poised. For a moment, she thought that Michael might be about to move, step forward, speak. Then she realized that he was crying, making no effort to disguise it, tears that curled around the corners of his mouth, ran without let or hindrance down his face.

21

"If there is one thing," the vicar continued, "we should remember most about the life of Deirdre Preston, it is that, no matter what the pain she suffered, no matter the magnitude of sorrow and sadness she was forced to face, she never once sank into despair, she never lost her faith.

"Now, in silence, let us each remember Deirdre in our own way, and let us pray for her soul, now and everlasting ..."

Lorraine and Michael, standing there together: Michael staring upward, the ceiling blurred by tears; Lorraine bent forward, eyes closed, long fingers winding restlessly in and out, sobbing. Happy.

Six

"I've already fucking told you," Billy Scalthorpe insisted, his voice a raw whine against the backdrop of overlapping conversations. "How many more fuckin' times?"

Carl Vincent shifted his weight on to his other foot. "How about once more?"

"Okay. Mark's walkin' out, right? Me and Adam, we're arguin' the toss up at the counter, Adam wants Coke without ice, and what they've give him is Coke with ice. Anyway, I turn me head, gonna shout to Mark to hang on, right? And there's these two blokes come at him from both sides and before you can fuckin' do anythin' they've shot him in the fuckin' head. Legged it out of here like they was in the fuckin' Olympics."

"Into a car, yes? There was a car waiting?"

Scalthorpe shook his head. "I didn't see no car."

Three different witnesses had spoken of a black four-door saloon, a Ford, most probably an Escort.

"But you saw them, the pair who attacked him?"

"Course I fuckin' saw 'em."

"You recognize them?"

"What?"

"These two, you knew who they were?"

"'Course I never."

"No?"

"No."

"Never seen them before?"

"I dunno."

"Then you might have?"

"Yeh, I might. S'pose I might."

23

"But you claimed not to have recognized them."

Scalthorpe shook his head in amazement. "They was fuckin' runnin' away. All I saw was the backs of their fuckin' heads, wa'n it? Fuckin' baseball caps, arse to front, like they all wear."

"All?"

"You know what I mean."

Scalthorpe held Vincent's stare for a moment, then blinked. A rosary of tiny white spots circled his mouth, mingling here and there with wisps of fledgling mustache. Vincent smiled: the two attackers were black, most probably a similar shade of black to himself. Yes, he knew what Scalthorpe meant. And if a leading sports commentator could claim, without embarrassment, not to be able to distinguish between one black soccer player and another, what else could he expect?

"You did get a good look, though," Vincent said, "at what they were wearing?"

"The one that shot him," Adam Bent was saying, "he had on this silver jacket, short, you know? Padded, maybe. Yeh, I think it was padded. Blue jeans. Trainers. Nike, maybe, I'm not sure. Blue. Blue and white."

"And a cap," Naylor prompted him, glancing up from his notebook. "You said something before about a cap."

"Oh, yeh. Dark blue with some sort of logo. Letterin', you know?"

Naylor nodded. "And his mate?"

"Sports gear. Green and white. Cap, too. Pulled back. Washington Redskins. I know that 'cause I used to have one meself. Lost it down Forest, larkin' around after the match. You don't go to Forest, do you?"

Naylor shook his head.

"Used to be a lot of your lot down there, Sat'days. Hanging round, outside the ground. Still, have to be in uniform, I s'pose, do something like that?"

Naylor nodded again. "The one who did the shooting," he said, "how much of a chance did you get to look at his face?"

◆◆◆

Either side of Burger King, a section of Upper Parliament Street was cordoned off with yellow tape. Traffic had slowed to a single line, snail-like, in each direction. A small crowd, mostly women and small children, had gathered outside the Disney shop opposite and stood gawking.

Millington switched off his mobile and went outside to where Resnick was standing on the pavement, talking to Sharon Garnett.

"Just spoke to the hospital," Millington said. "In surgery now, Ellis. Stable. That's all they'll say."

Resnick nodded. "Sharon's got a witness, woman who was passing, reckons she got a good look at one of them when they ran out to the car. Almost knocked her over. She's going to take her round to Central, take a look at some pictures."

Millington nodded. "Photofit, maybe."

"Maybe."

They were still standing there when a bulky man, dark-haired, wearing a leather jacket that might have fitted some years before, ducked under the tape and clasped Resnick by the shoulder.

"Charlie."

"Norman."

"It's a bugger."

"You could say."

"Bastards shooting one another in broad daylight."

"Yes."

Norman Mann was the head of the city's Drug Squad, a square-shouldered man with a reputation for calling a spade a fucking spade. He and Resnick were around the same age, had worked their way up through the Force more or less together, and treated each other with more than a little bonhomie and a careful respect.

"Let's talk, Charlie."

"Right." Resnick looked round at his sergeant. "Graham?"

"You get off. I'll hang on here."

They sat in the small bar of the Blue Bell, Mann with a pint of best and Resnick a tomato juice liberally laced with Worcestershire Sauce.

"This kid, Ellis," Mann said, "we've had our eyes on him for a while. Bits of low-level dealing, Clifton estate mostly. Out at Bulwell.

25

Amphetamines, Es. Once in a while, a little heroin. I thought you should know."

Resnick nodded. "You've never pulled him in?"

Mann supped his ale. "A little chat, nothing more. If he's dealing heroin, any quantity, he's got to have a line through to Planer, but we haven't figured out yet what it is."

Resnick knew there were two main suppliers in the city, Planer and Valentine. Something else Resnick knew: Planer was white and Valentine was black. With Planer, it was mostly pills and heroin; Valentine's fancy was more for marijuana, crack cocaine. But there was a lot of leeway in between. The pair of them had been targeted, questioned, arrested, grudgingly allowed back out on to the streets. Several of their minions had been successfully charged and convicted, and were now serving time. But not Planer, not Valentine.

"You think that's what this might be about?" Resnick said. "Drugs?"

Mann shifted his head to one side in a lazy shrug.

"There was a stabbing out at Jimmy Peters's place," Resnick said, "early hours of the morning."

"I heard."

"Youth as came off worse, Wayne Feraday. He's come your way too, I think."

"Rings a bell."

"Ellis, the one you've had an interest in—he was involved."

"You brought him in?"

Resnick nodded.

"And then let him walk?"

"Nothing to hold him."

Mann smiled with his eyes. "That's all right, Charlie. I know how it goes."

Resnick reached up to loosen his tie, but it had worked loose already. "Ellis, he was still under surveillance?"

"Like I say, Charlie, we had our eye on him, but no more than once in a while. Small potatoes. Nothing worth shelling out serious overtime."

"Beyond the obvious, you think there could be a connection

26

between him and Feraday? Something as makes this shooting more than tit for tat."

Mann gave it some thought. "I suppose it's a possibility."

"Nothing more?"

"Like I say, both of them pretty small beer. But, yeh, I'll ask around." He lit a cigarette. "Likely you'll do the same. Keep each other in the picture. That's why I came looking for you, soon as I heard."

"Right," Resnick drained his glass and slid it aside.

"Last thing we want, Charlie, that bitch from Major Crimes finding an excuse to muscle in." He winked. "Let's keep this one tight to ourselves."

Walking back down the street, the Theatre Royal at his back, Resnick thought about what Norman Mann had said. That bitch, as he called her, was Helen Siddons, the Detective Chief Inspector recently appointed to head the Major Crime Unit based in the city. When the post had been advertised, one of only three in the county, quite a few of Resnick's friends and colleagues had argued he should throw his name in the ring. But in the end, partly through a sense of loyalty to his existing team, partly a distaste for the whole appointments rigmarole, he had declined and Siddons had been offered the post.

One of her first actions had been to poach Lynn Kellogg, possibly Resnick's best officer, who had recently passed her sergeant's boards and was waiting for an opening.

Siddons was a high-flier, ambitious, hard as anthracite. Whatever Norman Mann wished to the contrary, if she wanted her squad involved in what was going on, when push came to shove, there was little he—or Resnick—could do about it.

Seven

Evan knew about wakes. His father—born and raised a Protestant in the midst of the Republic—a shining light, as he liked to put it, in the morass of that Catholic bog—had seen to it that the family kept the tradition alive wherever they happened to settle in England. Port Sunlight, Wolverhampton, Chester-le-Street, Wandsworth. Oh, not the weeping and wailing kind, four generations of toothless women in black, caterwauling like cats in heat; and not the fiddle tune and whiskey free-for-all that ended in fisticuffs and tears. No, what Evan's father advocated was a dignified coming together, serious not somber, never drunken but certainly not teetotal; a chance for all those mourning the deceased to recollect, remember, spin their favorite stories, raise their glasses in a dignified toast to the recently departed. It was how it had been when Evan's father had passed on three years before, sideswiped by a lorry plowing down the motorway in heavy rain, his father having pulled over to help someone who'd broken down and kneeling too near the edge of the hard shoulder, struggling to free the nuts on the rear wheel.

"You're serious, aren't you?" Wesley said, the two of them standing off to the one side, himself and Evan; Preston, his right arm secured again to Wesley's left, making the party up to three. Preston with his back turned toward the pair of them, as if the conversation they were heatedly engaged in was about somebody else and not himself.

"You know the instructions," Wesley was saying. "Straight up and back."

"Escort the prisoner to his mother's funeral and return him safely forthwith."

"Exactly."

"So what's your problem?" Evan asked.

Preston was watching Lorraine and Derek as they stood outside the chapel, talking to the vicar, doubtless thanking him. Lorraine conscious her brother was looking in her direction and not responding, trying not to, back in control of herself now, allowing just the single glance. Sandra and Sean watching him, too; fascinated, afraid to come too close. This man who was the uncle they'd never seen. Who'd killed their grandad. Killed him. It didn't seem possible.

When Preston took a half-pace toward Sandra and smiled, she turned away, head down, pushing Sean in front of her.

"My problem is ..." Wesley began, at pains to spell it out, as much for the prisoner as for Evan "... there's nothing there about taking him off to some bloody reception."

"Wake."

"What?"

"It's a wake."

"Whatever you want to call it, it's none of our concern."

Evan shaking his head, feeling his temper rising, but keeping it all under control. "Think of it this way, Wesley, the funeral, it's in two parts, right? The first, here at the crematorium, the second back at the house."

"Bollocks," Wesley said. "You're talking bollocks."

"Well, then, Wesley ..." Evan moving close now, lowering his voice. "I don't give a monkey's what you think, we're taking him anyway. So either you come with us or find something else to keep you occupied. Sit in the back of the car, maybe, and floss your teeth?"

The two reception rooms on the ground floor were separated by a pair of stripped-pine doors set into a wide arch, and these had been fastened back, allowing people to move freely between them. Glasses, borrowed from the off license, Derek and Sean had arranged on the low shelf unit, bottles alongside them—white wine, Lorraine had thought, along with some soda water in case anyone cared to make themselves a spritzer; orange juice, quite a few beers, cans of Coke and Fanta for the kids; no spirits, not in the middle of the day. The food, Sandra helping, Lorraine had set out on a long table near the French windows, which were open out into the garden.

It was one of those early summer days that had started off bright and fresh, then threatened to cloud over as it wore on; any breeze had dropped and now it was becoming decidedly muggy. Even though she'd taken off her suit jacket, Lorraine could feel her blouse sticking to her when she moved.

Preston's handcuffs had been removed as soon as they had arrived at the house and one or two people had come over to him, made a few remarks about his loss, then hurried away again, never pausing long enough for conversation. Sandra bravely brought over a plate of sausage rolls and held it out to him, avoiding his eyes; the moment he had taken one, she spun away, his thank you strangely gentle to her ears. Young Sean spent an age hovering, daring himself to ask questions that, in the end, remained unasked.

Lorraine aside, it was only Derek's sister, Maureen, who seemed at all comfortable in Michael's presence, leaning back against the wall after offering him a cigarette and encouraging him to tell her what it was like inside, being locked away like that with no, you know, women—Maureen flirting with him almost, that was how it seemed.

"Clock that?" Wesley said, nodding toward where Preston and Maureen were standing, Maureen laughing a little now, arching back her neck.

Evan nodded. He'd seen women like that before, visiting days, some bloke's reputation as a hard nut getting their hormones all in a tizzy.

"Keep that up," Wesley said, "get more'n she's bargained for."

Evan wandered across the room and fetched a couple more sandwiches. "You know your name?" he said. "Wesley."

"What about it?"

"I was thinking, are you named after Wesley Snipes or what?"

"Christ, man," Wesley exclaimed with a laugh. "You know how old I'd have to be to have been named after him? How long you think that guy's been around, huh? *White Men Can't Jump.* Nobody heard of him before that." He shook his head and laughed. "Wesley Snipes, my black arse!"

"So then, who?" Evan asked, unfazed.

"You know Wes Hall?"

Evan shook his head.

"Cricketer. Fast bowler, man. The best. Wes Hall and Charlie Griffiths. Played for the West Indies a long time back. Wes, he's from Barbados. Like my old man." Wesley laughed again. "These guys today, you think they quick, well, you slow to get your head out the way when Wes Hall bowl you a bouncer, wave your head goodbye."

Evan standing there, staring at him, eyes becoming glazed.

"You into cricket, Evan, or what?"

"Bunch of grown men standing round for days trying to hit a small red ball, that's what my dad used to say."

"Never mind your dad for once, it's you I'm asking. You appreciate the finer points of the game or not?"

"Not."

"Missing a lot, man. Grand game, cricket. Sport of kings."

Evan thought that was horse racing, but he saw no sense in arguing.

"Where's he gone?" Wesley said suddenly, pushing himself away from the wall.

"What? Who?"

"Preston, he's not there any more."

Evan staring at the spot where their prisoner had been moments before; no Maureen, no Michael Preston, just an empty glass on the floor.

He hadn't gone past them into the garden, they were sure of that; they checked the kitchen, then doubled back along the hallway, heading for the stairs. The first two doors were open, the kids' bedrooms, the third was locked. Evan hammered upon it with his fist. "Preston? You in there?"

"Yes, course I'm in here."

"Open the door."

"I can't."

"Open up now."

There was a shuffle of movement, followed by the small click of the bolt being pulled back and the door opened to reveal Preston standing there, underpants hoisted back up, but trousers still midway up his thighs, shirt flapping down.

"What's all the fuss about? I didn't know I had to ask permission to take a crap. Or maybe you just want to wipe my behind?"

Grim-faced, Evan closed the door firmly in Preston's face, far from appreciating the amusement in the man's eyes.

When he emerged five minutes later, Preston had recombed his hair and was smelling of somebody else's cologne. Evan was still standing outside the door, more or less to attention, Wesley sitting on the top stair, nursing a can of Coke and wishing it were Carlsberg.

"Thought I was doing a runner," Preston said.

"You were told to stay downstairs, within sight."

"Call of nature."

"I don't care."

"So okay, won't happen again."

"I know." Evan held out the cuffs and moved toward him.

"Look," Preston said. "There's a favor I got to ask."

"Forget it. No more favors."

"My sister, I just want to talk to her."

"You've been talking to her."

"No, alone."

Evan shook his head. "You heard what I said."

"Come on," Preston said, lowering his voice conspiratorially. "You got family of your own, right? Close. How'd you feel in my shoes?" He stared at Evan until Evan dropped his shoulders in a shrug.

"Be quick," Evan said, glancing along the landing. "In there, the bedroom. Ten minutes, tops. And remember, there'll be one of us out here, the other down in the garden—just in case you have a mind to do a Peter Pan."

"Okay," Preston said. "Thanks."

Evan stepped away. "You're wasting precious time," he said.

Five minutes later, Sean dogging his heels, Derek wandered over to where Wesley was standing in the garden, eyes flicking from time to time toward the bedroom window.

"You'll be on your way soon, I dare say," Derek said.

"Yeh. Just as soon as they're through."

"Through with what?"

"Preston and your wife, making their fond farewells upstairs."

Derek followed the direction of Wesley's gaze. "You stay here," he said to Sean. "Stay here and don't move."

"Dad …"

"Just stay."

On the upstairs landing, Evan moved to intercept him, but he was too slow. Three paces and Derek pushed the bedroom door all the way back so hard it rebounded from the edge of the dressing table with a hollow crack. Michael was sitting on the edge of the double bed, head bowed forward; Lorraine standing close in front of him, hand resting on his shoulder.

"What the hell's all this?"

Lorraine turned toward him. "Michael and I were just talking."

It had been silent in the room: neither she nor Michael had been saying a thing.

When Michael slowly moved his head away and sat back, Lorraine left her hand where it was. "Don't close the door, Derek," Lorraine said. "It's not allowed. Just leave it ajar, the way it was. All right?"

Flushed, Derek turned on his heel and pushed past Evan, taking the stairs two at a time. His sister Maureen was in the hallway with Sandra, but he swept on past, not speaking, pausing only to grab his car keys before slamming through the front door.

They were twenty miles shy of Leicester, heading south, the signs for East Midlands Airport just coming into view.

"Today," Preston said, surprising both Evan and Wesley by initiating a conversation. "You were both pretty decent. I hope you don't end up getting into trouble 'cause of what you did."

"Thanks," Evan said, with a slight turn of the head. "It'll be okay."

"Yeh," said Wesley grudgingly. "No problem." And he felt a sudden sensation, burning and sharp, along his arm.

Wesley's shout of surprise and pain merged with another from the front of the car, as Preston pressed the open edge of the razor-blade tight against the artery at the side of Evan's neck. They veered abruptly into the outside lane and drivers, cruising in excess of eighty, sounded their horns and flashed their lights in warning.

"I've just sliced your mate's wrist," Preston said. "Get him to a hospital fast and he'll be okay. You too." As yet, the blade had barely broken the surface of Evan's skin. "Now pull over on the hard shoulder. Do it now, don't even think."

"I don't know," Evan said aloud, as much to himself as anyone else.

Blood was spooling over Wesley's fingers as he gripped his wrist. "Evan," he said, "for Christ's sake, do what he says."

Evan started to swing in without indicating and almost brushed the side of a cattle lorry thundering off to Harwich and the Hook of Holland.

"Take it steady," Preston said, the hand holding the razor blade not wavering in the slightest. "Right, pull over. Over now." Before the car had stopped, he was holding his cuffed wrist out toward Wesley, the razor blade still fast against Evan's neck. "Unlock this."

Though the blood made it difficult to keep a grip on the key, Wesley did as he was told.

"Right," Preston said. "Now the car keys. Give them to me. Now!"

For a long time, Evan would remember what he saw in the mirror as he passed back the keys, the resolution bright and certain in Michael Preston's eyes. And moments later, Preston was running away from them, fast, across a field of rape.

Eight

Resnick had been close enough to the Victoria Centre to nip into the market for a quick espresso. Two quick espressos. He was on his way back down the escalator by the Emmett water sculpture when his mobile phone rang. The sound of Millington's voice immediately put him on the alert. "Graham, where are you?"

"Back at the station. Prisoner escaped on the motorway not far south of here. Category A."

"Our concern?"

"Our patch. Seems he was at his mother's funeral."

"Under escort?"

There was no hiding the sneer in the sergeant's tone. "Not so's you'd notice."

Resnick cursed. "Someone we know?"

"Preston. Michael Preston."

It had been a while back, Jack Skelton's case and not his, but Resnick remembered the details well enough. "Anyone hurt?"

"One of the prison officers as was with him. Getting himself patched in Queen's. Pal's there with him, holding his hand."

"Okay, you know the drill; airports, railway stations, buses, all the usual."

"In hand. And I made a quick check, wives, girlfriends, the like. Looks as if closest family he's got left's his sister. I've told Carl to get over there, soon as he can free himself up at Burger King. See what she's got to say for herself, nose around."

Resnick adjusted his step so as to avoid a heavily pregnant woman coming out of Boots. "How about the hospital?"

"Sharon's on her way there now."

"Tell her I'll meet her there, A and E. Ten minutes." Resnick

35

switched off his phone and cut through Jessops on to Mansfield Road in search of a cab.

Still a rarity in the Force, not only a woman detective, but also black, Sharon Garnett was doing her best to fill Lynn Kellogg's shoes.

Before joining the police in London, she had worked as both singer and actor—all the stereotypes, as she liked to say, it's a wonder I missed out on boxer—and had first met Resnick in the course of a murder inquiry when she was stationed in Lincoln. From there, it had been a comparatively short journey west across the Wolds.

She took the entrance into the hospital grounds just short of the University Park, left and left again, and within minutes she was inside and on the main floor, making her way between chairs and benches crowded with the city's walking wounded: young men with shaved heads and tattoos, and old men who cursed whenever the name called was not their own; women who by now could have walked in blindfold and sometimes did, eyes swollen and closed from too much crying, from the swing of an angry fist; babies who howled and toddlers who bawled, and kids who ran up and down the aisles until one or another slipped or someone's temper snapped and the tears they'd been warned it would end in finally arrived.

Resnick was standing near the inquiry desk, hands in the pockets of his shapeless gray suit.

"Third cubicle along," the harassed nurse said in response to his question, head turning away before the words were fully out.

Wesley was stretched out on a narrow bed, eyes closed. His left arm lay folded across his abdomen, bandaged and strapped. Evan, who had been sitting in a chair alongside, scrambled to his feet when Resnick and Sharon Garnett entered, mistaking them initially for medical staff, but quickly realizing the truth.

"How is he?" Resnick asked, nodding in the direction of the bed.

"Okay. He'll be, yeh, okay."

"Sleeping?"

"They gave him something, you know, for the pain."

"And you?"

36

Without willing it to, Evan's hand went to the plaster that had been taped across his neck after the small wound had been cleaned. "I'm fine."

"You're sure?"

"Yes, fine."

"Good. Let's find somewhere, get a cup of tea or something, and you can tell me what happened."

Avoiding Resnick's eyes, Evan nodded: it wasn't a prospect that filled him with enthusiasm.

"Sharon," Resnick said, pushing aside the curtain as they left the cubicle. "Perhaps you could have a word with the doctor on duty. Anything that might be useful. Catch up with us in the canteen."

"Sure." Sharon smiled. "Mine's coffee, black."

Evan had been running over the events in his mind, deliberating how much of the story he should tell, how much it was wise to hold back. Decisions he'd taken that at the time ... well, he wasn't stupid, he could imagine how they might sound to anyone outside, anyone who hadn't been in the actual situation. Think on your feet, son, his dad had liked to say, judge each case on its merits, that's what you've got to learn in this world. Which was what Evan had done, only he'd landed flat on his face from the edge of a high cliff.

In the cubicle earlier, waiting for the doctor to come and stitch up Wesley's wrist, Evan had asked him if they shouldn't agree beforehand on a version of events.

"Events, Evan? Only one event anyone's gonna give Jack shit about is we lost our prisoner. Okay? Far as the rest of it goes, you do the talking, right? You been doing it pretty good so far." And Wesley had turned his face away to the wall.

Gratitude, Evan thought, after me leaping out into that bloody motorway, risking life and limb flagging somebody down to get you to the hospital, instead of chasing off across the fields after sodding Preston. He supposed that had been wrong, too.

"Okay," Resnick said, having secured a table in the corner of the visitors' canteen. "Tell me what happened."

And, of course, Evan did. Every move in such detail that the party

37

still hadn't left the chapel when Sharon arrived and slid into the vacant seat.

By the time Evan had finished, his voice was little more than a whisper and Resnick's receptive listener's expression seemed to have frozen, immovable, to his face.

"Just one thing, er, Evan," Sharon said, breaking the silence. "Before you put the prisoner into the car for the last part of the journey, you didn't search him or anything?"

Evan succeeded in looking hurt. "Of course I did. We did. Wesley held him on the cuffs and I patted him down."

"Patted him down."

"All right, it wasn't a strip search, I agree. But then I didn't see any need. But it was thorough, I did a proper job."

"Yet he had a blade," Resnick said.

"Yes."

"A razor blade."

"Yes."

"When you searched him. Thoroughly."

There were tears welling at the back of Evan's eyes. "Okay, Evan," Resnick said, pushing himself to his feet.

"If we need to talk to you again, we'll be in touch."

The sun was surprisingly bright for so late in the afternoon and angling steeply in toward them as they crossed the car park, forcing Sharon to squint up her eyes while she fished her sunglasses from her bag.

"So what did he do?" Sharon asked. "This Michael Preston."

"Strangled his father with his bare hands, then beat him round the head with a car jack for good measure."

Sharon was quiet till they arrived at the car.

They were turning at the Derby Road roundabout, trailing a pair of green City buses, when she asked Resnick what else he knew about Preston.

"Hard man. Villain. Father ran a bookie's, one of the few independents left. Been taken over now, like everything else. Preston started out doing a bit of collecting for him. Got a taste. Graduated to armed robbery. Couple of post offices, building societies and the like. Served a little time, but not as much as he should. Liked him for a big wages job, I remember, but he was alibied up and no one was prepared to drop him in it."

Sharon grinned. "Guilty, though?"

"As sin." Resnick laughed.

"What he did today, Preston, you wouldn't say it was out of character?"

Resnick shook his head. "Sounds as if he was pretty much in control. He's cool, certainly. Used to be."

"Odd thing to say about someone who's killed his father."

Resnick nodded. "That was impulsive, irrational … not his normal pattern at all."

"Twelve years inside, it changes a man."

Resnick nodded. "A man like Preston, makes him harder."

They were passing the Three Wheatsheaves and about to drive over the railway bridge this side of Lenton Recreation Ground. Resnick had a glimpse of teams in white, men and women, playing crown bowls; kids on the roundabouts and swings; Asian families sitting in abstract circles on the grass, women with the children, the men a way off, playing cards.

"Still seeing your lady?" Sharon asked.

"Mmm," Resnick said, uncertain. "Sort of. Both been kind of busy lately. You know how it is."

Hannah Campbell lived in one of the Victorian terraced houses toward the end of the promenade overlooking the recreation ground from the other side. Sharon had met her on a number of occasions now, formal and informal, and quite liked her, enjoyed talking to her, more laid-back than most of the teachers she'd had at school. A good companion for Resnick, she thought, while wondering why it was they never seemed quite at ease in one another's company. Still, maybe that was just the way they were and anyway, who was she to judge? Stand the other halves of my relationships side by side, Sharon thought, one early sad marriage included, and you'd have enough for a basketball team and some to spare. Too much brawn and too little brain, that was what it came down to; too much concern with good pecs and muscle tone. A great body, though—oh God!—hormones in the ascendant, that could be difficult to resist. But right now she was sticking to volley-ball, the ladies' league, and sweating her way through a single life.

"How long is it now, anyway," she asked, "you and Hannah?"

"Oh," said Resnick, "must be a year or more."

"You don't know?"

"Not exactly, no." Which wasn't quite the truth.

Sharon laughed. "How d'you go on about anniversaries then, stuff like that?"

Resnick shook his head. Hannah had surprised him with rack of lamb for dinner, champagne, a three-CD set by Stan Getz she'd seen reviewed in the *Guardian*, a card showing a painting by a black American painter named William H. Johnson, on which she'd written *Twelve months, two days, who's counting? Love, Hannah.* The next day he had gone to one of the stalls in the market and bought a large mixed bouquet of flowers, but by then it had been too late.

Sharon turned right off Derby Road and down the slope in the police station car park. "What d'you think?" she asked, sliding the vehicle into a vacant space. "Preston—you reckon we'll catch him?"

Resnick shook his head. "Ask me again this time tomorrow." Releasing his seat belt, he swiveled out of the car. "He's a career criminal, dangerous—nobody's fool. If he's still around, not made a run for it, we'd best get him and fast."

Nine

Lorraine Jacobs's address was in a part of the city Carl Vincent didn't yet know well, a newish development tucked away to the west of the Hucknall Road. Three- and four-bedroom houses set back from a hilly maze of winding streets, lined with newly planted trees; some of the houses beginning to look shabby, no longer wearing the glossy sheen of the three-color brochures that had graced estate agents' offices. Well, Vincent mused, this close to the city center you could do a lot worse.

The Jacobs' house was number twenty-four, situated at the end of one short street, another branching off from it at a right angle and running up a steady slope toward the southwest. Its position meant a larger than average front garden, set to lawn with low shrubs at the edges and a tall hedge separating it from number twenty-two. One path, paved, led to the front door, another, graveled over, ran to the garage on the farther side. Through the garage door, which was partly raised, Vincent could see the lower half of a Volkswagen Polo, color blue. Ten to fifteen meters past the garage was a metal fence and beyond that, unlikely as it seemed, an expanse of open ground, more or less a regular field, in which a pair of horses stood, necks bent, grazing, occasionally flicking their tails at what Vincent assumed were importuning flies.

He walked to the front door and rang the bell.

The woman who answered was wearing a white cotton robe, decorated here and there with blue flowers; a pink towel was wrapped around what was clearly wet hair and her feet were bare. Thirty-seven, maybe, Vincent thought, thirty-eight; anything over forty and she's looking especially good, taking care of herself well.

"Mrs. Jacobs?"

41

Lorraine glanced at the warrant card in Vincent's hand.

"Detective Constable Vincent, CID."

"How can I help you?" A few drops of water shook themselves free from a stray strand of hair and fell on to Lorraine's sleeve.

After the last guest had gone and it had become clear that Derek was intent upon giving her the hurt and silent treatment, Lorraine had found a largely untouched bottle of unoaked Chardonnay and busied herself with clearing away the remains of the strange, strange afternoon. Now Derek and the children were off somewhere in his car, most probably carting empty bottles to the dump.

"Just a few questions."

"About what?" With one hand she pulled at an end of the towel and as it came free, shook her head so that her hair, still damp, rose, then fell slowly back across her neck and shoulders.

"Your brother."

"What about him?"

"He was at your mother's funeral earlier today, I believe?"

"Yes, but ..."

"And afterward?"

"We all came back here, family and friends. Michael stayed until he ... until he had to go back." She looked at Vincent defiantly. "Back to prison."

"And that would be the last time you saw him?"

"Yes."

"Mrs. Jacobs, you're sure?"

Lorraine pulled her robe tighter. "Look, what's all this about?" A flush had risen from the base of her throat. "Has something happened? If something's happened to Michael, I want to know."

"Your brother absconded, Mrs. Jacobs. He attacked the officers guarding him and escaped."

Vincent couldn't tell if it were joy or fear bringing the shine to Lorraine's eyes.

When Derek arrived back with the children ten minutes later, instead of his wife, he found Carl Vincent in the living room. Vincent looking none too idly at the family photographs lining the shelf above the fireplace.

42

"Who are you?" Derek wanted to know.

As Vincent was introducing himself, Lorraine came into the room, dressed in blue jeans and a loose gray sweatshirt, hair pinned up. "Michael's got away," she said.

"What?"

"Run off, escaped, done a bunk. Ask him, he knows."

"You two," Derek said to the children, who had entered on their mother's heels, "off you go upstairs for a bit and leave us to talk."

"Dad," complained Sandra. "You never let us in on anything."

"Uncle Michael," Sean said, addressing Vincent, "did he beat up the guards? Did he? Them two as was here? Did he kill someone?"

"Out! Both of you, out now. Sandra, get him out of here."

Without bothering to ask anyone else if they wanted to join her, Lorraine was standing by the drinks cabinet, fixing herself a stiff gin.

"Did he hurt anyone?" Derek asked.

"Cut one of the officers pretty badly, I believe," Vincent said. "He's being treated now in Queen's."

"Cut?" Derek repeated. "He had a knife?"

"A razor blade, apparently."

Derek flashed a glance toward Lorraine, which Carl Vincent couldn't miss. "You wouldn't know anything about that, either of you?" Vincent asked. "How he might have got hold of a blade?"

"No, why would we?" Lorraine said. She carried her drink over to the settee and sat down, the two men watching her all the way.

"I imagine he went to the bathroom, for instance," Vincent said, "while he was here?"

"I imagine he did."

"I doubt if there are any blades there," Derek said. "I use an electric, have done for years."

"So do I," said Lorraine with what was close to a giggle. How much has she been putting away, Vincent wondered? A regular habit or simply the strain of the funeral? "What does it matter," Lorraine asked, "where Michael got it from? Unless you think one of us slipped it into his hand."

"And did you?" Vincent asked lightly.

"Oh, yes. Of course." Lorraine drank some more of her gin and tonic. "In fact, Derek and I planned the whole thing."

43

"You'll know where he is now, then." Vincent smiled, playing along. "Michael."

Lorraine smiled back at him over the top of her glass. "Upstairs. Under the bed."

"Lorraine, for God's sake ... My wife isn't being serious," Derek said. "It's been a trying day. I hope you realize ..."

"Oh, yes," Vincent said. "Yes, of course. I do have to ask you, though, both of you, if there was anything Michael said today that might have given you the idea he was considering absconding?"

Derek's head started to turn toward Lorraine, but he checked himself and looked at the floor instead; Lorraine continued to stare at Carl Vincent over her glass. "What sort of thing?" she asked.

"Anything to make you think he was planning to do something like this."

"Nothing," Lorraine said, perhaps a touch too quickly. "Certainly not to me. Derek, he didn't say anything to you, did he?"

"I doubt if we exchanged more than a dozen words the whole time."

"Yourself and Mr. Preston, then," Vincent queried, looking at Derek, "you weren't on what you'd call friendly terms?"

"I wouldn't say that."

"Wouldn't you, Derek?" Lorraine swiveled on the sofa, reaching out with her free hand to steady herself. "Really? Well, of course, that's just because you're too polite—Derek being polite, you see, gentlemanly. Quite big on the old-fashioned virtues, Derek, standing back and opening doors, always walking on the outside of the pavement so that ... Why is that exactly, Derek, I forget? To protect me from anyone wanting to snatch my bag from a passing car or bike, or is it something to do with not getting splashed?"

Derek's face drawn now, thin lips pursed tight; his hands, Vincent noticed, were closed into fists upon his thighs, their knuckles white. He was a small-boned man, wiry; if someone had said he had been an athlete when he was younger, middle distance most likely, Vincent would not have been surprised. Probably still played tennis in the summer, went swimming with the kids.

"He doesn't like to give offense, you see," Lorraine was saying, "Derek. Not to anybody. And not to me especially, this being such a delicate time. The funeral and then seeing Michael again after all that while …" Shifting position, Lorraine slid forward on the cushions of the settee, the tall glass wobbling in her hand till Vincent ducked forward quickly and took hold of it, easing it from her fingers and setting it on the floor.

Pushing a hand up through her hair, Lorraine gave Vincent a long look. "The truth of it—you want to hear the truth—is that Derek doesn't like Michael one bit, he never did. Not ever."

"That's not true," Derek exclaimed, looking at Lorraine for a moment, then away. "That's just not true."

"Of course it's true. What's the matter with you? Can't you own up to a single bloody emotion, even if it means admitting you hate somebody's guts?" Lorraine was leaning toward him, eager and alive; the brightness Vincent had noticed in her eyes before had returned.

"I don't hate anyone."

"Oh, Derek." Lorraine reached down and recovered her glass. "You might keep it locked away inside, but that doesn't mean it's not there, festering away. All that ill will, gurgling around down there in your gut, growing …"

Before she could finish, Derek was on his feet and heading for the door. A smile on her face, Lorraine lifted her glass high, toasting him on his way. Footsteps faded, then stopped. Vincent was conscious of the clock ticking on the wall, of the glass tilting dangerously in Lorraine's hand. Somewhere in the house, a door slammed.

Ten

Until he had fallen from grace into the arms of Helen Siddons some two years previously, Resnick's immediate superior, Jack Skelton, had been an evangelist in the cause of cleanliness and Godliness, healthy bodies making healthy minds. "That man," as Resnick's colleague Reg Cossall had been heard to say, "doesn't just think he's holier than Jesus Christ; he thinks, given a standing start, he could take him over fifteen hundred meters."

But the affair with Siddons pulled Skelton's life apart. His daughter already off the rails in the way of teenage kids half the world over, his wife, Alice, had started doing her drinking and hollering in public, instead of in the privacy of their four-bedroom detached. For her part, Siddons tried easing herself out of the relationship and, when Skelton wouldn't let go easily, she dumped him flat. Fitness regime abandoned, private life the stuff of canteen gossip, Skelton began turning in for work later and later and, on occasion, not at all. Only a sixth sense of survival, allied to some unofficial counseling from his colleagues, pulled him back from the brink.

At his age, not so far short of his statutory thirty years service, Skelton was never going to get back the taut trimness he once had; but the surplus fat that for a while had hung around his gut and pouched out his face had disappeared, his shirts were crisp and white once more, suits clean and pressed, every paper clip and piece of paper on his desk knew its exact place.

When Resnick knocked and walked into the superintendent's office that evening, it was almost as if nothing had ever happened to throw Skelton's life off course; except they both knew that it had.

"Jesus, Charlie, why didn't they tell us?"

"Sir?"

"Prison Service, letting someone with Preston's record home for the day, you'd have thought somebody would have had the nous to let us know. Pick up the telephone, fax, send a bloody e-mail—this is the communications age, or so we're told—but no, nothing, not a sodding word. Didn't even occur to them to request assistance, I suppose."

Resnick shrugged. "Likely knew what headquarters'd say, low priority, staff shortages, look after your own."

"They still could have asked."

"Maybe."

"Damn it, Charlie, think of all the hours it's going to cost us now. As if we didn't have enough on our plate with a bloody range war building up out there. What's the latest on all that, anyway? This shooting and what went on at the club—linked, is that what we're thinking?"

"Looks that way."

"I'll need a report, Charlie. The Chief's been hollering down the phone."

Resnick nodded. There was nothing like a bit of media activity for stirring interest from way on high.

Skelton eased his chair back from his desk and reached into a side drawer. "This other business—I pulled Preston's file."

"It was your case."

"Preston and three mates," Skelton continued, "they took off a wages van in Kimberley. New supermarket. One of the security guards fancied earning his money for a change. Soft bastard. Got himself whacked half to death with an iron bar."

"That wasn't Preston?"

Skelton shook his head. "Frost. Frank Frost. That sort of mindless violence was much more his mark. But Preston had been the fixer; he'd put the team together, laid it out. Organize, he could do that. And what he had besides, his old man's betting shop—a better place for laundering cash'd be hard to find."

Plucking at the seam of his gray suit trousers, Skelton recrossed his legs. "Had him in for it. Twice. Three times. Him and his running mates. Nearest we came, talked Gerry O'Connell into saying he'd supplied Preston with the guns direct, which was more or less the truth. Couple of days later, O'Connell's cut himself shaving, thirty or so stitches till the surgeon stopped counting. Severe case of amnesia, O'Connell, after that."

"And Preston walked away."

"Cocky bastard. Came up to Reg Cossall and myself in the side bar of the Borlace Warren, says how he's heard poor Gerry O'Connell's had a nasty little accident and would we like to chip something in toward a collection he's getting up, send O'Connell some flowers maybe. Buy him a week in Skeggy. Convalescence."

Resnick smiled. "I can see Reg loving that."

"Came close to head-butting Preston there and then. Told him he was so full of shite, it wasn't any wonder every time he opened his mouth that was what came pouring out. Preston laughed in his face and slapped a tenner down on the bar, told Reg the next round was on him. Still laughing when he went through the door." Skelton slipped a pack of Silk Cut from his pocket, took out a cigarette, and rolled it between his fingers before pushing it back again, sliding the packet toward the corner of the desk and farther from temptation. "Next time I saw him, Preston, he was sitting back of the counter of the betting shop, place all closed up, sitting there with a bottle of scotch between his legs, two-thirds empty; his old man was in the garage out back with his head stove in."

"You must have asked yourself why he didn't make a run for it, try and get away?"

Skelton squinted up his eyes, remembering. "When we got there, seemed as if Preston had been waiting for us. "Some of your handiwork?" I asked him, and he turned to me and said, "The best day's work I ever fucking done. Only I should've done it a bastard time ago." And that was that, pretty much. I tapped him on the shoulder and told him he was under arrest and all he did was take another long belt at the scotch, then get to his feet with both hands outstretched. It was about as much as he ever said about it again, at the trial or before. Well, you know, you were around."

Resnick nodded. "For some of it, yes."

"Best we could figure out," Skelton said, "his father had been

48

cheating on him, money he was laundering; holding back, siphoning off the top. Michael fronted him out with it and that was the result. Truth or not, likely we'll never know. Not that it matters, not to us. He went down for it and that's enough."

"Till now," Resnick said.

"Anything by way of a sighting?" Skelton asked.

"One, unconfirmed. Leicester station, round the beginning of the rush hour. Quarter to five. There's a London train, leaves Leicester just past the hour."

"We've informed the Met?"

"Photo and description, faxed down."

Skelton folded his hands, one across the other. "All we can do."

Resnick nodded. "I'm putting a watch on the sister's place. Just for tonight. If Preston's looking for somewhere to hide out, it might be there. Carl Vincent was round there earlier, some sort of aggravation between Preston's sister and her husband ..."

"Lorraine," Skelton said, remembering. "That her name?"

"Yes. Sounds as if she and her brother were pretty close."

"After what happened with the old man," Skelton said, "it's hard to see her welcoming him back with open arms."

"Families," Resnick said ruefully, "who's to say?"

"Well," Skelton rose to his feet, signaling the meeting was over, "forty-eight hours, Charlie. You know the drill. If he hasn't come crawling home by then, it's doubtful he ever will. No reason to think Preston'll be any different to the rest."

Kevin Naylor was sitting alone in the front of a nondescript Ford Sierra, some seventy meters back along the street facing the Jacobs' house. Ben Fowles was covering the side and rear from the vantage point of the field, which he shared with a pair of ghostly horses and whatever unseen creatures startled him from time to time, scuffling through the grass close by his feet. The sky above was never quite dark, burning with the dull orange blur of cities, the moon a muted curl of white shadowed by slow cloud.

Naylor had a pair of binoculars resting in his lap and from time to time he would train them on the upstairs windows, where the curtains had been pulled across since well this side of midnight.

Most of the other houses were the same. Since one o'clock, not a single car had passed either way. A good, law-abiding neighborhood, Naylor thought, everyone tucked up in bed early, thinking pure thoughts. It was difficult, sitting there in the darkness, fidgeting a little to avoid getting a cramp, for his own thoughts not to wander off to where Debbie was curled up inside their bed back home, one of her hands lightly grasping her opposite shoulder, the other resting, innocently enough, between her legs. With any luck she'd still be there in the early hours and he could sneak under the covers without waking her; without her waking until she felt him pressing up against her.

In the field, Fowles checked the position of the hands on his watch and checked again, sure they must have stopped. There was no more than a shake of coffee left in the bottom of the flask in the side pocket of his anorak and he was rationing himself through the final hours. He'd tried singing all the old Clash songs he could remember, shouting out the lyrics silently inside his head, and now he was starting on The Jam. Songs he'd learned from his older brothers. He broke off at a movement back along the line of the fence, near a small thicket of trees: just a fox, treading its almost dainty way from one dustbin to the next.

At a little after two, one of the lights suddenly went on upstairs and both men were instantly on the alert, but not so many minutes later it went out again; most probably one of the children, Naylor thought, woken by a dream and needing to take a sleepy pee.

By the time they were relieved, a false dawn was rising behind the shadows of the buildings and a low mist was curling, silvery gray, above the gardens and their neatly trimmed hedges. All too soon, the hum of traffic that had never quite faded to silence would accelerate them into a new day.

Eleven

When Lorraine slid back into the bed in the early hours, Derek had moaned a little and stirred, turning toward her, one arm pushed across her body. Only gradually had she pushed it back. After that she lay there, unable to sleep, listening to the almost unbroken monotony of Derek's breathing. Since their row in front of the policeman, when she had let the alcohol and her tongue get the better of her, neither she nor Derek had spoken about what had happened. Both Sean and Sandra had walked round them on tenterhooks, unnaturally quiet, aware, as kids usually are, that something important was going on, without understanding exactly what it was.

Lorraine eased herself out from under the covers and into her slippers and dressing gown. Outside, it was breaking light. She set the kettle to boil and made tea. After yesterday's drinking, her head wasn't aching as much as it should. She tried to imagine Michael and where he was—hiding somewhere, hungry and cold, desperate—but no clear picture came to her mind. She remembered the look that had come to his eyes when he held her. Anger and something she didn't want to recognize. "You don't love him, do you? Derek. Even if you ever did, you don't love him any more. I can tell."

Then Derek himself had burst into the room, and Michael had been led away and she had not known when she might see him again. She still didn't know. He could be a hundred meters from the house or less; he could be a hundred, a thousand miles away. She didn't know.

She heard footsteps, Derek's, at the top of the stairs.

✦✦✦

51

Since his old Saab had given up the ghost, Resnick had been loath to replace it with something new. In need of transport, he either borrowed a vehicle from the station car pool or used one of the city's many taxis; mornings like this—crisp and clear, the sky a pale wash of blue—he opted for shank's pony.

Walking through the Arboretum, rose gardens rising to his left, Resnick realized he was thinking about Preston. Though he couldn't bring to mind the exact statistic, he knew close to nine hundred prisoners absconded every year. Knew, too, common wisdom said most of those not recaptured during the first few days remained at large. A surprisingly small number managed to leave the country, a handful more changed their identity and settled into a quiet, law-abiding life; most went underground and in the fullness of time resumed the same criminal activities as before. If they were caught, most often it was chance, simple coincidence, or because they were arrested for some new crime.

The prevailing police attitude, as Skelton had suggested, was we did our job once, nicked and tried and put away: if they get out again, not down to us; why waste the energy, bust our balls doing it all again?

Resnick waited for a gap in the morning traffic and crossed Waverley Street into the cemetery and the wavering path that would take him up through a succession of ornate Victorian tomb-stones and out on to Canning Circus and the Alfreton Road.

There were things about the escape he wanted to know. Had it been simply opportunist or planned? And, if the latter, who had helped and why?

He stopped off at the deli in the middle of the Circus for a coffee and an apple Danish, and carried them across and up the shallow steps into the station.

Millington was moments ahead of him, entering from the rear car park and waiting for Resnick at the foot of the stairs.

"Morning, Graham."

"Aye. For some. Came by way of the hospital, thought I'd see how the casualty list was shaping."

"And?"

"Ellis, lucky bastard, bullet passed right through without as much

52

as touching a vein. Damage to the jawbone, nothing major. Some plastic surgeon working on him right now, patching up his face with the skin off his arse." Millington laughed: "Be talking out his backside for real. But he'll live. More's the pity, maybe."

Resnick shot him a look, but said nothing.

"As for the rest of 'em," Millington continued, oblivious. "Feraday's out of intensive care, making good progress, apparently."

"And the chap from the prison service, Wesley?"

"Patched up pretty good, on his way out today."

Millington pushed open the door to the CID room and stepped back to let Resnick through. Sharon Garnett and Carl Vincent were at their desks; Naylor and Fowles sleeping off their apparently wasted night on observation.

"Sharon," Resnick said, "how d'you get on with that woman from outside Burger King, reckoned she got a good look at one of the suspects when they ran past her?"

Sharon made a face. "Went through all the likely faces down at Central. Didn't recognize a single one."

"Worth trying her again?"

"I don't think so."

Resnick sighed. "How about the other witnesses? Anything there?"

"I've been going back over the statements," Vincent said. "There's a few it might be worth talking to again. We ought to be able to get more on the car, at least."

"Okay, keep working on it. It's all we can do." Two phones rang almost simultaneously, and Garnett and Vincent moved to answer them.

"How about Preston, Graham? Any news?"

Millington shook his head. "Nothing at the sister's place last night. Quiet as the proverbial. There was one report come in late on, looked useful, bloke trying to charter a private plane, Tollerton Airport. When we checked it out, it was just some chap from Trent Water, executive, looking to fly to Guernsey for a bit of rest and relaxation. Worn out from carrying his wallet, I don't doubt."

Resnick grinned. "No follow-up to the sighting at Leicester station?"

"Nothing from the Met. Arranged for leaflets to be given out to passengers making the same journey today, the London train." Millington arched his eyebrows. "I shouldn't hold your breath."

"We're checking his old running mates?"

"I'll set Kev and young Fowles on to it when they come in."

Carl Vincent was on his feet, one hand over the mouthpiece of his phone. "One of the prison officers, sir. Evan. Wants to know can you spare him ten minutes before he shoots off back to London?"

Resnick glanced at his watch. "Tell him he stops by in half an hour, I'll give him five."

Lorraine had sent Sean back three times to change what he was wearing, Sandra sitting there in her school skirt and blouse, kicking her heels against the living-room carpet, waiting.

"Why can't you take us?" Sean asked. "Why do we have to go now? Take us on your way to work like you always do."

"Your mother's not going to work," Derek said, buttoning his jacket. "Not today, anyway."

"Aren't you, Mum?" Sean said. "Why not? Why not?"

"Are you okay, Mum?" Sandra asked. "You're not ill or anything?"

"No." Lorraine smiled, pushing the fringe back from her daughter's eyes. "I'm just a bit tired, that's all."

"After yesterday?"

"Yes, I expect so. I might go in later, anyway."

"You'll meet us after school?" Sean asked.

"Yes, don't worry, I'll meet you after school."

Derek was standing with his briefcase in one hand, car keys in the other, stranded between the children and the front door. Lorraine sensed him looking at her and raised her head, returning his gaze.

"You'll be okay?" he asked.

She nodded. "I'll be fine."

"I only need to make a few quick calls when I get in, no meetings, I could take a couple of hours off, come back ..."

The look in her eyes told him what he didn't want to know.

"As long as you're sure?"

"I'm sure." She kissed the children and bundled them out the door.

Evan looked more hangdog, if possible, than the day before. Guilty about what had happened and certain that he was returning to a reprimand at best, a suspension more than likely, he could scarcely bring himself to look Resnick in the eye. "I was wondering, you know, if there was any news? About Preston?"

Resnick shook his head. "Nothing definite."

"I see. I just thought that if, you know, you'd caught him, like, had an idea where he was, well it might … make things easier, I suppose that's what I meant."

"I'm sorry," Resnick said, Evan looking so pathetic he almost meant it.

"If you do … find him, I mean. I don't suppose you could let me know?"

"It'd be passed on," Resnick said. "The appropriate channels."

Evan blinked. "I see."

"Maybe, Evan," Resnick said, "there's something you can tell me. Preston, yesterday. At the funeral and after. You've been thinking about it, bound to have. Is there anyone special you remember him talking to? Off on their own, maybe?"

Of course Evan had been thinking about it; he'd been thinking of practically nothing else. Now he thought about it some more. "Only the sister, that's all, really. Worked up about that, he was. Important. He asked us specially, me and Wes. If he could talk to her alone. Just the two of them, you know."

"And you said …"

"I said okay. I didn't see the harm. I mean, I was outside the door all the time."

"Close enough to hear what they were talking about?"

Evan shook his head. "No. No, I'm afraid not." He looked at Resnick anxiously. "Was it important, d'you think?"

Resnick stared back at him. "Probably."

Thirty minutes later Resnick was on his way back out of the station, heading down into the center of the city.

Twelve

Resnick nodded thanks as Aldo slid the small cup of espresso along the counter toward him. The early edition of the *Post* lay folded against the till and Resnick pulled it toward him. It was strangely quiet in the market that morning, only a couple of middle-aged women sitting at the far side of the coffee stall with tea and cigarettes, chatting about prices and last night's TV.

The article on Preston's escape filled the whole page, raking up details of his father's murder and the subsequent trial. Underneath an old file photograph of Preston himself, grim-faced, being led into court, were the words of the judge: *It is almost beyond comprehension in a civilized society that any man would turn against his own flesh and blood with such violence and without apparent provocation.*

Provocation: an argument over money, Skelton had suggested, the siphoning off of Preston's ill-gotten gains. Well, maybe.

Realizing that, almost without noticing, he had finished his first espresso, Resnick ordered another.

For the first half-hour, Lorraine wandered slowly from room to room, enjoying the silence, willing herself not to look at the clock, the telephone. Without exactly daring to admit it to herself, she knew that what she wanted was for Michael to call, though she was unsure what she might say if he did.

Unable to settle to the *Mail*, she went into the living room and hoovered and dusted, tidying their few records and CDs, making neat piles of magazines. Upstairs in Sean's room, she collected up stray socks and fetid sportswear, filched a fold-out pin-up of Pamela Anderson from underneath the bed and Blu-tacked it neatly to the wall alongside Sean's team picture of Manchester United and above the one of Ryan Giggs. Along the landing, Sandra's room was pristine in comparison, everything folded, hanging, shelved; pony books stood alongside Mills and Boon romances and *Pride and Prejudice*; they'd watched that together on the television, agreeing, despite Sean's sneers, how gorgeous Colin Firth was as Darcy. A Greenpeace wall chart showing endangered species shared space with the Spice Girls and Gary Barlow from his days with Take That.

Lorraine sat on her daughter's bed and closed her eyes. "*You don't love him, do you? Even if you ever did, you don't love him any more. I can tell.*"

When the phone rang, she gasped and it was as if, for a moment, her heart stopped. The receiver was cold as she fumbled it to her face. "Hello?"

"It's me. I was just wondering how you were."

Eyes closed, she rested her head against the wall. "Derek, I'm fine."

"You're sure? 'Cause like I said, I can always …"

"No, I'm … Derek, it's sweet of you, but really, I'm okay. I just need a little time, that's all."

Silence at the other end of the line.

"Derek?"

"Yes?"

"You do understand?"

"Yes. Yes, of course. Only …"

"Only what?"

Another silence. Then, "It doesn't matter."

"Derek …"

"No, really. As long as you're okay. I'll see you this evening, yes? Take care." And the connection was broken.

Slowly, Lorraine replaced the receiver and turned away.

Cutting through toward the Jacobs' house, Resnick glanced at the well-tended shrubs and borders, and wondered what had been there before. Other houses, smaller, a spread of terraced back-to-backs perhaps, workers' homes so-called? Or had it all been open

57

ground, sprawling north from printing works and bakery, allotments possibly? Prize marrows, dahlias, runner beans.

For a couple of years, maybe more, his father had shared an allotment with another family from the Polish community. Resnick remembered watching him settle his cap on his head before setting out early on a weekend morning, trundling his wheelbarrow through half-deserted streets, fork and spade rattling against the rim. On lucky days, inside a sack, his father would be carrying manure, claimed swiftly from outside their house whenever the rag-and-bone cart had passed by; yellow-brown loaves of shit that lay steaming on the road's smooth surface and crumbled open at the spade's first touch.

Sometimes Resnick had gone with him, helped to dig shallow trenches, forked over brittle earth, watched as his father bent and prodded and poked. After an hour, he would become bored and wander off, constructing elaborate daydreams detailing how he would run away and where: the adventures that would be his if and when he left, wiped the dust of the city from his feet. Thirty or so years later, it still clogged his pores, veiled his eyes, clung to his skin.

And he regretted, looking back, all those times he had scorned his father's company, shunned his presence—times that could never now be recovered or replaced.

As Resnick pushed open the gate of number twenty-four, he glanced up and saw, framed for an instant in one of the upstairs windows, a woman with dark hair pulled back from the pale oval of her face, staring down.

Lorraine was wearing black trousers and a blue shirt, faded, which hung loose over her hips; pale tan moccasins on her feet. No trace of makeup on her face. The skin around her eyes was puffed and dark, the tiny lines at their corners etched deep. She offered Resnick coffee and he followed her past the foot of the stairs into the first of two reception rooms, the dining-room, he supposed; connecting doors partly opened into the living room beyond—a leather sofa, deep armchairs, cut flowers in a tall glass vase. Everything smelled of polish, wax, spray-on shine.

"Why don't you go on through?" she said. "I won't be long."

Where he had anticipated hostility, without knowing exactly why, the way she had greeted him had been pleasant enough, cordial, almost as though she had been expecting him. Well, Resnick thought, she had been expecting someone.

There was a photograph album on the coffee table, a pattern of red and gray diamonds across its padded front and a decorative tassel hanging from its side. Bending forward, Resnick looked inside: babies in prams, babes in arms, toddlers at the seaside, the park, the swings. Birthdays and Christmases, Sunday treats. A pair of dark-haired kids in T-shirts and shorts, check shirts and jeans. Michael—or was it Lorraine?—holding up a fish, a bat, a silver cup. Five, six, seven, eight. Inseparable, or so it seemed.

"That was Mum's," Lorraine said from the doorway. "Photo mad." She was carrying a tray with cups, a jug of milk, sugar, coffee in a cafetière. "Shunt it out of the way, will you? Then I can put this lot down."

She set down the tray on the table, gestured for Resnick to sit on the sofa, and took a seat opposite him in one of the armchairs.

"Funny, isn't it? All those snaps of me and Michael as kids—I suppose you don't think about it at the time, too busy having fun—but they must have been forever sticking that camera in our faces. Mum and Dad. Smile. Say cheese. But then, Derek and I, I expect we're the same with our two. Except for Derek, it's his video camera." She favored Resnick with a quick, uncertain smile. "You should see the number of tapes he's got stashed away."

Resnick nodded; made no reply.

"You've got kids of your own, I dare say."

He shook his head. "No."

She looked at him. "Not married, then?"

"Not any more."

It hung there, like motes of dust, still in the afternoon light.

"At the door," Lorraine said, "you said there wasn't any news about Michael."

"That's right."

"You've still no idea ..."

"Not really, no."

It was quiet: the ticking of a clock from the dining room, the faint whirr of someone's mower away up the street, the dull residue of traffic.

"I expect this is ready by now," Lorraine said, pointing at the cafetière. Reaching forward, she eased the plunger slowly down toward the bottom of the jar.

Used to being offered coffee which bore little resemblance to the real thing, pale watery cups of bland brown liquid made from instant coffee granules, worse still, powder, Resnick was pleasantly surprised that this looked dark and strong.

"Milk?"

"No, thanks. This is fine."

"When the other officer was here yesterday, I got the impression—he didn't say anything, mind—but I got this sense that he—you—knew where Michael might be. Hiding, or whatever."

Resnick shook his head. "I only wish we did."

Lorraine sipped at her coffee, put in sugar, half a teaspoon, enough to take off the edge. "I expect you're watching this place, aren't you?" she said.

The slightest of hesitations before Resnick said, "Yes."

"He'd be a fool to come here, then, wouldn't he? I mean, he'd know. He's not stupid."

"He might consider it worth taking the risk."

Lorraine staring at him now, trying to figure out how much he was guessing, how much, if anything, he really knew. "That's not too strong for you?"

"Just right. How I like it."

"Good. Good."

Out in the hallway, where Resnick had noted it attached by a bracket to the wall, a small table close by, pad and pen for noting down calls, the telephone began to ring. Eyes fixed on Resnick, Lorraine made no attempt to move. After six rings, it stopped.

"The officer yesterday ... Carl, I think you said ... he asked me about Michael at Mum's funeral ... if, when we were talking, he'd said anything, you know, about escaping."

Resnick looked at her encouragingly.

"I told him, no. Nothing. He didn't even mention it. Nothing at all."

"And that was the truth?"

"Of course. What do you think? I was as surprised as anyone." She leaned back a fraction on the settee. "If he had asked me, I'd have said, no, don't be so stupid. You'll only make things worse for yourself, that's all."

"But you didn't ..."

"What?"

"Say that. Tell him ..."

"No, of course not. How could I?"

"You didn't know."

"No."

Her eyes held Resnick's for a moment longer before she lowered her cup and saucer back on to the tray.

"And the blade? The razor blade?"

"What about it?"

He smiled at her with his eyes. "It came from your bathroom, I imagine."

It was difficult not to smile back. "I imagine it did."

"You told the officer ..."

"I said I didn't use them. Didn't use a razor. I don't, not any more. But I used to. My legs, you know." She did smile then, almost a grin. "I think there were some spare blades. Left over."

"You think?"

"All right. There were."

"And Michael took one."

"Like I said, I suppose so."

"And like you said, you don't know for sure?"

Lorraine shook her head.

"And that's the truth?"

"Yes."

Resnick nodded. He thought he believed her; about that, at least. He drank some more coffee; it was good. Not bitter. "I was wondering," he said, "if there was anybody special your brother was seeing before he went to prison? Someone he might have kept in touch with, perhaps?"

"Special? You mean, like a girlfriend?"

"I suppose so, yes."

She thought for several moments, or pretended to. "I don't think so."

"Nobody at all?"

"Nobody who meant anything special, no."

"He wasn't a monk."

Lorraine laughed with her eyes. "Michael?"

"So tell me."

"Look, Michael had women. Had them trailing round after him from the time he was sixteen, seventeen. He went to bed with them, of course he did, fooled around. But none of them were important, that's what I'm saying. None of them meant anything. Not really. Not ever."

"And you'd have known."

Head down for that moment, she glanced back up at him, sharp. "Of course I would."

Resnick reached toward the album: one photograph showing the pair of them, Lorraine and Michael, cross-legged on a patch of bleached grass; Michael, hair cut in a pudding-basin fringe and wearing a plaid short-sleeved shirt, watching Lorraine as she balances plastic skittles, four of them, unsteady on the palm of one hand; another, perhaps a year or two later, early teens, standing with arms around each other's shoulders, heads together, staring out, smiling.

"You were close."

"As kids, yes."

"Not since?"

"You know what happened."

"To your father, yes."

"I haven't spoken to Michael since before the trial, haven't seen him. Not once."

"Until yesterday."

"Of course."

"You blame him?"

For a moment, doubt crossed her eyes. "For killing my father? He did it; he was the one. Who else is there to blame?"

Resnick was looking at the photographs again, side by side where he'd placed them. "At first I wasn't sure, but you're the older."

"A year, that's all."

"He looked up to you, admired you."

"Not especially."

"Wanted to protect you."

"Against what?"

"Anything. Everything."

"Do you want some more of this coffee," Lorraine said, "before it gets cold?"

Resnick shook his head. "No, thanks."

She bundled the cups and saucers back on to the tray and took it to the kitchen. When she returned, Resnick was standing at the French windows, gazing out. Near the foot of the garden, where it met the cluster of trees, a robin was hopping around on a patch of recently disturbed earth, hopeful for grubs and perhaps the occasional worm.

He turned his head as Lorraine came to stand beside him. "You're lucky. Having all that open space. So close."

"I suppose so. There's a family up the street, keeps a couple of horses in the field. They let our Sandra ride one sometimes, but, of course, she wants one of her own."

"You're not so keen."

"I don't know. It's a lot of trouble and expense."

They were facing one another now, Lorraine quite tall, her head level with his shoulder. "It's a nice place," Resnick said. "You've done well. Your mum would have been pleased."

"You knew her?"

"A little. On account of your dad, mainly. We crossed paths a few times when he was alive. Professional reasons, I suppose you might say. I met Deirdre then. She seemed a nice woman. I liked her. Somehow she'd hung on to her sense of humor."

Lorraine smiled.

"No picnic, living with your dad, I imagine."

"How d'you mean?"

"Too used to getting his own way."

"He'd a mind of his own, yes."

"Michael, too, I dare say."

She shook her head and took a step away. "All that's over now.

63

Dead and buried." Catching herself, she laughed. "Those things we say, all the time, no thought to what they mean. And then one day they're not just stupid little sayings any more, they're true."

For a moment, he touched her arm at the fold of her cuff and was surprised by the coldness of her skin. "I was sorry to hear about your mum."

She nodded. "Thank you."

In the hallway he hesitated beside the phone, almost willing it to ring again.

"If Michael gets in touch ..." he began.

Lorraine was standing at the front door, holding it open. "I don't think he will."

"But if he does, you'll let us know. Let me know."

She held his gaze. "He won't. I'm certain."

Resnick stepped past her, out on to the paved path. Somewhere, hidden from plain sight, someone was watching them through binoculars, most likely bored, waiting to be relieved.

"Maybe we'll talk again," Resnick said.

"Maybe."

Before he had reached the gate, Lorraine had closed the front door and turned the key in the lock.

Thirteen

Michael Preston's known criminal associates were four: Frost, O'Connell, Forbes, and Cassady. Frost, Crazy Frank, was safely locked away in Broadmoor, living up to his name. Gerry O'Connell had followed a family connection to Manchester and got himself shot for his pains, twice through the back of the head. Two down, two to go.

Naylor and Fowles went looking for Millington and found him in the canteen with the remains of double egg, beans, and chips. Late lunch or early supper.

"This Arthur Forbes, sarge," Naylor said. "According to the file, you did him for burglary, five years back."

Millington grinned through his mustache. "Arthur Quentin Forbes, reformed character these days. Wandered into the Church of Divine Revelations Pentecostal mission down in Sneinton, more than half out of his head on a cocktail of crack cocaine, ecstasy, and Spanish brandy. Seems the Holy Ghost stepped in to claim what was left. You can find him most days, preaching the gospel in the Old Market Square or parading up and down Angel Row strapped into sandwich boards proclaiming the Word." Millington lit a cigarette. "I doubt if he and Preston've set up in business again, if that's what you're thinking."

"Which leaves Cassady," Naylor said.

Millington nodded. "Cassady, Liam H. Blagged his way on to some Government start-up scheme, set himself up in the security line."

"Gold Standard," Fowles said. "The outfit Jimmy Peters uses. Coincidence, d'you reckon? Nothing more?"

"Doubt it," Millington said. "Cassady's outfit must provide security for a good third of the clubs in the city."

"Worth talking to, though," Naylor said, "where Preston's concerned?"

Millington glanced up at the canteen clock. "Get your skates on, you'll catch him now with time to spare. Always assuming it's regular office hours he's working."

"Right, sarge."

Millington leaned back to enjoy his cigarette and ponder the possibility of rhubarb crumble and custard.

Liam Cassady had been born on the north side of Dublin, his father and his uncles working across the water for months at a time, sometimes remembering to send money home, sometimes not. When he was fourteen, Liam stowed away on the Dun Laoghaire-Holyhead ferry and found his old dad behind a pint of Guinness in a Cricklewood pub, one tattooed arm round the shoulders of a dark-haired woman who definitely wasn't his mum. His father swore him to secrecy, boxed his ears, and sent him back home. When Liam tried the same dodge three years later, his dad stood him a pint and a large Bushmills to boot, introduced him to all his mates and, within a matter of days, had set him up with a slow-witted girl from County Mayo, working as a chambermaid in a hotel near King's Cross.

Cassady soon fell in with a bunch of tearaways who did their drinking in the Archway Tavern. After chucking-out time, they'd amuse themselves by picking fights in the Irish dance hall on the Holloway Road, or doing a bit of breaking and entering in the quieter streets between Hornsey and Palmers Green. Quite a bit.

Soon Liam had money and didn't mind spending it. His girlfriend now was a would-be photographic model with a Scottish mother and a Trinidadian father. When Liam decided his patch of north London was getting too hot for comfort, the law having carried off three of his mates to the local nick in as many weeks, she followed him north to Liverpool. And Warrington. And Leeds. Jacky, that was her name, though Liam liked to call her Jack.

He still saw her from time to time, even after two abortions, a miscarriage, two marriages—one each—one divorce—hers—and two children—his and Jean's.

Jean, Cassady had met after he'd arrived in the East Midlands and was doing the occasional spot of casual laboring by day, hanging out with the lads at night. Michael Preston and the rest. Great days. Five jobs they'd pulled off, five in eighteen months and though the law had their suspicions, when it came to hard evidence they didn't have jack shit.

And Jean, Cassady thought, was different. They got married and moved into a house in the Meadows, intent on settling down. Jean: he liked to call her Jeanie. It was all a long time ago.

They were still married, though; two boys, Jimmy and Dan. After the second, Jean had turned away from him and now Liam met Jacky every month or so, always a hotel, always out of town. Jacky was living in Sheffield and they tried to find somewhere in between. Jean knew, of course, though it was nothing they ever discussed; she knew and in a way she was happy; if he was getting what he wanted from Jacky, it took the pressure off her. Live and let live, it was the best way.

Fowles had given himself a final check-over in the mirror of the gents before leaving the station: chinos, button-down Ben Sherman shirt, blue zip-up jacket with leather facing on the collar, brown leather shoes with a heavy lugged sole. Alongside Naylor, who was sporting one of his suits from Man at C&A, he looked a regular fashion item.

"Just remember," Naylor warned, "no going in heavy."

"As if."

"Ben, I'm serious."

"I know, I know."

Gold Standard Security had its office on the first floor of a postwar building close to the Ice Stadium. Pale brick and iron bars across the windows on the ground floor. Fowles winked and pressed his finger to the bell.

They were buzzed up into a single room that stretched from front to back, with a tall walk-in cupboard to the left of the door. There were two desks: one near the rear window and unoccupied now, was used by the woman who came in three afternoons a week and issued invoices, made payments, did what she could to keep things in order; Cassady himself looked up from behind the other and smiled a lopsided smile. "Gentlemen ..."

Shelves behind Cassady's desk were mostly taken up by box files, cartons, telephone directories, and a few paperback thrillers—Grisham, Dick Francis, Tom Clancy. A television set stood on a low table within Cassady's easy range of vision. The security monitor was at one side of his desk, a computer on the other.

"This will be about the other night," Cassady offered. "That business at the Hot Spot."

"Will it?" Fowles said.

"What else? I gave our man a right bollocking, you can imagine. One more cock-up like that and he's out. Not the way to handle things at all." He looked serious for a moment, then grinned. "Pull over a couple of them chairs, why don't you? Take the weight off your feet."

Neither man moved.

"Michael Preston," Naylor said.

Cassady's brow furrowed. "Preston?"

Fowles shook his head. "Your mate, Michael Preston. That's who we're looking for."

"Who?"

Fowles laughed out loud. "What's that meant to be? A joke? Good crack? See that, Kev? Straight-faced. Clever. Natural comedians, the Irish. You are Irish? Flair for language, it's well known. James Joyce. The Pogues. You've not got *Ulysses* on your shelves, I see. No, well, better kept at home. Bedtime reading. He was a filthy old sod, Joyce, but then what can you expect from a man who never left the house without his collection of women's dirty knickers. We'd have had him locked up for it, no two ways. Where is he, then, Michael Preston? And don't tell us you don't know."

"I don't know."

"But you know who I mean?"

"Yes, of course."

"You've seen him," Fowles said.

"I have not."

"Heard from him?"

"Not a word. Not for years."

"How often did you visit him in prison?" Fowles asked, toward the window.

"I didn't."

"We can check."

"Half a dozen times, no more than that."

"How come? I mean, I thought you were close, went back quite a way?"

"He didn't want it, didn't want any visitors."

"You know why?"

Cassady hunched his shoulders forward. "He found it easier. You know, to do his time."

Fowles took three strides toward the cupboard and rapped smartly on the door. "It's okay, Michael, we know you're in there. You can come on out now."

"Is he always like this?" Cassady asked.

Naylor shook his head.

"You don't mind if I take a look?" Fowles said, giving the handle a deft tug.

"Help yourself."

"No, it's all right." Stepping away, Fowles peered down at the papers piled on the accountant's desk.

"You're saying you've no idea ..." Naylor began.

Fowles interrupted him with a shrill whistle. "Is this all they get?" He was holding up a sheet of headed notepaper, high in front of his face. "Your blokes. Fiver an hour? Maintaining peace and tranquility among the night-clubbing classes. Turning their backs on the sale of a few Es. Don't seem much."

"Are you looking for work yourself, then?" Cassady asked. "Is that it?"

"He will be," Naylor muttered.

"Moonlighting," Cassady said, "that's the thing. I've more than a few of your fellers on my books already."

"Your opinion," Naylor said, "Preston. You know him. Used to. Where would you say he is now?"

"After twelve years?" Cassady shook his head. "Out of the country. Far as he can. Somewhere you can't get your hands on him and good luck. He's served his time."

"Not exactly."

"Will there be many more questions?" Cassady asked, leaning back a little in his chair. "Only I've a couple of inquiries to reply to and then a site I need to go off and inspect. Theft from building works, heavy equipment—kind of thing we're being called on to deal with more and more."

Reaching toward the computer, Fowles pressed a button and Cassady's screen saver disappeared instantly from sight. "When he sends you a postcard," he said, "Rio, wherever. You might just let us see it, check the postmark, put our minds at rest."

"Well," Fowles said, as they stepped back out on to the street, "don't know about you, Kev, but I thought that went pretty well myself."

Kevin Naylor didn't say a thing. Just watched as Fowles slid out into the light one of the sheets of paper he'd purloined from the top of Cassady's assistant's desk.

"List of all the blokes he's had working for his outfit in the past six months," Fowles explained. "Run it through records, compare and contrast. What's the betting it throws up one or two interesting names?"

Sharon Garnett and Carl Vincent were getting nowhere sifting through the witnesses to the Ellis shooting. So when Resnick asked Sharon if she could find the time to run a check on Lorraine's—and Michael's—family, she was glad of the diversion.

Resnick was ready to pack it in for the day and considering a quick half over the road before heading home when Sharon knocked on his door.

"Preston, sir. Now that his mother's dead, there's only the one sister, Lorraine, close family anyway. She works for this small printer's, part-time, ordering supplies, accounts, that sort of thing. Derek, her husband, he's a divisional sales manager for a paper suppliers." Sharon grinned. "More than likely how they met. But anyway, nothing out of line, not as much as an unpaid parking fine between them. Surprising, maybe, the kind of example Michael and his father had set. In fact, the only one who seems to have blotted her copy-book's the husband's sister, Maureen. Runs a clothes shop off Bridlesmith Gate. By Design. Second-hand, but pricey. Out of my league, anyway. She's had a couple of warnings from the Inland Revenue, discrepancies in her VAT returns. And once what looks like a fairly serious inquiry about handling stolen goods."

Resnick perked up and looked interested.

"Seems this customer went in and found several pieces that had been nicked from her place in the Park just the week before. Jean Muir skirt, one or two things like that. Hanging there on the rail marked 'New Arrivals.'"

"She wasn't charged?"

"No. Gave the clothes back, profuse apologies, offers of fifty per cent off. You can imagine. Claimed she'd bought the stuff in all innocence from someone who walked in off the street." Sharon shrugged. "Well, who's to say? It's the kind of business she's in."

Resnick shuffled papers on his desk. "I don't really see how it fits in. With Preston, I mean."

"Maybe not. I just thought, if you reckoned it worthwhile, I could call round, have a word."

Resnick shook his head. "I don't think so. Get back on the shooting. But thanks, anyway.

"Right, sir." Sharon was thinking she might drop in there some time anyway. By Design. She might come across a bargain, you never knew till you looked.

Resnick and Millington were in the old public bar of the Partridge, the pair of them savoring Speckled Hen on draught.

"You'd best watch out," Millington said, something of a gleam in his eye.

"How's that?"

Millington nodded at the pint glass in Resnick's hand. "I'll have you enjoying a decent ale yet."

Resnick laughed. "Instead of that Eastern European muck, you mean?"

"You said it, not me."

"Young Fowles," Resnick said a few moment later. "How d'you reckon he's settling in?"

"Ben? Bit of a motormouth, given half the chance. Fancies himself maybe a mite too much. But plane away a few raw edges, he'll do fine."

Resnick sank another inch of his pint. "Someone likely said that about Mark Divine a few years back."

"Aye, you and me both."

"And we'd have been wrong."

"Some things you can't allow for; some people."

"Seen anything of him lately? Mark?"

Millington shook his head. "Rang him a few weeks back—well, tell the truth, must be a month or more—you know he's got that new place, top of St. Ann's, not that far from you—anyway, hear him tell it, life couldn't be better."

"Working?"

"Driving job; one of these overnight delivery places. Got him rushing all over. Doubt the pay's great, but at least it's something. Keeps his mind off things."

Resnick was thoughtful; there were times since Divine had left the Force when he'd wondered if there weren't more he could have done; but the odd meal, the occasional drink aside, Divine had made it clear handouts were not what he was looking for. Intervention, however well-meaning, was not to be encouraged.

"Another?" Millington asked, holding up an empty glass.

"Best not."

"Hannah?"

Resnick shook his head.

The cats were waiting, patiently or impatiently, depending on temperament. There were dark beans in the freezer ready to be ground, pepper salami, blue cheese, cos lettuce, and cherry tomatoes in the fridge, light rye with caraway in a plastic bag on the side. Also in the fridge, a bottle of Czech Budvar that had survived three whole days. Next to the stereo in the front room, there was a CD of tracks by the clarinettist Sandy Brown, which Resnick had picked up at the record shop in the West End Arcade but not yet had the chance to play.

He had heard Brown once live, a studiously irascible Scotsman equipped with a withering tongue and rich, biting tone on the clarinet, which he made sound, with his dramatic whoops and glides up and down the register, like no other jazz player Resnick had ever heard. The Gallery Club, that's where it had been, the place up in Canton Bill Kinnell held together for a while with promises and sealing wax. "Splanky," Resnick remembered, and, more especially, "In the Evening," Brown's blues-edged voice so raw you could have used it to sharpen a pair of shears.

Brown had died in nineteen seventy-five, too many years short of fifty.

Resnick played the CD while he was eating his sandwich, sinking his beer, stroking the ears of the smallest cat, the photograph he had seen at Lorraine Jacobs's house drifting unbidden into his mind. Young Preston watching his sister with what? Pride? Admiration? Love?

When Resnick finally went upstairs, he fell asleep before remembering to set the alarm. In the event, it didn't matter.

Fourteen

Five forty-five. In his dream, Resnick is shackled into an old-fashioned pair of stocks in front of a full complement of constabulary and ordered to explain exactly how he will reorganize policing in the city after the millennium. Sweat lies slick along his back.

It took him several moments to recognize the voice of Anil Khan, now a member of Helen Siddons's Major Crime Squad. "This escaped prisoner," Khan was saying, "something just came through, I thought you might be interested."

"What? A sighting?"

"Not that definite. An incident out at Field Head; small village, apparently, north of the A50. Out past Charnwood Forest, according to the map. Anyway, a man was attacked as he was backing his car through the gate, and the car stolen. The man was tied up with baling wire, taped across the mouth and eyes, and dumped in his own barn. Took him the best part of two days to get free."

"Hurt?"

"Not too badly, apparently. Shaken up more, I think. Hungry. Dehydrated."

Resnick was on his feet now, blinking himself fully awake. "What else was taken?"

"Aside from the car? Sixty pounds or so, all the cash he had with him. Keys, of course. Doesn't have a credit card. Oh, and it looks as though whoever it was helped himself from the kitchen."

"And you think it might have been Preston?"

"Right area, sir. Got to be a possibility."

Resnick was trying to ignore one of the cats, nudging against him with its head. "How long ago was this reported?"

"Three this morning, Leicester. Someone a little slow perhaps, putting two and two together. Came through to us in error. I thought I should call you."

"Okay. Thanks, Anil. I'll get myself over there."

"There's a couple of officers out there from the local station. I told them you might be on your way."

"Right, thanks. Oh, and the car, you've had it listed as missing?"

"Priority. Toyota estate, eight years old, maroon."

"Good. And Anil, one more favor. Give it an hour or so, then ring Graham Millington at home. Tell him what's happened and ask him to hold the fort till I get back."

Resnick thanked him again and hung up. Before sticking his head under the shower, he called Carl Vincent and was slightly thrown when it was Vincent's partner who first answered the phone. "Rise and shine," Resnick said when Vincent himself came on the line. "May be nothing in it, but it might just be Preston has shown himself. Charnwood Forest. Down near your old patch, isn't it? You can pick me up on the way."

PC Kenny Rothwell was pale-faced, ginger-haired, his tie askew and the top two buttons of his uniform shirt undone. He made a poor attempt at fastening them as Resnick and Vincent approached.

"What's the situation?" Resnick asked, identifying himself.

"Victim's in there, sir. Winscale. Harry, I think. WPC Clive is with him."

"Shouldn't he be at the hospital?"

"He says not, sir."

The house was small, most likely an old farm laborer's cottage, once white plaster walls now various shades of patchy gray; small square windows with rusting metal frames. To the rear there was a large vegetable plot, a smaller one to the side and beyond this a chicken coop in need of some repair, and a low barn with a slanting roof. Reddish brown hens skittered half drunk, pecking hopefully at the hard ground.

"Whoever it was," Resnick said, "he went in the house?"

"Looks like it, sir, yes. There's food missing and ..."

"So it's been dusted for prints?"

"Not yet, sir, no. Scene of Crime are still on their way." Rothwell managed to look guilty of tardiness on their behalf.

"No danger of anyone running round in there, getting their clammy hands all over everything?"

"No, sir. Mary … WPC Clive'll make certain of that."

Resnick looked past Rothwell toward the barn, where a small pile of logs had been stacked since winter. The early morning air was decidedly balmy, promising another warm day. "That's where he was tied up?"

"Back there, sir, the barn, yes. Nothing's been touched."

"Okay. Carl, why don't you and the constable go and take a look? I'll talk to … Winscale, is that what you said?"

Rothwell confirmed that it was and Resnick walked past him toward the cottage.

The ceilings were low and even though Resnick negotiated the first beam successfully, he fell foul of the next. Standing in the small living room in her uniform skirt and blouse, WPC Mary Clive winced on his behalf.

Harry Winscale was sitting at a square, gate-leg table, head down, dark hair falling toward his eyes, cradling a mug of tea in his hands; he was wearing an old brown jacket over a green shirt, collar pushed up at one side. Resnick put him at between fifty and sixty years old.

"There's tea in the pot," Mary Clive said. "I could freshen it up."

"Thanks."

So far, Winscale had scarcely lifted his head. Resnick pulled out a chair from the near side of the table and sat down. When the man did finally look at him, Resnick inquired how he was, then asked him to tell what had happened in his own words, taking his time.

Winscale took a slow drink of tea. "It was ten, ten-thirty, I was coming back from the pub. Drove in, where I always stick the motor, up alongside the house. Bugger hits me, don't know what with, but I doubt it were his fist. 'Fore I can get any balance, he's grabbed ahold o'me, smacked my head a few times agin the roof of the car." There was a scab, ridged, behind his ear, blood matted into his hair. "I recall him draggin' me across into the barn, maybe he hit us

76

again after, I don't know. Next thing, it's dark as buggery, like being down bloody pit, and I'm trussed up like a Christmas roast, some old bit of cloth stuffed in me mouth and taped across." His eyes held Resnick's. "Not a lot else I can say."

"The man, what did he look like?"

"He were a big bugger, I'll tell you that." And then, as the WPC appeared at Resnick's shoulder, "Beggin' your pardon."

"Tall," Resnick asked. "Heavy—what?"

Winscale studied Resnick for some moments. "Tall as you, I'd say; close enough, anyway. Not near as fat." Standing behind Resnick, Mary Clive suppressed a giggle. "Like running smack into a wall of anthracite, I'll tell you that."

"How about his face?"

"Not got a clue. Not really. Don't forget it was coming fast dark. 'Sides which, it all happened so quick."

"If I showed you a photograph ..."

"Be wastin' your time."

"And the voice? He did speak?"

"A little, aye. Hard, you know. Like he was used to snapping out orders. Army, maybe, something of the sort."

"Any kind of an accent?"

Winscale gave it some thought. "Nothing strong. Not as jumped out. If you'd said he was local, I'd not be surprised. Closer to Yorkshire than here, mind. Sheffield, say."

"And there's nothing else about him you can remember?"

"Isn't that enough?" Winscale spread his hands on the table. "Seems to me, you got an idea, pretty much, as to who the bastard is already."

Resnick pushed the chair back from the table. Whatever Mary Clive had done to the tea, it still tasted stewed, stewed and slightly sweet, but anything at that hour of the morning was welcome enough. "Your car," he said to Winscale, "if you're right and this is who we think, my guess is it'll get dumped, likely not come to any harm. We'll need to check it over, if and when that happens, but you'll get it back in one piece."

Winscale chuckled. "Best thing as could happen, far as I'm concerned, bastard thing gets wrapped around a tree somewhere, written off. Insurance can buy me some kind of van, four-wheel drive."

"Don't count your chickens," Resnick said.

"Christ!" Winscale laughed. "Don't tell me the bugger's had them away as well."

"Seems to be snapping out of it well enough," Resnick observed, "considering."

They were standing outside the front door of the cottage, the skies brightening around them, mist still waiting to be burned off the ground.

"Told me he was trapped beneath ground once," Mary Clive said, "working down at the face. Some sort of cave-in, apparently. Sixty-two hours before anyone tunneled through wide enough to drag them out. This would have been a picnic compared to that."

Resnick glanced round at the close rows of vegetables, potatoes, cabbages, arched sticks of runner beans, tomatoes under a cold frame, the ragged gaggle of hens. He'd noticed a sign propped inside, ready to set out on the road: *Fresh Farm Produce, Free Range Eggs.* "Bought this with his redundancy money, I dare say. Put it to better use than some."

"His wife left him after the strike. He bought this place soon after. Just enough for one, or so he says."

Resnick smiled. She was a plain-faced young woman in her late twenties, stockily built; she had a ready smile and twice the confidence of her colleague.

"You seem to have got on with him pretty well," Resnick said, nodding in the direction of the cottage. "Life story, almost."

"Glad for someone to talk to after what he's been through."

"See if you can't talk him into going to accident and emergency, have that wound checked out. Put a call through for an ambulance; better still, drive him yourself. He should have an X-ray, at least."

She smiled back with her eyes. "I'll see what I can do." Contacts, Resnick thought, tinted blue.

Carl Vincent was standing a short way off, talking to Rothwell. He broke off what he was saying and walked across toward Resnick. "What d'you think, sir? Our man or not?"

"Could well be."

"But why make his move when he does? Why not wait till he's farther down the motorway, closer to London?"

Resnick had been thinking about that. "Not so far from East Midlands Airport. Maybe fancies his chances of getting out of the country more from there, rather than getting caught up in all that extra security at Gatwick or Heathrow."

"Need a passport, though, just the same."

"Not so difficult," Resnick said. "Even inside. Couple of thousand, that was the last price I heard quoted. Get you a passport so well put together you'd be hard put to tell the difference." He smiled wryly. "No need to stop there, either. National Insurance number, credit account, invent yourself a new life for the right money. University degree, if it's what you fancy."

"And you think Preston would've been able to lay his hands on that kind of money?"

"I think he might. From what little I know, he could be the careful sort, keep a little stashed away."

"He'd need help, then. Someone on the outside he could trust."

"No doubt." Resnick scuffed at the ground with the toe of his shoe, checked his watch. "Not a lot more we can do here. And no sense hanging around till Scene of Crime've tipped themselves out of bed. Too much like waiting for the kettle to boil. If they come up with anything, they'll be in touch soon enough. We'd be best occupied closer to home." He grinned. "Move now, we should have time to stop for a bit of breakfast on the way."

Vincent smiled back, thinking, is that the motorway services, then, or the Little Chef on the A49? Two Early Starters, bacon crispy and well done, coffees, brown toast.

Fifteen

They were six miles short of the city when a message came through on Resnick's mobile: meet Sharon Garnett at Queen's Medical as soon as possible. Resnick was getting to feel more like a hospital consultant every day.

Vincent dropped him by the main entrance. Sharon was waiting just inside the doors, tired skin pouched around her eyes. "Getting to be a habit," she said.

Resnick nodded. "Fill me in."

They started walking along the central corridor.

"Forest Recreation Ground," Sharon said, "early hours. Jason Johnson drove in there with his girlfriend, Sheena Snape. Jason's sister, Diane, along with them. They'd been there a while when this fire-red Porsche convertible drives up, parks nearby. Just the one person inside." Sharon took a beat. "None other than Anthony Drew Valentine. Not just a Premier League pimp but, if the rumors are to be believed, a major drug dealer of this parish."

Resnick steadied his pace. "What happened?"

Sharon smiled. "The details are still open to question. But the net result's this—Johnson's in Intensive Care with a bullet wound to the neck and Valentine's in a private room on the floor below, a stab wound in the groin."

"Weapons?"

"The knife was easy enough to find; one of the paramedics took it out of Valentine's leg. No sign of the gun. There'll be a search party in there now."

They walked on toward the lifts. "Jason's been on the critical list since they brought him in," Sharon said. "They rate his chances as sixty-forty. He lost a lot of blood, but I don't know if it's just that. Maybe there's some infection. They're being cagey, not saying."

"Any possibility of talking to him?"

Sharon shook her head. "They'll page me if it looks like he's rallying round."

"And Valentine?"

Sharon laughed and rolled her eyes. "Fat bastard! I know him from when I was working vice. The kind who'll piss all over your boots and tell you it's raining."

"What's his story about putting a bullet in Jason Johnson's neck?"

Sharon laughed. "According to him, he'd driven in there looking for a bit of peace and quiet. I think the actual phrase he used was 'nocturnal meditation.'" She laughed again, caustically. "Talk about a little education being a dangerous thing. Specially for a nigger like Drew Valentine."

Resnick looked at her sharply; he knew that if he'd used the word himself, Sharon would, at best, have reported him, at worst, taken a punch and then reported him.

"So according to this particular story," she went on, "he's chilling out under the stars, Jason and these two girls are up to who knows what in the comfort of their Sierra and then this other guy suddenly appears …"

"Other guy?"

"Exactly. This other guy appears through the trees—you'll like this, it gets better—runs toward Jason's car and bangs on the window. There's a mess of shouting before Jason slides down his window and pow! Stranger pulls a gun and shoots Jason at close range."

"Valentine have any suggestions as to what all this was about?"

Sharon shook her head. "He's still figuring that out. What he does say, soon as he hears the shot, he jumps out of his car, the gunman runs off, and then, humane character that he is, Valentine hurries over to see if he can be of any assistance. Maybe he did St. John Ambulance when he was a kid in the Meadows. What he gets for his trouble is stabbed in the leg. I told him, Drew, that's all the thanks you get for coming to the rescue like a good citizen."

"And Jason, at the moment he's in no position to give his version?"

"Not a word."

"How about the girls?"

"So far, not saying a thing. Maybe a night in the cells will loosen their tongues. There were drugs in the car and Diane's already got one charge of possession. We might be able to hold that over her, force some kind of a deal."

The lift emptied out and Resnick and Sharon got in.

"Diane," Sharon said. "You know Jason turned her out on the street when she was fourteen?"

"His own sister?"

"I asked him about that, one time when I had him in for pimping. Starts singing at me, 'Family Affair'—you know that?"

Resnick shook his head.

"Sly and the Family Stone. Anyway, he tells me what he's doing— proud of it, right?—helping his little sister get on in the world. And then he says, 'Besides, she's the only one of my whores ain't ever holding out on me, not as much as a penny.'"

"You think he had Sheena working the street, too?"

"I don't know. But to my knowledge, no."

Resnick stood for a while, his head in his hands, fingers rubbing across his eyes. "Him and Valentine, quite a couple."

"Yeah, true meeting of minds."

"And Valentine's story, you believe it?"

"If it was inscribed on tablets of stone," Sharon said, "handed down from heaven with a choir singing, I wouldn't believe it."

Drew Valentine was in a private room with a uniformed officer sitting outside the door. Valentine was propped up against four or five pillows wearing a yellow Ted Baker shirt unbuttoned to the level of the sheets, his hair tied back in a ponytail. He was leafing through the pages of a style magazine, listening to music on his Walkman.

He grinned at Sharon as soon as she entered, choosing to ignore Resnick for as long as he was able. A small diamond in the shape of a star shone from his left ear, catching the overhead light.

"Hey, sister," Valentine called over the sounds tearing at his ears, "how you doing?"

82

Sharon reached down, disregarding the hand stretched palm up toward her, and tugged the headphone jack from the machine.

"Hey! That's Puccini, girl. *La Bohème.* You can't do that."

"I've brought someone to meet you, Drew," Sharon said, reaching for a chair. "Detective Inspector Resnick, my boss. And don't call me 'girl.'"

"Charlie, yeh." He gave Resnick a swift appraisal. "Heard of you, man. Seen your picture in the paper."

Resnick sat down at the opposite side of the bed. "So what gives?" Valentine said. "I mean, I don't see no grapes or nothin'."

"How about telling us what went on," Resnick said, "out on the Forest? You and Jason?"

"Oh, man, I already told her that shit."

"Your word, not mine." Resnick leaned in closer. "Now, the truth, okay?"

"I'm tired," Valentine said. "I shouldn't be answerin' no questions. You check with my doctor, see if that ain't what he says. No stress, no hassle. I have to rest."

"All in good time."

"Man, this is harassment, no other word for it." He eased himself back against his pillows. "You guys, always the same. Pulling the same old shit."

"And I suppose you're not," Sharon said.

"Hey, girl ..."

"I warned you not to call me 'girl.'"

Valentine ran the tip of his tongue slowly along his lower lip.

"You could save yourself a lot of aggravation," Resnick said, "if you came up with a story that fits the facts."

But Valentine was reaching under his pillows for his mobile phone. "Or I can call my brief and he'll be here in fifteen. And you know what his advice is gonna to be: nigger, button your lip."

"You forget," Resnick said, "whatever Jason says when he comes round ..."

"If he comes round."

"There are two other witnesses ..."

"Whores."

"Two witnesses who saw everything ..."

"Out of their sad heads and, besides, they ain't gonna tell you nothing."

"There's always the gun, Drew," Sharon said. "Interesting if it turns up with your prints on it."

Valentine's face widened into the broadest of smiles. "That gun, yeh—interestin' if it turn up at all."

Resnick leaned in suddenly close, his face inches away. "I want you to think about this: one way or another we're going to find out what actually happened. So which is easier? If we hear it from you first, or have to drag you in kicking and screaming once we've got all the facts? Maybe you should ask your brief that. Oh, and if I were you, I'd be praying Jason pulls through, or you may find you're facing a murder charge."

He got to his feet and Sharon followed suit. "Puccini, hmm?" Sharon grinned, dangling the wires of Valentine's headset from her hand. "Tupac a little too strong for you these days, Drew? Big bad man, getting off on 'Your Tiny Hand is Frozen.'"

As soon as he returned from the hospital, Resnick popped his head round the door of the holding cell where Sheena Snape was waiting to be interviewed.

He had good reason to know the Snape family well. The mother, Norma, struggling to bring up three kids more or less on her own, had already lost two sons: the youngest, Nicky, had been found hanging in his room while in local authority care; Shane, the eldest, was serving a life sentence for murder. Which left Sheena—and since Nicky's death, Sheena had been running pretty wild.

When he entered the room she was sitting stubbornly on the floor by the far wall, knees hugged against her chest, pale skin blotchy and hair a tangled mess, wearing Doc Martens, from which the laces had been removed, and a skimpy orange dress.

"Are you okay?" Resnick asked.

No answer.

"Sheena, are you okay?" he asked again.

"What do you think? Or fucking care?"

"Is there anything I can do? Your mum, does she know you're here?"

"Only if she's been looking in her crystal ball."

"Do you want me to tell her?"

Sheena spun her head like an angry cat. "Enjoy that, will you?"

"No."

But Sheena was already looking away again, staring at the floor. "Do what you fucking like."

Resnick went off and came back a few minutes later with a blanket, which he laid across the back of the solitary chair, where it remained, untouched. The uniformed officer relocked the door and shook his head. "Wants her mouth washed out. Ungrateful little cow."

"She's got," Resnick said, suddenly angry, jabbing a finger against the man's chest, "precious little to be grateful for. Something you might do well to remember."

It was close to midday, and Resnick was eating a sandwich on the run when a fax came through from the Scene of Crime team that had gone out to Field Head. There were prints, mostly partial, but one clear forefinger, smack on the fridge door, and it matched, without question, that of Michael Preston.

Two hours later, Resnick about to leave his office for a twice-postponed meeting with Jack Skelton, a call was patched through to him from Central station; the security staff at Birmingham International Airport had found a maroon Toyota with badly rusted bodywork and a missing offside rear light, seemingly abandoned in the short-stay car park.

Sixteen

Resnick knocked on the door of Skelton's office and went in.

Helen Siddons was standing, stony-faced, in front of the super-intendent's desk. She was wearing a blue-black suit with deep lapels, a black shot-silk shirt, and shoes with a definite heel. Her dark-brown hair was pulled back from her face and held with a large clip.

"Busy couple of days for you, Charlie, by all accounts."

"Busy enough."

Siddons's mouth, Resnick realized, was the startling red of his damson jam.

"Helen's been explaining her anxieties ..." Skelton began.

"I've been telling Jack what's going on's a bloody farce. A bunch of cowboys using one another for target practice and where's the fucking posse?"

"Helen's proposing ..."

"I'm sending a memo, with Jack's support, to the Chief Constable, suggesting in the strongest terms he sets up a special Task Force to deal with drug-related shootings."

"If that's what ..." Resnick began.

"Oh, come on, Charlie, what the hell else are they? And if we don't do something now, we're going to fetch up like Manchester or Bristol and worse."

Resnick exchanged a glance with Skelton and neither man said anything. Siddons took a cigarette from her bag and lit it with a silver lighter. "What I want to see, pro-tem, while we're waiting for the terms of reference of this Task Force to get sorted, is some sort of informal arrangement. Major Crimes, Drug Squad, yourselves—pool knowledge, act in conjunction where possible." She blew

86

smoke down her nose. "Nip these bastards in the bud." Slowly, she looked from one man to the other.

"Helen would ..."

"My squad could act as liaison ..."

"You want the investigation run through you?" Resnick said.

Siddons angled her head backward. "Someone has to coordinate, else we're all pissing in the wind." She almost smiled. "We have the technology."

"You've talked to Norman Mann about this?" Resnick asked.

"Not yet."

"You think he'll fall in?"

Siddons glanced toward Skelton's desk and Skelton took an ashtray from a drawer and slid it toward her. "The kind of success rate his squad's had recently, he should be taking help from the Brownies and grateful for it." She stubbed out the long end of cigarette and hitched the strap of her bag higher on to her shoulder. "Thanks, Jack. Charlie. I'll be in touch."

Siddons outside the room, Skelton leaned his chair back till it was resting on its hind legs and, for a moment, pressed both hands hard against his cheeks.

"You don't reckon maybe she's biting off more than she can chew?" Resnick said.

Skelton rocked forward. "Her specialty, Charlie. Spit 'em out later."

Resnick pulled up a chair and filled the superintendent in on developments. Despite a seemingly thorough search, no gun had been found on the Forest. Diane Johnson and Sheena Snape were still refusing to say anything.

"That sodding family, Charlie. Women like that—what's her name?"

"Norma," Resnick said quietly.

"Norma. Walking argument for bloody sterilization."

Resnick tensed himself to argue back, but knew there was little point: a lecture from the super about the evils of single-parent families, about the last thing he needed.

Skelton got to his feet and turned to the window, looking out through the tops of the trees toward the tennis courts in the upper

87

valley of the Park. Resnick wondered if the session was over, but no. "How about Preston, then?" Skelton said, turning. "This car at the airport, Birmingham. You think he's off sunning himself somewhere, some beach in Spain?"

"Points that way."

"You want to know what I think, Charlie? And I've seen him, remember, Preston. Spent time with him, too much." Skelton had settled on one corner of his desk and was leaning forward, his face close enough for Resnick to catch the mixture of peppermint and tobacco on his breath. "He's the kind who looks after himself, confident; thinks you can't ever get to him, not here." Skelton tapping his fingers briskly against his chest. "Not inside. The money from those robberies, I doubt he would've passed it all through his old man. I think he'd have kept something stashed away somewhere, invested even. When he went down, he'd have had somebody on the outside keeping it safe, keeping an eye. Passport, tickets, travel money—that's what he'd have used for those."

"I was thinking maybe the sister," Resnick said.

"You've talked to her recently, I'm not in the best position to judge. After what happened to the father, though, she'd not be the most likely. Not to my way of thinking. More likely someone he used to run with."

"Cassady's the only possibility there, far as we know. And then there's nothing to connect them, not recent."

Skelton stood away from the desk. "Fly bastard, by all accounts. But as for Preston himself, I were a betting man I'd say he's long gone, laughing at us from afar."

It made, Resnick thought, heading back toward his own office, absolute sense. Why then, deep in his gut, didn't it feel right?

Norma Snape's kitchen looked out on to a square of garden which had once been grassed, but was overrun now with weeds and littered with empty burger boxes and cans, tossed across the back fence by whoever was using the rear alley as a cut-through. When Shane had still been there, he would occasionally bestir himself from watching the afternoon racing on TV and set it to rights. Now it was simply another of Norma's good intentions, somewhere between persuading that bloke she'd been chatting with in the pub to bring round his tools and fix the boiler and getting something done about the leak in the front roof, something more permanent than the bucket she'd put out to catch the drips.

Several of the houses close by, Resnick noticed, were boarded up; one had been burned out, another stripped of all the tiles from its roof.

Norma answered the door wearing baggy sweat-pants and a white blouse that had been through the wash too many times, old tennis shoes on her feet. If Resnick hadn't known she was still under forty, he would have put her at ten years older.

"Sugar's on the side," she said, lifting the tea bag out of Resnick's mug before passing it across. "If you want it, that is."

Resnick was sitting at the melamine-topped kitchen table, doing his best to ignore the sandy-colored mongrel dog that was alternately nuzzling its head against his groin and biting at his shoes.

"Push him out of it, if he's a nuisance," Norma said encouragingly.

"No, it's okay. He's fine."

Norma reached over and took a whack at him anyway, the dog reacting with a snap at her hand and a low whine. "It's cats you've got, i'n't it? Remember you told me once."

Resnick nodded.

"Least they're not slobbering round you all hours, either that or carrying on to be let out, then barking to be let back in again. More of a mind of their own, I suppose you'd say. Independent." Norma sipped at her tea and made a face. "Gnat's piss!"

Resnick grinned. "I've tasted worse."

"We had a cat, you know. Nicky's it was, really. Well, it was him as brought it home. Buggered off after he ... you know, after what happened. Thought maybe it'd got run over, something of the sort. No such soddin' thing. Found itself a better home, couple of streets away. This old girl as feeds it bits of fish and chicken, bought it a fancy cushion to sleep on." Norma reached for her packet of Silk Cut and shook one loose. "Like bastard men, cats are. Always on the lookout for a better hole."

Leaning back, she lit her cigarette and, wafting away the first release of smoke, looked Resnick square in the eye. "It's our Sheena, i'n't it? Got to be. Only poor sod left."

Resnick told her the details, as much as she needed to hear, one man getting shot, another wounded, a quantity of drugs found in the car, more maybe than could be for personal use.

"Well," Norma said, when he'd finished, "least she'll not be able to say I never warned her. That lot she's been hanging out with, I knew it'd come to something bad. I told her. Told her she'd end up going the same way as her brothers and all she did was stick two fingers in my face and laugh. Well, now she'll be laughing on the other side of her own."

"You'll be wanting to go and see her."

"Will I, buggeration! Let her stew for a bit. Come sneakin' back with her tail between her legs. If she'll not learn her lesson from this lot, she never will. Next time, it'll be her they're draggin' out of some motor on the Forest with a bullet in her. Too late to say she's scutterin' sorry then."

Resnick swallowed down some more tea. "I don't know for certain what'll happen. Looks as if it'll not be my case. But I doubt they'll hold her, not more than overnight."

"They bloody should."

"Most likely she'll get police bail in the morning, it depends. At the moment she's not co-operating ..."

"Grassing, you mean."

"She was witness to a serious incident, a shooting ..."

"Oh, right." Norma pushing herself back from the table, up on her feet. "I've got it now. This is what it's all about, you comin' round here, butterin' me up. Mr. Sympathy. Oh, yeah. What you're after is me going down there, talking her into grassing up her own. Well, I'll not do it. I'll not and that's a fact." Norma glared at him, arms folded across her chest; the dog over by the back door growling, alerted by the change of tone in Norma's voice.

"Norma, I've told you," Resnick said, "it's not my inquiry."

"It's you that's bloody here."

"You had to be told what had happened. I thought it might be better if you heard it from me."

"You what? Why the fuck would you think that? Eh? You think I like having you here? Detective Inspector high-and-mighty Resnick. Slipping round here. Supping tea. How d'you think that makes me look up and down this street? Bastard police traipsing in and out. But no, you're too full of your own bloody puffed-up self to think of that."

With a slow sigh, Resnick rose to his feet, automatically taking his half-empty mug toward the sink.

"Bastard!" Norma struck the mug from his hand and it shattered on the floor. The dog braced itself on its hind legs and started to bark. "You think I like having you here in this house? Yeah? Do you? You really think I'd rather bad news came from out of your mouth? Norma, that lad of yours, we've got him locked up for murder. Norma, that bairn of yours, he's took his own life, hanged hisself, we just this minute finished cutting him down. Oh, yes, you can bet your days I love it when Mr. Charlie sodding Resnick comes round here, up to his armpits in bad news. I thought you'd rather hear it from me, Norma. Well, what I'd wish," Norma close to him now, pushing him back with the force of her words, "I'd never set eyes on your fat prick of a face at my door!"

Resnick held his ground for five long seconds before turning on his heels and walking out into the passageway, past the open living-room door, out through the front, and across to where four skinny kids with pinched faces and short cropped hair were loitering round the unmarked Ford he'd borrowed from the pool.

"Give us twenty pee, mister."

"Give us a fag."

When Resnick drove off, they raced after him, making signs mimicking masturbation, shouting abuse.

Seventeen

Early evening. Hannah Campbell stood in her small front garden, looking out across the expanse of the recreation ground opposite, its grass no longer the peculiarly vibrant green of midday or even mid-afternoon, but calming now into the softer shade that reminded Hannah of a particular dress her mother used to wear, muted and warm. The shadows of the railings and the trees standing close alongside them were soft and slowly lengthening and, from the middle distance, the cries of children clambering over the playground swings were faint, even musical. Off and on, scenes from Hannah's own childhood had been picking at the edges of her brain all day, and she knew the reason lay in the letter, French-postmarked, from her father: *My dearest Hannah, I hope you will understand …*

She stood a while longer outside the late-Victorian terraced house, with hanging baskets beside its blue door. She had bought the house several years ago, at a figure she could ill afford; but its position, traffic-free, so close to open space, yet near the center of the city, made it worth its price and more. Now she felt settled there, more so than anywhere since she had left her family home to go to university, not quite nineteen. At her next birthday she would be thirty-seven, nearing forty.

Preoccupied, she was startled to see Resnick, hands in pockets, turn into the path which led toward the front of the house. Was it two weeks since he had called round unannounced, or three?

They sat in the L-shaped kitchen-dining room at the back of the house, Resnick at the scrubbed pine table, his back toward the old range which Hannah never used, but kept for appearances. Hannah was moving between the table and the narrow strip of kitchen, washing greens for a salad, shaking lemon oil and vinegar together for a dressing, cutting cubes of cheese, spooning hummus into an earthenware bowl, heating ciabatta in the oven.

"Are you going to stick with beer, Charlie, or d'you fancy some of this wine?"

Resnick raised his glass. "Beer's fine."

Salad bowl in hand, Hannah paused before the table and smiled. "There's some work I have to do later, I hope you don't mind."

"No, why should I mind?"

"I just didn't want you to think ..." She shrugged. "You know."

"That I was going to stay the night?"

"Yes, I suppose ..."

He had followed her from the table and when she turned it was almost into his arms.

"That wasn't why I came, you know."

"A bit of sex."

"Yes."

"Slip back into the old routine."

"Is that what it was? Routine?"

She looked into his face. "Sometimes, yes, I think so. Don't you?"

"Maybe that's what happens."

"This soon?"

Resnick shrugged. His shirt was crumpled and his tie had been pulled off and draped across the same chair back as his jacket. His hair was something of a mess.

Hannah touched his wrist and felt the veins running under the cuff of his sleeve. "Why did you come round?" she asked.

"I wanted to see you," he said, but the pause before speaking was too long.

"The truth." Smiling at him all the same.

"I don't know. Does there have to be a reason? I don't know."

"Oh, Charlie ..."

"What?"

Reaching up, she kissed him close to the corner of his mouth. "You had a bad day."

"It wasn't good."

"You had a bad day and you didn't want to sit with the rest of your team in the pub and you didn't fancy going home to that barn of an empty house with nothing there but the cats, so you came here instead. You wanted company, comfort; someone, maybe, to hold your hand." She was holding his hand. "Charlie, it's okay. I understand. I just don't want to go to bed with you, not tonight. I don't want to make love. Is that all right?"

"Yes. Yes, of course."

After they'd eaten, Resnick wandered into the front of the house and switched on the light by the shelf where Hannah kept her small stack of CDs. He toyed with the idea of Billie singing "This Year's Kisses"—the ones which no longer meant the same; or the knowing irony with which she leaned back upon the beat and sang "Getting Some Fun Out of Life"; Lester Young's tenor saxophone adding its dry commentary to "Foolin' Myself."

Was that what he was doing? What both he and Hannah had been guilty of? The simple truth—Resnick caught himself smiling—the simple truth rarely existed outside of fairy-tales and thirty-two bars of popular song. And even then ... his mind went back to Hansel and Gretel, Little Red Riding Hood. Nothing simple there.

He slipped the Billie Holiday back into place and pulled out the Cowboy Junkies. Not exactly cheery stuff, but somehow, he knew, Hannah seemed to find consolation in the almost forlorn, floating pessimism of their songs—"Murder, Tonight, in the Trailer Park"; "This Street, That Man, This Life."

Sitting in the armchair, Hannah with her legs up on the settee, Resnick told her about his meeting with Norma Snape. Feeling sympathy for them both, Hannah listened: it was easy to understand why Resnick, acting out of all the best intentions, should feel hurt, rebuffed, misunderstood; but Norma—and she knew, from her work, many women whose situations, while less extreme, were not so far removed from Norma's—Hannah could feel her helplessness and frustration, a life lived forever at the mercy of circumstance and patronizing authority.

94

"What will happen to her, Charlie? The girl."

"Sheena? Maybe nothing much, not this time. But in the future ..."

"I remember her, you know. She was in my class at school. Just for a year. And in all that time she barely spoke, other than to her mates. Did as little work as possible, enough to steer clear of trouble. And I don't think we did anything—I did anything—in the whole three terms that engaged her imagination one scrap." Leaning sideways, Hannah retrieved her glass of wine. "I didn't do anything about it, Charlie. I didn't even try. All my energies, they went on the dozen or so who could be real pains if you gave them half a chance, them and the few who were really good, genuinely interested, off writing poems in their spare time, plays, borrowing the tape-recorder to make a documentary about where they lived. Those were the kids I really bothered about. That's what was rewarding, that kind of response. As long as Sheena showed up and shut up, I didn't care."

"What's all this?" Resnick said, setting down his own glass and moving across to the settee to sit beside her. "Taking on my guilt to make me feel better?"

Hannah smiled and brushed her hair away from her eyes. "Not really. Not consciously."

"You're not to blame for whatever's going wrong in Sheena's life."

"Aren't I?"

"No." Resnick's arm was resting on Hannah's leg, his hand on her knee. "No more than we all are."

"And we punish her for our mistakes."

Resnick shook his head. "That's too easy."

"Why?"

"She may not be academically bright, but she's not stupid. She has to take some responsibility for her own actions."

"Yes. I know."

There had been a moment, crossing the room, and later, when Resnick had thought he might kiss her, but now it had gone. He was looking at his watch.

"Busy day tomorrow," Hannah said.

"You or me?"

"Both."

At the door, she slipped her hand around his waist enjoying, however briefly, the solidity of his body, the inward curve of his back. She kissed him on the mouth, but before he could respond she had stepped away again and was wishing him goodnight. "Call me, Charlie."

"Of course."

"No, I mean it."

"Yes. I know." Resnick walking, crablike, down the path.

At the railings, he raised a hand and in the failing light she smiled. Inside, she leaned back against the door, his footsteps faint and growing fainter till they disappeared. Some months before, happy, half-drunk, turned on, she had asked him to join in the fantasy that was playing, unbidden, through her mind; the man heavy on top of her as she struggled, pinning her arms to the bed with his knees; a voice she barely recognized as her own, shouting, "Hold me, Charlie! Hold me down!" For Resnick, it had been too close to the realities of his working life: power, force, aggression. Neither of them had talked about it since. But it had been the first wedge between them; nothing afterward had been quite the same.

Hannah carried the glasses through into the kitchen and rinsed them under the tap. Not so far short of eleven; too late, she reasoned, to phone her mother now. Her father's letter was where she had left it, out of reach if not out of mind. She stood for a while at the upstairs window, gazing out into the dark. Denying the impulse to call Resnick, tell him she'd been stupid, jump in a cab, come on round. Her father's writing was oddly small, squirrelly. She had needed to read the words twice before their meaning became clear. *Robyn and I have decided ... never imagined I'd want to get married again ... important to both of us ... writing to you before I say anything to your mother ... easier coming from you ... I hope you will understand.* He had even tried for a joke: *now Robyn's reached the grand old age of thirty, I think she wants to settle down.* And what, Hannah thought? Sell the place in the French countryside Robyn and her father had spent years doing up

96

and buy somewhere larger? Move back to England? Write another best-selling novel? Have children? A child.

She didn't realize until it was done that she had torn the letter into smaller and smaller pieces, which went fluttering like confetti down around her feet where she stood.

Eighteen

It was early enough still for Resnick to rub his hands together for warmth as he walked. Mist was wreathed faintly around the trees edging the grounds of the university and, off to the east of the city, the sun showed only as an orange smear above the waters of the Trent. He had considered wearing a topcoat, before deciding against it, and the material of his gray suit was feeling not only shiny but thin.

Parker's café was facing him now across the boulevard and he waited for a pause in the traffic swishing off the Dunkirk round-about before hurrying toward it. In younger days, Parker's had been an informal meeting place for Resnick and a clutch of his fellow officers, and for Norman Mann it seemed it still was.

There was steam on the insides of the windows and the heat struck Resnick, not unpleasantly, as he entered. Heat and cigarette smoke, the savory smell of bacon frying. For several moments, he wondered why he had stayed away so long.

Mann was on his feet, leaning over one of the other tables, joking with two men in dark overalls. As usual, there were a number of fire officers from the station next door, uniform jackets unbuttoned, celebrating the beginning or end of a shift with oversized mugs of tea.

"Charlie." Breaking off his conversation, Mann greeted him with a strong handshake and slap on the shoulder. "Let's sit over here. This corner. I've already ordered mine. Sort out your poison and we'll talk."

At the counter, old habits quarreled with new-fangled ways, his own leanings toward moderation linked to Hannah's lectures about healthy eating and coronary failure. In addition to coffee, no sugar, no milk, he settled for a sausage sandwich with brown sauce and grilled tomatoes on the side. Set against Mann's full breakfast with black pudding and fried bread, it looked positively frugal. But then, Resnick told himself, it wasn't his stomach that was straining shirt buttons to the last thread, or needing a strongly buckled belt to hold it aloft.

"Cutting down, Charlie?" Mann asked, pointing across the table with his knife.

Resnick shrugged.

"Only live once, Charlie. Enjoy it. That's my motto. And bollocks to anyone who says different. Present company always excepted."

For several minutes, they ate and said nothing, the blur of conversation rising and falling around them. How many wives was it now, Resnick wondered? The third Mrs. Mann or possibly the fourth? Each of them, those Resnick had seen, no taller than Norman's shoulder, dark-haired, dark-eyed, soft-spoken; submissive, seemingly, until the day those eyes were opened and they packed their bags and walked away. He didn't change and neither did they.

Mann balanced his cigarette on the rim of the ashtray and broke off a piece of fried bread with his fingers. "Siddons, Charlie, I know she's been on to you as well as me. You and Jack. Getting her knickers in a rare old twist about this business with Valentine. Looking to poke her skinny nose in." He broke the surface of his egg with a corner of the bread, dipping it first in tomato sauce, then mustard, before lifting it to his mouth.

"Fucking Valentine, we've been after that black bastard for fucking months. Run a tap on his phones, stripped that fancy Porsche of his down to the chassis, got more intimate with the inside of his house than a fucking death-watch beetle. Never come up with anything more than a couple of spliffs and a packet of Neurofen."

A sliver of reddish yellow slid, unimpeded, round the side of Mann's chin.

"He is dealing?" Resnick said.

Mann laughed and wiped a paper napkin across his face. "'Course he's bloody dealing. Even he can't live that way on social bloody security. But, try as we may, we've never been able to lay a hand on him. Not one that counts."

Resnick sipped his coffee. "So what? Lucky? Clever? What?"

"Fuck knows, Charlie. I don't." Mann speared a circle of black pudding. "Best thing could've happened, that youth'd been a bit more on target with his knife, lopped Valentine's tackle off and slung it out to the dogs. As it is, he'll get patched up good as new and that'll be the end of it."

"He shot somebody in the head."

"According to who? You've got witnesses, reliable? A couple of tarts with less brains between them than the average cockroach. And how about the weapon? Even if it does turn up, which I tend to doubt, you reckon it's going to have our man's prints all over it, nice and sharp? No, Charlie, it's a waste of time. My way of thinking, let Siddons flap around like she's running the show, keep her sweet. Comes up empty-handed, it's her bloody fault and not yours or mine."

Resnick cut the remaining half of his sausage sandwich into quarters and chewed thoughtfully.

"Moved, Charlie, don't know if I ever told you. Place out the other side of Arnold. New. You must come out some time. Bring that woman of yours. Teacher, isn't she? Gloria'd like that. Someone new to show it off to, rabbit with. You know what they're like."

Resnick nodded and not so many minutes later Mann looked at his watch. "Time I wasn't here." He scraped back his chair, slurped down a last mouthful of tea, and started toward the door. "Drop you anywhere?"

Resnick shook his head. "I'll walk."

"Got you under the thumb, has she? This woman of yours. Lose weight. Exercise. Have you down the gym next. One of them standing bicycles. Treadmill. Waste of energy, Charlie. All that effort and it never gets you anywhere."

Diane Johnson was having problems bringing the cigarette to her mouth. Her hands were shaking so much that after the fourth attempt Sharon Garnett reached across the table and steadied them with her own. For a moment, Diane looked Sharon in the eye before blinking away.

There were four of them in the interview room: Sharon and Carl

Vincent, Diane and her solicitor. A wooden table, a metal ashtray, stackable chairs. Attached to the wall was a tape machine with a twin deck and, above that, a clock. The duty solicitor, dandruff, spectacles, bored, angled away from his client, legs crossed, crosshatching doodles on his pad. Sharon sat up to the table, facing Diane, Vincent alongside her, his chair pushed back, taking the secondary role.

The only window was the small square of frosted glass reinforced with wire that was set into the door. Above their heads, the single strip of neon gave off a low, off-key hum. The air was stale and second-hand.

There were lines around Diane's eyes, small scab marks close to her mouth, dark on her dark skin. Her hair was a tangle of tight curls. It had been a long time since she had slept, slept well; a night on the skimpy mattress of the police cell hadn't helped.

Sharon handed Diane a box of matches and she snapped the first two, finally managed to light her cigarette from the third. She drew down hard and, eyes closed, let the smoke drift from her nose. After several more drags, her hands were still shaking, but not quite as much.

"I need my medicine," she said, a crack in her voice.

"You mean your drugs," Sharon said.

"My medicine."

"For which you've got a prescription."

"'Course I've got a fuckin' prescription."

Sharon's eyebrow rose.

"Temazepam, i'n'it? For my fuckin' nerves."

"One hundred and five capsules," Vincent said, speaking for the first time.

"What?"

"Jellies, Diane," Sharon said. "Over a hundred of them stuffed into a plastic bag under the front seat of the car. That's to say nothing of the hash in the glove compartment."

"What compartment? What car?"

"The one you and your mate, Sheena, were in when your brother got himself shot."

Diane screwed up her face and folded her arms tight across her chest. "I don't know nothin' 'bout that."

"The Temazepam or the shooting?"

"Neither." There were goosebumps down Diane's arms and her fingers rubbed her skin below her T-shirt sleeves.

Vincent eased forward. "Come on, Diane. You were there when it happened."

"Yeh, well, I was out my fuckin' head, right? No use asking me anythin'. Just forget it, right? Forget it."

"Diane ..."

"An' I want to see my brother."

"Jason can't see anybody at the moment," Sharon said. "He's in no fit state."

"I don't care. I want to see him."

"As soon as the hospital says it's okay for him to have visitors, then you can. But for now, you know, I've told you, he's still in intensive care. He's not seeing anyone."

"He'll see me."

"Diane, will you ever listen?"

"I'm his next of fuckin' kin."

There were tears close to her eyes. Sharon reached out for her hand and Diane pulled it away. The solicitor lifted his head from his doodling long enough to give both officers a warning glance.

"There." Sharon took her pager from her pocket and placed it on the table between them. "The hospital, they've promised they'll call me the moment Jason comes round. And when he does we'll go straight there, you and me. You can be the first to see him, Diane, okay?"

Diane was staring at the cigarette, burning down in her hand.

"Diane? Is that okay?"

Her voice was little more than a whisper. "Yeh, I suppose so."

"I think perhaps," the solicitor said, leaning forward, "it would be a good idea if my client had a drink, a cup of tea."

"Diane," Sharon said, "would you like something to drink?"

"No," Diane said.

Diane Johnson had been excluded from school for much of her final year-and-a-half: open insolence, bullying, bringing alcohol onto the school premises; finally, slapping her home economics teacher round the face and calling her a jumped-up white whore. She had been cautioned by the police on several occasions for suspected shoplifting, before being brought up in front of the juvenile court and given a conditional discharge on two counts of theft, another of receiving stolen goods. As she'd entered in her defense at the time, round where she lived what other kinds of goods were there?

Diane's mother had gone off the day before her daughter's thirteenth birthday, leaving a five-pound note in an envelope and a greeting card on which she'd scratched out Merry Christmas and scrawled Happy Birthday in its place. Two phone calls aside, during one of which her mother had seemed so wrecked by alcohol and remorse it had scarcely been possible to understand a word she'd said, Diane had had no contact with her since.

Her father, who had been pushing drugs with only moderate success for years, never close enough to the top of the chain, spending too much of the profit feeding habits of his own, was doing fifteen in Lincoln for shooting a rival dealer in the face in a dispute over territory.

Apart from Diane's older sister, the only person in the world she had been close to, growing up, was her friend Dee Dee. And when Dee Dee fell pregnant, her father, a devout Christian, beat her with a strap, then prayed for her soul, while her mother took her to the hospital to arrange a termination. In sympathy, Diane had unprotected sex with several men until she, too, became pregnant, only to miscarry after two months. A while later, she was more successful and the baby—healthy, coffee-skinned, and strong—was named Melvin. Now Diane's sister looked after him most of the time; it was either that or hand him over to social services. Foster parents. Children's homes.

"While we're waiting to hear from the hospital," Carl Vincent said, "how about telling us whatever you can?"

"What is it?" Diane scoffed. "You an' her together. Pair of black coppers. S'posed to make me feel better, is it. Trust you, like?" Diane laughed. "Talk about fuckin' obvious. You must think I'm stupid or something. Mental."

Vincent rested one forearm on the edge of the table. "Would you prefer to talk to a white officer, Diane, is that what you're saying?

103

I'm sure we could arrange it, if that's what you'd prefer. Of course, what with people being busy and everything, it may take a little time, but if that's what you really want …"

"Shove it," Diane said. "What's the difference? You're all the fuckin' same." She took a final pull on her cigarette and stubbed it out in the ashtray.

"How's the baby, Diane?" Sharon asked. "Melvin, isn't that his name?"

Diane stared back at her, saying nothing.

"He must be nearly walking by now."

"What's it to you?"

Sharon smiled. "Just trying to be pleasant, that's all."

"Don't bother."

"Wondering what would happen to him, the baby, if you went to jail."

"I i'n't goin' to no fuckin' jail."

"Diane," the solicitor said half-heartedly, "it won't help if you allow yourself to get excited."

"Look, Diane," Sharon said, "that amount of drugs in your possession …"

"They wasn't in my possession …"

"As good as. And no court's going to believe that was all for personal use. Which means dealing, you understand that, Diane. That's serious. You'd be in breach of your conditional discharge. This time, you could go to prison, you really could. Which might mean Melvin being taken into care."

"That's not right," Diane said. "They're not taking no kid of mine into care." She looked at them defiantly, biting her bottom lip.

Sharon offered her another cigarette, and this time Diane got it lit without a problem. "Okay," she said, "start at the beginning and tell us as much as you can about what happened. From when you drove on to the Forest to when Jason was shot. There's no rush. Take your own time."

The story, when it came, was not so very different from the one Millington dragged slowly, faltering syllable by faltering syllable, from the mouth of Sheena Snape.

After an evening that had begun in the pub and moved on to a club, they had fetched up, the three of them, in Jason's flat, smoking hashish and drinking vodka and Pepsi Cola. Around one in the morning, Jason had decided to call on some mates who lived north of Gregory Boulevard, but when they'd arrived there was nobody home. So they'd driven up on to the Forest instead.

"What for?"

"A bit of a laugh."

After smoking a few spliffs, Diane had curled up on the back seat and pretty much fallen asleep; Sheena and Jason had fooled around a little, nothing too heavy; all of them pretty much out of it when someone started hammering on the car window.

Whoever it was shot Jason in the face, neither girl had the least idea. It had been sudden and dark. One thing they were careful not to do was point the finger at Drew Valentine. If Jason had stuck a knife into him, and neither of them was saying that he had, then it had to be because he was confused, mistaken. Of any argument between the two men, any exchange of words, neither Sheena nor Diane remembered a thing.

Perhaps Norman Mann had been right, Resnick thought after listening to the reports, maybe the best thing was to chuck it all at Helen Siddons and let her make of it what she could. But the thought of stepping aside still stuck in his craw and what he didn't understand was the ease with which Mann was prepared to do the same. Was there less, then, Resnick thought, than met the eye, or was there more?

He dialed the number for Major Crime Unit and asked to speak to Sergeant Lynn Kellogg.

Nineteen

The ice-cream van just inside the Castle grounds was doing a brisk trade and the teachers steering a ragged crocodile of primary school kids through the turnstile were going to have trouble containing them until after their visit to the museum. Thirty or so nine-year-olds, some of the boys wearing baseball caps, some turbans, the girls—half of them at least—kitted out in their junior Spice Girls gear, all carrying cans of pop, packed lunches, and patchily copied worksheets.

Resnick was sitting on one of the benches lining the avenue of trees that stretched toward the bandstand. Now that the sun had broken through the cloud cover, it was warm enough for him to have removed his jacket and draped it across the bench, tugged his tie toward half-mast. Half turned toward the entrance, he shielded his eyes from the sun and watched Lynn Kellogg walk toward him; Lynn with her dark hair cut short and shaped to her head, wearing a deep-red cotton top tucked down into black denims, boots with a low heel. A soft leather bag hung from one shoulder.

"Sorry I'm so late."

"Not to worry."

"So much going on, it was difficult to get away."

Resnick nodded to show he understood and shifted back along the bench. "Chance to soak up some sun. Bit of a change from earlier."

Lynn dropped her bag between them and sat down. Close to, she looked tired; dark, purplish shadows around her eyes. She seemed to have lost weight also; her face was less full, cheekbones hard against the skin.

"Are you okay?" Resnick asked.

"Fine."

"You look a bit ... well ..."

"It's that woman. Siddons. Slave-driver isn't in it."

"Not like me, then?" Resnick grinned.

"Expects everybody to work a thirteen-hour day *and* keep pace with her afterward in the bar. Glad it's her liver and not mine."

"As long as it gets results."

Lynn sighed. "I suppose."

"You're not regretting it?"

"Transferring to Major Crimes?"

"Yes."

"No."

The gates at the far end of the drive swung open and a single-decker bus chartered by one of the local day centers nosed slowly in. On the bench opposite where Resnick and Lynn were sitting, a couple in his-and-hers pin-stripe suits were opening Tupperware containers and settling into an early lunch.

"I talked to Norman Mann earlier," Resnick said, "about your boss's involvement in this firearms business out on the Forest. He's a sight less fussed about it than I thought he'd be."

Lynn didn't answer for some little time. "Maybe that's not too wise. From his point of view, at least."

Resnick looked at her questioningly.

"There's rumors going round someone in his squad's dirty ..."

"Norman ... that's daft. Whatever he is, he's not crooked." He looked at Lynn and she looked away. Behind her, a phalanx of half a dozen wheelchairs were being pushed in slow formation past the ornate flower municipal beds, up toward the Castle.

Lynn drew a deep breath. "All the reports we've seen—Open Doors, people on the Crack Awareness team, the APA—they all say drug use in the city is up. Eighteen months to a year. Heroin. Crack cocaine. During the same period, even though arrests for possession have risen in roughly the same proportion, arrests for dealing have stayed pretty much the same. And convictions have actually fallen."

"Maybe the dealers are getting better organized?"

Lynn pushed her fingers up through her hair, then brushed it down flat. "Siddons has got Anil going back through cases where there's been an acquittal, or where the bench has just thrown it out of court, no case to answer. Seems there's a handful of instances where blame could be laid at the door of the officers concerned— poor preparation, evidence mislaid, you can imagine the kind of thing."

"But a pattern?"

"Not so far. If it was just one or two, the same names cropping up again and again, that would be easy." Lynn shifted position, leaning back against the bench. "What's interesting is who's getting pulled in, who isn't. You go through the interviews with users, low-level dealers, and the same suppliers get mentioned over and over again. Valentine. Planer. But look for those names on the arrest reports and what do you find? No mention of them. Hardly at all."

"That couldn't be because they're keeping it all at arm's length, not getting themselves involved?"

Lynn nodded. "They all use runners, sure. And what the runners do, in turn, is dilute it down, get the stuff rebagged, send it out on the street with runners of their own. Kids, for the most part. Same as it's always been. But that doesn't mean nobody knows who's back of it all, bringing the stuff in; they're just not touching them, that's all."

"And your boss thinks it's her business to know why?"

"Somebody must. There's people under thirty-five, no visible means of support, driving round the clubs in brand-new scarlet Porsches, Mercedes convertibles. They're wearing Versace gear and more gold than you'd see in Samuels's shop window. They didn't all win the Lottery. And if they're dealing, getting away scot-free, they've got to be buying protection. What else can it be?"

"That's what Siddons thinks, too?"

Lynn looked back at him, serious-faced. "Probably."

"And you think Norman Mann knows all about this? You can't think he's actually involved?"

"Involved, I don't know. It's too early to say. But if he doesn't know, then he's lost all track of what's going on in his team."

"And if he does, he's got to be turning a blind eye."

"At least."

"If any of this is true, then there ought to be an inquiry. Official. Someone from an outside force. Whatever evidence Major Crimes gets should be handed over to them."

Lynn smiled and shook her head. "Maybe it will. In the end. But only after Siddons has got what I think she wants. The dealers in one hand, whoever they're buying off in the other. Twice the arrests, twice the glory. She wants it all."

Resnick was thinking about Norman Mann, cases they'd worked on together, bars that in their younger days they'd closed down. All those marriages, three kids, a new house apparently; something going on with one of his younger DCs, or so Resnick had heard. Not without his prejudices, Norman, not above doling out the odd backhander if he thought it might speed up inquiries and there wouldn't be any bruising, but, all that aside, as honest, Resnick would have thought, as the proverbial day was long.

"Come on," Lynn said, getting to her feet. "Let's walk."

They were leaning on the parapet, gazing out over the slow waters of the canal and across the Meadows toward the Trent when she told him what else was preoccupying her mind, stopping her from sleeping. "It's my dad," she said. And suddenly, from nowhere, there were tears at the corners of her eyes. "The cancer. It's come back. I'm afraid he's going to die."

Resnick reached for her hand to give it a consoling squeeze, but fumbled and missed; finally, embarrassed, he flung an arm around her shoulder and settled for a clumsy hug. "Lynn, I'm sorry. Really sorry."

"It's okay. No, no. It's okay. I'm … I'm fine."

In the brief moment he had held her close against him, her tears had left dark patches on his shirt.

"Lynn, look …"

She cried now, without attempting to stop herself or hide what she was doing; Resnick looking on, helpless, hands in his pockets, stranded in his own awkward uncertainty.

It was twenty minutes later and they were in the cafeteria, drinking coffee at a corner table shy of visitors. Lynn had ordered a sandwich and, after two small bites, it lay unwanted on its plate. The hum of conversation rose and fell around them.

"Your dad," Resnick said, "when did you hear?"

She didn't answer straightaway, but took another sip at her coffee, already growing cold. "Last weekend. I was meant to be driving over, you know, going home. Then pretty much at the last minute I canceled. Phoned Mum and said something had come up at work, overtime. It wasn't even true. And the peculiar thing is, I don't even know why. It wasn't as if there was anything going on here, anything special. Oh, Sharon was planning to go out on the Saturday, girls' night out sort of thing, asked me to come along. But it wasn't that, I just didn't … I just didn't want to go. So I lied.

"Mum said all right and that she understood; she sounded a bit down, but I thought that was because she'd been, you know, looking forward to me being there. Then she rang me back on the Sunday morning when Dad was out with the hens and told me. He'd been having a lot of pain again, down in his gut where it all happened before. Bleeding when he went to the toilet. His doctor made an appointment for him to see the specialist at the Norfolk and Norwich."

There was a catch in her voice and for a moment Resnick thought she might be about to cry again. But she carried on. "Colorectal cancer, that's what it's called. Cancer of the bowel. Last time, two years ago now, more, they cut away part of the intestine. That was supposed to have dealt with it, once and for all. 'Clean bill of health,' that's what the doctor said. 'You don't have to worry about your father, young lady, he'll live till he's a hundred.' Patronizing bastard. Liar, too."

"It's returned," Resnick said.

"Worse than before. He's had X-rays, another endoscopy. Given the spread and the state of Dad's health, they're not keen on operating again."

"There must be something they can do?"

"Chemotherapy. Large doses. The only thing they can promise for certain is it'll make him feel like shit: it might not do any good."

"But if they don't do that?" Resnick asked.

Lynn shook her head and made a sound somewhere between a

laugh and a groan. "Treat the pain and let nature take its course. Mum says they started talking to him about going into a hospice and he told them all to bugger off. Said he'd rather die at home with his hens."

Resnick had a vision of the poultry farm he had never seen; row after row of wooden huts, chicken wire, and husks of grain. "You've been over?" he asked.

She shook her head. "This weekend. Sunday."

Resnick covered her hands in his. "I am sorry."

She nodded, not raising her head. Not wanting to look at him, not then.

"If there's anything I can do …"

"No, I don't think so." A quick smile. "But thanks." What she wanted him to do was fold her in his arms and hold her tight. The illusion that if he did, somehow, it would be all right.

Back outside the castle grounds, a party of Japanese tourists all but blocked the cobbled forecourt, photographing everything in sight. Robin Hood, Resnick thought, had a lot to answer for.

He and Lynn steered a path between them, crossing toward the corner of Hounds Gate and up the hill past the entrance to the Rutland Hotel, heading in the direction of the Ropewalk and Canning Circus. Across the street from the old hospital, Resnick paused. "Thanks."

"What for?"

"Telling me what you did."

"You won't …"

He shook his head and smiled. "Not a word."

Lynn took a pace away and Resnick reached out and touched her arm. "Your dad. Sunday. I hope it goes well. You never know, it might not be as bad as you fear."

"Yes. Maybe. Thanks, anyway."

"You'll let me know."

"Yes, of course."

Before she had reached the main doors, Resnick was well on his way toward his own building, hands in pockets, head down, stride lengthening.

111

Twenty

Lorraine had gone in to work earlier, thinking she needed at least to show her face; stay, at most, half the day. But after a couple of hours listlessly flicking through ledgers, pulling out the most over-due bills and passing them through for payment, making a call or two chasing paper supplies, she went into the general manager's office and told him she was sorry, she just couldn't carry on. Her concentration was shot. She'd try again after the weekend. He nodded sympathetically and assured her he understood: things like that—meaning her mother's funeral—sometimes they hit you harder than you think. Take all the time you need, come back when you're good and ready. Someone of Lorraine's experience, moti-vated by more than the decidedly average wage he paid her, he knew she wouldn't be easy to replace.

Insofar as she'd thought at all, Lorraine had reckoned on going back home, settling into a bath, occupying herself with another bout of mindless housework, tidying up the garden. As she was backing the car out on to the road that wound through the center of the industrial estate, she realized that wasn't what she was going to do at all.

Wollaton Park was reasonably close to the city center, just the other side of Derby Road from the university. Turning off the ring road, past that sixties pub that looked like a great goldfish bowl, she drove slowly through the main entrance and along the narrow, uneven track, headed toward the ornate pile at the center. A mass of stairways and statues, high-arched doorways and elongated turrets, the Hall had long since been turned into a museum, and Lorraine remembered herself and Michael as children, pointing with momentary curiosity at stuffed birds behind dusty glass, before running off and sliding after one another down broad banisters and along polished floors.

Now she skirted the building itself to stroll through the gardens, winding back and forth along the geometrically arranged paths with their precise sets of shrubs and flowers. Everything in its place. Perfect. Crossing the trench that ran around the grounds, she sat on a bench and looked down over the broad swathe of grass toward the lake at the bottom of the slope.

How old had Michael been when he fell in? Eight? Nine? Chasing a ball their father had kicked, punted high and heedless into the air, calling, "Catch it! Catch it! Catch!"

In those moments that followed, everyone but Michael had seen what was about to happen. Only Michael, head tilted upwards, eyes fixed on the white blur of plastic, had not noticed how close he was running to the edge until, oblivious to the shouts of warning, his legs had carried him over and into the water—a sudden splash that had scattered unsuspecting ducks and reduced Lorraine to screaming. Shrill screams of fear as her father threw off his jacket, pulled at his shoes, and jumped in through the reeds to where Michael's arms were flailing, his head appearing, then disappearing, till finally he was lifted clear, water streaming off him, and held high above his father's head. Lorraine's screams faded to tears then, her body shaking as she watched the smile broaden on her father's face as he waded back toward the shore, triumphant, Michael safe in his arms.

How she loved them then, at that moment: loved both of them. Without question.

Feeling a shiver run through her, Lorraine looked up to the sky, but it was still an unblemished blue, echoing the unbroken water below. Rising to her feet, arms wound tight across her chest, she shivered again. She had been so certain, when she heard he had escaped, that Michael would find a way of coming to her. Not for long, she understood that, but once at least, before he ran. She had been convinced of it. *You don't love him, do you?* She had been wrong about so many things.

◆◆◆

The Pentecostal church in which former robber and general ne'er-do-well Arthur Forbes found salvation was primarily of Afro-Caribbean descent in its congregation; its spiritual leader was a white-haired Antiguan who had first heard the calling on a windswept boat threatened with forty-foot waves crossing the Windward Passage between Haiti and Santiago, Cuba. In truth, the man's hair had not been white until that transforming experience, rather, jet-black, a happening from which he had been known to extract the maximum symbolic resonance at the pulpit. Macon, Georgia; Charlotte, Virginia; Chattanooga, Tennessee—the minister learned his preaching in the best, the steamiest of circles, his oratory suffused with a richness of Southern gospel traditions. So that now, when he threw back his head and raised his voice to praise the Lord in accents which mingled the East Midlands and the West Indies with the American South, those gathered together in the makeshift breeze-block building in Sneinton found it easy to believe it was indeed the Holy Ghost descending on their bowed heads, rather than dust and dirt dislodged from the ceiling by a passing train.

Arthur Forbes, forever lamenting his past ways, had chosen public avowal and humiliation as his penance. Wearing a discarded head waiter's frock-coat and a pair of striped trousers several sizes too large and held together by staples, he paraded the streets and public places of the city center, preaching the word, singing psalms, and bearing a sandwich board which he used to fend off the sour fruit and empty lager cans that were propelled in his direction by the Godless youth of the city.

Forbes was easing off his boots, prior to immersing his feet in the waters of one of the Old Market Square fountains, when he saw Millington approaching.

"Oh, where were you, brother," Forbes began singing, "when they crucified my Lord? Where were you, oh sinner, when they nailed him to a tree?"

"Never laid a hand on him," Millington said, "and if he says anything different, he's a liar."

"Is that in your notebook, sergeant?"

"Gospel."

"Aah," Forbes exclaimed, sliding his right foot down into the bubbling water. "Isn't that blissful?"

"It's probably contravening several bylaws. Polluting a public place, for one."

"But you're not here to arrest me?"

Millington lit a Lambert and Butler and pushed the rest of the packet down into Forbes's jacket pocket.

"What you're after," Forbes said, rubbing an index finger down between his toes, "will cost you more than that."

"And what would that be? This thing that I'm after."

"You want to know if I've seen hide or hair of Michael Preston. Even though they have it on the news that he's away."

"And you're saying they're wrong?"

Forbes changed feet. "I've not had so much as a smell of him. He's not been near. What was in the paper, for all I can tell you otherwise, it's true."

"Shame, Arthur." Millington patted the wallet inside his jacket pocket. "Might've found a little something for the collection box."

Forbes's eyes sparkled. "How little?"

"Depends on what you had to sell."

Easing himself back on the stonework, Forbes began to dry his feet on a large and grubby handkerchief. "Rumor has it you've been looking for a gun. Something to do with Anthony Valentine."

Millington stood closer. "You know where it is?"

Forbes shook his head. "Just where it came from."

Millington folded two ten-pound notes and pressed them down into Forbes's outstretched hand.

"You know a boy name of Gary Prince?" Forbes said.

Millington's mind was racing. The only Gary Prince he knew was a small-time crook with little ambition and less talent—for thieving or anything else. Maybe he'd been going to night school. Extra lessons. Not, in all probability, Byron and the Late Romantics.

"What's that little toe-rag got to do with anything?"

"The man's growing, got responsibilities."

"And he's peddling guns, that what you're saying?"

Forbes squeezed his feet back into his boots and tied careful double knots in his string laces. "I'm saying what Valentine was carrying that night, our Gary's where it come from. Now, if you'll excuse me, I'll be on my way. The Lord's work, you know, it's never done."

No more's bloody mine, Millington thought as he headed back through the square. Jason Johnson was still not talking, Valentine himself was hiding behind his well-paid brief; all of their efforts to uncover a witness who could identify the Burger King shooter had proved fruitless. Gary Prince might not be much of a lead, but it was a start.

At a little past two that morning, Lorraine had found herself in her dressing gown looking at the children. Sandra had thrown both the pillows out of her bed and was lying in a perfect diagonal, covered only by the sheet, a frown crossing her sleeping face as Lorraine watched. Sean had twisted himself almost upside down, one leg sticking out over the edge of the mattress, the other pushed up against the wall. Like a cat's paw, one arm rested across his face, covering his eyes.

Whatever else, Lorraine thought, I have these.

Careful to avoid the boards that squeaked, she padded downstairs. Probably on purpose, Derek had not replaced the empty bottle of gin. She remembered a bottle of vodka, Russian, in the freezer. Standing at the French windows, glass cold between her fingers, she stared out into the almost dark. She was still there when she heard Derek's feet on the stairs, saw his reflection coming slowly closer. His hand, warm on her arm.

"Can't sleep?"

She shook her head.

For some moments, he didn't speak and Lorraine could feel his breath against her neck, his hand moving lightly above and below her elbow, tips of his fingers pushing down into her palm.

"However long you stand here waiting, watching, he's not going to come."

Leaning forward, Lorraine closed her eyes.

"Not now. You know that, don't you? Lorraine, sweetheart, don't you?"

"Yes." Her voice so faint that, even close, he wasn't certain she had spoken at all.

"Lorraine?"

"Yes. Yes, I said, yes."

Derek stroked her hair. "Sooner or later, you've got to face it, love. The kind of man he is. He didn't come to your mother's funeral out of respect for her. Affection. He didn't even come to see you. He came because it was his chance; his chance to escape and that's what he's done."

There were tears running down Lorraine's face and she was starting to shake. Before she dropped it, Derek took the empty glass from her hand.

"I'm your husband, Lorraine. Those children upstairs, they're yours and mine. This is our family. Ours. And I love you, remember that. I love you, no matter what."

Twenty-one

"Are you planning to stay there all morning or what?"

At the sound of his mother's voice, Evan woke, blearily breaking out of a dream in which he was somehow back home again in his old room, until he realized it wasn't any dream.

"It's almost ten o'clock. There's tea downstairs in the pot. I'm just off out to the shops." A pause, then: "You make sure you're out of there by the time I get back."

Evan lay listening to his mother's footsteps receding along the narrow passageway and down the stairs, just as he had for so many years, all of the years he had been at school. After the front door had clicked shut, he threw back the sheet he'd been sleeping under and swung his legs round toward the floor. He'd opened the window last night before getting into bed, but not enough; his hair was plastered to his scalp with sweat. The pillow wasn't merely damp, but wet.

When he'd moved back home, not so many weeks before, he hadn't told any of the people he worked with, for fear of what they might say. But the place Evan had been renting, a second floor out by Hackney Marshes, had become a liability. The bloke he'd been sharing with, another officer from the prison, had proved congenitally unable to deal with money. Bills had rolled in and either remained unpaid or Evan had stretched what little he had and settled the whole thing from his own account. Having the phone cut off hadn't been too bad, he could have lived with that, but then the landlord took to pushing all those notes through the door, threatening to take them both to the small claims court for nonpayment of rent, and the crux had come when Evan had stumbled down into the communal hall one morning to find a gas board official searching for the mains so he could cut off their supply.

"You know you can always come back here for a bit," his mother had said, "that old room of yours isn't doing anything but collecting dust. Just till you get sorted, mind. You cluttering up the place all hours, getting under my feet, that's the last thing I want."

So Evan had agreed, a couple of weeks while he looked around for something else. He wouldn't expect his mum to do it for nothing, of course, he'd see her right; a few extra quid in her purse would more than likely not go amiss and besides, most probably she'd welcome having somebody else about the place, living on her own there since his dad had died. "There" being a flat-fronted two-story terraced house with a raised ground floor in east London, Clapton; Evan's folks had moved in not so far short of thirty years back and now theirs were the only white faces on the street.

Evan padded downstairs in his boxer shorts and into the kitchen, where the cat, a ginger-and-black tom with a nasty temper and one badly chewed ear, was busily scratching round in its tray, spraying gray cat litter over the floor in its efforts to cover up what it had just left behind. Jesus! Evan thought. Why is it with a garden out there, at least one open window, to say nothing of a cat flap, you still have to crap in the house? Unlocking the rear door, he shooed the animal down the metal steps leading to the narrow strip of grass, the flower beds his mum was clearly letting go, a stumpy fruit tree that bore no fruit.

He poured himself a mug of tea, strong enough by now for the spoon to stand up in, tipped some cornflakes into a bowl with sugar and milk, and sat down with his mum's *Express*. Thumbing through twice, he could see nothing about Michael Preston's escape. Yesterday's news, and even then, down there in the smoke, it had rated no more than a couple of paragraphs, *Murderer Escapes After Mother's Funeral, convicted killer still on the loose.*

He had tried ringing to find out how Wesley was getting along, now that he'd been released from the hospital, and someone with a voice like ready-mixed concrete, one of Wesley's brothers he supposed, had told him in no uncertain terms to keep his face out of Wesley's business unless he fancied getting it rearranged. As if it were his fault Wes had lost a liter or so of blood and was sporting a neat line in stitches. All right, he'd been the one who'd actually patted Preston down, but he hadn't exactly been acting on his own. Wesley had been there all along. And who'd let his attention wander sufficiently in the back seat of the car that his prisoner was able to transfer the razor blade from wherever he'd been hiding it out into his hand?

"You stand up for yourself, Evan," his mother had said, when he told her there was going to be an internal inquiry. "Don't always be so keen to take the blame. Soft, you are, that's your trouble, like your dad. And see where it got him, God bless him. No, you want to look out for yourself for once in your life. Don't let them push you around."

Suspended from duty on full pay. "All you can expect," his union delegate had said. "Sod off down the coast for a couple of days, why don't you? No family hanging round you. Me, I'd get in a bit of fishing."

Evan looked across at the clock on the cooker, quarter to twelve. He'd go up and throw some water on his face, clean his teeth, pull on some clothes, and go for a walk to clear his head, maybe along by the filter beds.

When he stepped on to the pavement twenty minutes later, the black guy who lived to the right was outside again, tinkering with his motor, doors flung wide open, radio blaring—the man himself not doing a thing but leaning back against his front railings, stripped to the waist save for the gold chain round his neck, so heavy you'd have to wonder he could hold his head straight. "Morning," Evan said, walking past him. "Nice again." No harm in being friendly. The man silent behind his shades, as if Evan had never opened his mouth.

Maybe a bit later I'll give Wesley a bell, Evan was thinking, see if he hasn't calmed down a little.

Sitting on the end of one of the desks in the CID room, Resnick and Millington, Naylor and Sharon Garnett as audience, Ben Fowles flipped open his notebook and cleared his throat. Millington had put Kevin and himself on to checking out Gary Prince.

"Past form's pretty much what you'd expect," Fowles began. "Small-time thieving as a kid, truanting, suspended from school for what they called persistent anti-social behavior; one care order, too many last warnings. Young offenders' center by when he was sixteen. Celebrated his eighteenth with a six-month stay at Lincoln. Various bits and pieces of probation. Longest sentence so far, eighteen months for handling stolen goods, of which he served just about half. That was almost two years ago. As far as records go, he's been clean since."

"And no suggestion," Resnick asked, "of him being involved with guns?"

Fowles shook his head. "Credit cards, watches, jewelry, that's more his mark."

"Kevin," Millington said, "you've got some more?"

Naylor took a quick swallow from his mug of lukewarm tea. "Our Gary's twenty-eight. Finally moved out from his mum's, February of this year. Bought himself a place near Corporation Oaks. Three bedrooms, garage, newish, nothing fancy. Paid close to sixty thousand, all the same. Round about the same time, he started seeing this Vanessa Parlour. Some kind of model. Promotions, the odd commercials, nothing too high-powered." He grinned. "Pulled a couple of photos of her from the *Post*'s files. Pretty classy stuff."

"I wonder what she sees in Prince?" Millington asked.

Sharon smiled. "Perhaps our Gary's got hidden charms."

"Like the guy in *The Full Monty*," Ben Fowles suggested. "Whips off his Y-fronts and there's this thud as the end of his dick hits the ground."

"The woman," Resnick said, "maybe she's the one responsible for Prince finding a little more ambition? Moving himself up in the world?"

"Guns," Sharon said. "It's possible. For some women there's something very sexy about guns."

Fowles laughed. "Tell us about it, Sharon."

"In your dreams."

"One other thing," Naylor said. "He's got this lock-up garage, near his mum's place in Sneinton. Still uses it, as far as I can tell."

"Be nice to get a look around inside," Millington said wistfully.

Resnick scraped back his chair as he rose to his feet. "Bit more patience, Graham, maybe we will. I'll have a word with the boss, see if he can't stir up a warrant."

Coming up out of the underground into Brixton, Evan thought, was like stepping out into another country. Not simply the preponderance of black faces, he was used enough to that where his mother lived, after all; here, the air, the whole atmosphere, were different. In Dalston, no matter how many there were, black or Asian, it was as if they were living, cuckoo-like, on sufferance in a white world. But here, these people with their dreadlocks and multicolored woolen hats and that lazy, strutting way they walked, no, they owned this place, these streets. And Evan, blinking to readjust his eyes after traveling below ground, he was the stranger in a foreign land.

"Hey, man!" And there was Wesley pushing through the crowd, grinning, holding out his hand.

First time in his life Evan had known Wesley pleased to see him. Half a dozen calls it had taken before the man would agree to meet him at all.

"How you doin'? Okay? No problem gettin' here?"

Evan nodded, fine, fine.

"Di'n't forget your passport, right?" Wesley laughing at Evan's discomfort. "Come on." Nodding his head up toward the Ritzy cinema at the foot of Brixton Hill. "Let's get something to eat. Famished, yeah?"

Evan followed Wesley along the broad pavement and into one of the entrances to the covered market.

"Where we going, anyway?"

"Franco's. Best pizza in town. Best pizza anywhere." And he laughed again. "What? You think all we eat is jerk chicken and sweet potato? Curried goat? Anyway, look around, you'll feel at home."

There was a line of tables clustered close together out front, all occupied. Most of the customers were white, youngish, casually dressed, sitting there with acres of newsprint spread out before them.

"Yuppie types," Wesley said. "Think it's cool, hang outside

Franco's, watch the world go by. We'll go inside, quieter there."

They took a table near the back and Wesley ordered a Coke, Evan a beer. The menu was long and seemed to include every pizza topping Evan had heard of and several he hadn't thought possible.

"So," Wesley said, "what's up?"

Evan shrugged, temporarily lost for words.

"Something's bugging you, the way you was on the phone."

"No, it's just ..."

"Just this Michael Preston shit, right?"

"I suppose so, I ..."

"Listen, man, if it's what happened to me, getting cut an' all, okay, I was plenty mad at you at the time, but I'm through that now. It's cool. Nothing to reproach yourself for, okay? Evan, okay?"

Evan nodded uncertainly. "Yeh, okay."

"Good. Now let's order us some food, I'm starvin'."

Evan played safe with the basic pizza, ham, mozzarella cheese, and tomato; Wesley tucking into aubergine, anchovy, and pepperoni sausage.

"How is it, anyway?" Evan asked between mouthfuls. "Where he cut you? Still giving you any pain or what?"

Wesley shook his head as he chewed. "Once in a while, maybe. Just, you know, a little niggle. But, hey, like I told you, you got to quit worryin' 'bout it."

"I just feel guilty, that's all."

"Weren't none of your fault, man. Well, not exactly none of your fault, but, you know, what's done's done. That crazy fucker, Preston, he's the one to blame, he's the one cut me, right? An' he sunnin' hisself right now on some beach in Spain or Greece, stickin' his finger up at the world. You think he care about us, spare us a second thought? Okay, so you don't waste your mind on him. Forget him, right? Get on with your life."

"This inquiry ..."

"Inquiry be fine. Stay cool, chill out. You see."

Evan cut off another strip of pizza—every bit as good as Wesley'd said it would be, no more contented evenings in Pizza Hut after this—and washed it down with a swig of beer.

"What it is, Wesley," he said, leaning forward a little, lowering his voice, "all this stuff about him buying false papers, getting on some flight abroad, I don't believe none of it."

Wesley laid down his knife and fork and looked at him, curious.

"I reckon that's all bollocks. A blind."

"How come?"

"I don't know how come, just a feeling. But I can't, you know, shake it. I think he's still there, where we took him."

"What?" Laughing. "Camped out in some field alongside the motorway?"

Evan shook his head. "Back in the city."

"Easiest way to get caught, he'd know that better'n anyone."

"Maybe," Evan said, not really meaning it. "Anyhow, I reckon I might take a trip up there, you know. Look around."

"Look around?" Wesley echoed, amazed. "What the hell for?"

Evan cut away a piece more pizza. "See if I can't find him."

Wesley staring at him now, open-mouthed. "Find him, you sayin'? Find him? Evan, man, you crazy or what? You think the police didn't try to find him? You think you can do somethin' they can't?"

"No." Evan shaking his head. "I don't think they give a monkey's about Michael Preston. I don't think they care."

"And you do?"

"Yes, what's wrong with that? My responsibility, right? You said yourself, down to me more than you. So, okay, I'll find him."

Wesley laughing except that it wasn't funny, it was pathetic, that's what it was. Evan as Batman, the Lone Ranger.

"What? What's the big joke?"

"You, you're the joke. You think you are, some kind of vigilante?"

Evan looked back at him and didn't say anything.

"Suppose you do find him, right, what then?"

"Bring him back."

"You ..." Wesley pointing at him with his knife. "You a little soft in the head, you know that, don't you?"

"Okay," Evan said. "Okay." He was this close to standing up and walking out of there. "I wish I'd never said anything, right? You made your point. Now I don't want to hear any more about it. Okay? Yeh, Wesley, okay?"

Wesley rattled the last of the ice cubes round in his glass, sucked on the slice of lemon, lifted up a sliver of anchovy between fore-finger and thumb, and deposited it on his tongue. "Evan," he said a few moments later. "You are one crazy fucker, you know that, don't you?"

What Evan knew was what his father had taught him, if you want to earn respect in this world, you have to be responsible for your own actions; and if you want to be able to respect yourself, you have to acknowledge your mistakes and then do everything in your power to set them right.

Fowles was standing pretty much to attention in front of Resnick's desk, hands clasped behind him. The list of Gold Standard employees lay between them.

"Tell me again how you got hold of this," Resnick said.

Fowles told him.

"You realize if we wanted to use this, needed to, in court, Cassady's brief could most likely get it thrown out?"

Fowles was avoiding Resnick's eye. "Yes, sir."

Resnick let him stew a little longer.

"The names, sir. I've been running a check on them as and when I could. Cassady, we could have him over a barrel if we wanted. Three men he's employed, got criminal records as security guards, two with convictions for aggravated assault. And this one ..." Fowles jabbed a finger down on to the list. "Bloke been done for house burglary, out patrolling this estate nights, Wilford way."

"Write it up," Resnick said. "And next time, think before you pull a stunt like this."

"Yes, sir." Fowles didn't move.

"There's more?"

"Yes, sir. Three of our lot, moonlighting. Couple of uniforms and a sergeant out the Drug Squad."

"Name?" Resnick asked sharply. "The sergeant."

"Finney, sir. Paul Finney."

Resnick half remembered a thirtyish man with strong, dark hair and an open face. He'd met him a few times in the company of Norman Mann and others; Finney mostly quiet, friendly. Spoke only when he was spoken to.

"Right," Resnick said. "Leave this with me."

Fowles closed the door quietly behind him and Resnick eased forward in his chair. Finney, Finney. There was something about him he couldn't put his finger on and then he could. Greyhounds. Wasn't Finney part of a syndicate that owned a couple of greyhounds? Raced them. Norman Mann had tried to talk him into going along one evening, Resnick remembered. Colwick. One of those occasions he'd said maybe and then stayed home. He thought about calling Mann and dialed Siddons's number instead.

Twenty-two

The youth with a ring through his nose was sitting cross-legged on sheets of cardboard in the estate agent's doorway, a sandy-haired dog coiled close alongside. As Resnick approached, he held out a hand and pleaded for change.

You and the rest of us, Resnick thought. There were a couple of pound coins in the side pocket of Resnick's coat, a smattering of silver. "Here."

The dog growled, low in its throat, and the youth wished Resnick a good night.

The restaurant was at the other end of the pedestrianized street and Resnick had passed it many times without being tempted inside. The menu, attached discreetly to the wall, had faded to the point where it was difficult to read. Antipasto ... risotto ... pescatore. Resnick climbed the lean flight of stairs and found himself in an almost empty room with an extravagant mural along one wall, somewhere Mediterranean where the sea was always blue and the sun never set. Vines, presumably plastic, dangled from a trellis overhead. On each table, empty chianti bottles sat garlanded in dusty candle wax.

By one of the windows, a couple, married but not, Resnick instinctively felt, to each other, maintained a silent vigil over their linguine al alfredo. Near the far wall, a middle-aged man sat toying with his spaghetti and reading from a fat book he seemed almost to have finished. The night's other customers had long gone.

A waiter wearing regulation black and white, his apron, unstained, tied high above his waist, moved to intercept Resnick and addressed him by name. "Your friend, she is already here."

Resnick followed him past the entrance to the kitchen, along a little dog-leg corridor and up another short set of stairs into a second room.

Chairs were stacked on all the tables save one.

"Charlie, good. You found it, then. I was just beginning to wonder." Helen Siddons, hair pinned up, little makeup, a shirt buttoned to the neck, gestured toward the empty chair and as Resnick was sitting, filled his glass. "Barolo. Not bad for the price."

Resnick nodded and, shrugging off his suit jacket, hung it from the back of his chair.

"It was good of you to ring me."

He shrugged. "I thought it was the way you wanted it played."

"Even so ..." Half smiling, she swiveled the single menu in Resnick's direction. "Why don't we order first? It's all pretty much your bog-standard Italian. But if you value your lower bowel, steer clear of the prawns."

Once the waiter had disappeared, Resnick told her about Valentine and Gary Prince.

"That's it?" she said when he'd finished. "Beginning to end, that's all you've got?"

"So far."

Siddons shook her head. "Rumor and conjecture, Charlie. And not a lot of either."

"But if we can link Valentine through Prince to the gun ..."

"If. If. The last I heard, the gun was still missing."

Resnick leaned closer. "We have to work with what we've got."

"You'll turn Prince over?"

"First thing."

Siddons lifted her wineglass. "You might strike lucky."

"If we can link Valentine to the weapon that shot Johnson ..."

"Big if, Charlie."

"Johnson's just about fit enough to answer questions."

"And you think he might dump Valentine right in it?"

"If someone had just put a bullet through my head, I think I would, don't you?"

Siddons cut into her veal. "That would depend if I thought he was going to do it again."

For some minutes, they ate in silence.

"Those two girls," Siddons said, "Jason's sister and her mate, did you ever get anything out of them?"

"A lot of abuse, not much else."

"They're not still in custody?"

Resnick shook his head. "Didn't seem a lot of point."

Siddons pushed her plate aside and lit a cigarette. "There's more?"

Resnick drank some more wine and told her about Paul Finney. She liked what she was hearing, he could tell. A Drug Squad officer on Cassady's payroll and Cassady providing security for clubs where so much illegal drug activity went down: it was a start, a way in, a weak link in the chain.

"Anything else, Charlie? Coffee, dessert?"

"I'll have an espresso, double. Thanks."

"Join me in a brandy?"

Resnick shook his head.

Fifteen minutes later, Helen Siddons slid her credit card between the folded halves of the bill. "Your shout next time, Charlie, okay?"

The youth and his dog were curled against each other, sleeping in the doorway.

"Poor bastard," Siddons said, nodding in the boy's direction.

"Amen to that."

"Got your car, Charlie?"

Resnick shook his head.

"Come on then, mine's just round the corner. I'll give you a lift."

As they turned on to the Woodborough Road, Siddons leaned a little to the left and rested her hand on Resnick's knee. "I know you could have gone elsewhere with this. Norman Mann, for instance. You're pals. I know that. And I'm grateful. I'll not forget it."

Resnick sat there wondering exactly what his friend Norman would think of this particular evening's work. Siddons changed gear sharply, signaling right. Maybe it was the brandy, but whatever the reason, she was driving too fast. Probably she always did. In just a few minutes, they were pulling up outside Resnick's house, its shape bulked dark against the night sky.

129

Resnick opened the door and got out on to the pavement and, with a pert trill, Dizzy jumped down off the stone wall and trotted toward him.

"A sight more than some of us get," Siddons said wryly, "someone to greet us at the front door when we get home of a night. Even if the first thing they do is stick their arse in our face." She laughed. "Sweet dreams, Charlie. Have one on me."

Resnick raised a hand as the car pulled away from the curb and then, bending low, he listened until the sound of the engine had faded beneath Dizzy's insistent purr.

Twenty-three

Gary Prince was awake early, as it happened, needing the lavatory shy of five and then deciding to stay up for a while, fancying a cup of tea and a smoke; something distinctly savory about sitting up to the breakfast bar he'd had installed in his own kitchen, while the gorgeous woman he'd been shagging less than half a dozen hours before lay upstairs sleeping in his bed. Though in truth, technically speaking, it had been Vanessa who'd been shagging him. Now he was a little older, Gary found he liked it that way. Preferred it even. One of those welcome signs of maturity, he reckoned, along with his first gray hair and moving out from his mum's.

Yes—Gary stubbed out his cigarette and, without thinking, lit another—about the best thing he'd ever done, buying this place. Nothing fancy, not one of those fake Tudor places out at Edwalton some he knew aspired to as soon as they'd got a quid or two in their pocket, a few TESSAs in the bank. This place was nothing flash, discreet even, unlikely to draw the unwelcome attentions of Resnick and the like, well within his means.

Though if things progressed with Vanessa the way he thought they might, there'd have to be improvements made, money spent.

Vanessa was currently sharing a flat in the Park with two pals in the same line as herself, corporate videos, a little photographic modeling, sales promotion. Gary had first met her, in fact, when she was using her leopard skin bikini to show off the lines of the new Sierra in the forecourt of the Broad Marsh Centre. Gary himself there on security duty thanks to his pal, Cassady; stop any bastard scratching the paintwork, kids running off with scads of brochures, only to toss them over the balcony like overweight confetti. They'd struck up a conversation over something Gary couldn't remember

131

and before you could say prawn cocktail, steak and chips, he'd been asking her out to dinner.

He'd dropped one or two hints about her chucking up her flat, moving in full time, but so far she hadn't bitten. What he ought to do, Gary reckoned, get her more involved in his plans for the house, that way she'd come to see it more as something they shared. And besides, a girl like Vanessa, she'd have ideas about style, color. All manner of things. Adding a conservatory, maybe. Patio doors.

The tea was stewed, but he squeezed out another cup anyway. Someone like Vanessa moving in, that would really say something about him, add a definite tone. A dog, too, Gary thought, he might get one of those. A pair of them. Alsatians. Rottweilers. Living where he was, St. Ann's, you couldn't be too careful.

Gary thought he'd go back up and see if Vanessa was anything like awake, but when he stripped down to his boxer shorts and slid back under the covers she was stretched out at an angle across the bed, mouth slightly open, snoring gently. He wriggled himself close against her and, not thinking he would actually go back to sleep, closed his eyes. When the noise woke him, almost an hour later, his first thought was that it was burglars, but not his second.

Bastards! He knew if he didn't get down there double quick they'd have the front door off with a pair of sledgehammers.

"Gary Prince?"

"What about it?"

"CID."

There were three of them; two fast in his face the second he opened up, sports gear, trainers, so pumped up he could smell the adrenaline. The third one, older, a little mustache, sports jacket and slacks as if he were taking a morning stroll. Standing there in his boxers, Gary was feeling decidedly underdressed.

"How about the thieving bastard formerly known as Prince?" Ben Fowles said. "More your fancy?"

"Fuck off!"

"Not bloody likely."

They went past him, the first two, like they'd just heard the pistol at the start of the hundred meters.

"You've got a warrant?" Gary asked.

Millington grinned a particularly malicious grin. "More warrants than you could fit up your arse between now and Sunday."

"You'll not find anything, you know."

"Oh, well, least it gives the lads a chance to chuck things about for a spell. All good practice."

A muffled shriek from above told him all the racket had hauled Vanessa out of bed.

Gary was on his way when Millington detained him with a hand tight on his upper arm. "Gary, Gary, no sense going off at half cock."

"If they lay a hand …"

"Don't worry. House-trained the pair of them."

A succession of sharp thumps seemed to give the lie to that, drawers being pulled free, their contents tumbled to the floor.

"Gary," Vanessa called, "whatever's going on?"

"Pack her off into the kitchen," Millington advised, "tell her to make us all a nice cup of tea. Unless yours is one of them liberated relationships, of course. Non-gender specific in the domestic-task area—I think that's what the wife calls it. In which case, Gary, mine's Yorkshire if you've got it, common or garden PG Tips if you've not. Oh, and one sugar, easy on the milk."

"Bollocks," Gary said, halfway up the stairs.

"Ah, it'll be the little woman then, after all."

The little woman, all five feet nine of her, was standing at the entrance to the master bedroom, wearing a pair of high-sided lace briefs and the residue of last night's Obsession. Ben Fowles, in the hallway directly in front of her, was doing his level best not to stare.

"If you'd like to get dressed," he said, "put something on, like, we need to get into the bedroom."

"What for?"

"We have reason to believe a considerable amount of stolen property is on the premises," Fowles said, eyes flickering nervously in the face of the most perfect set of breasts it had been his good fortune to encounter in the flesh.

"Gary," Vanessa said, as he arrived at Fowles's shoulder. "What's all this about?"

"Nothing, nothing. It's all a mistake."

133

"Gary …"

"Look," Gary said, backing her toward the bedroom, "maybe you should get yourself covered up, yeh? And then … well, you don't suppose you could slip the kettle on …"

"Fuck off, Gary," she said and slammed the door in his face.

Ben Fowles snorted with laughter and went off to help Naylor going through the treasures of the spare room. Whistling while he worked, Millington sallied off in search of the kitchen; if they were going to be there a while, he might as well mash the tea himself.

At Gary Prince's lock-up, Carl Vincent and Sharon Garnett stared into a twenty-four by seventeen meter space liberally filled with boxes, while two uniformed officers made a detailed inventory of sundry cordless telephones, compact disc players, carefully bubble-wrapped and probably imitation Rolex Tudor Chronograph watches, and what looked like several hundred copies of the new Madonna CD. What they had not found, any of them, was a lethal barreled weapon of any description from which any shot, bullet, or other missile might be discharged, nor, Robin Hood territory or not, a single item relevant under the Crossbows Act of 1987.

"You reckon he's got receipts for this lot?" Sharon asked. Standing a little way off, she took a pack of Marlboro Lights from her bag and offered one to Carl before lighting up herself.

"Bound to," Vincent said with a wry smile. "VAT invoices, the lot."

Sharon shook her head. "You imagine the work involved, checking this lot against stolen property?"

Vincent shrugged. "At least we're not coming away empty-handed."

"You think that'll sweeten the boss's temper?"

"I doubt it."

Sharon drew on her cigarette, released the smoke slowly and smiled. "You want to give him a call, or shall I?"

Resnick's stomach was noisily reminding him that, two cups of coffee aside, he'd skipped breakfast. Millington, who'd feasted on two Shredded Wheat with an added sprinkling of wheatgerm and bran, didn't look any happier.

"We got nothing," Resnick said. It wasn't a question.

Millington's jacket smelled faintly of dry-cleaning, his trousers, pale-gray, had a definite crease down the front. Casual but smart. Resnick was reminded of the men he saw in the Viccy Centre on Saturday mornings, waiting patiently outside Jessops or Boots for their wives. "I wouldn't say altogether nothing." For once, he wasn't looking Resnick squarely in the eye.

"Nothing that links Prince with the gun, any gun."

A quick shake of the head. "No."

"So your pal, Forbes ..."

"Arthur Forbes is going to be meeting his maker a lot sooner'n he wants when I've got shot of him."

"And we're no closer to Valentine."

"No."

Silent, they were conscious of the constant thrum of traffic on the Derby Road, the shrill sigh of brakes as lorries slowed for the long left turn around Canning Circus.

"There is all that stuff in his lock-up." Millington said. "Even a good brief's not going to talk him out of that. You never know, pile up the questioning, he might let something slip."

"Yes," Resnick said. "Happen he will."

Neither of them believed it.

Outside, in the CID room, telephones rang and were answered, rang and were not.

Twenty-four

Sometimes, Maureen thought what her sister-in-law needed was a good seeing-to. Someone to get a firm hold of her and shake all that mardiness out of her, once and for all. A quick slap around the face, even, if that was what it took. She smiled at herself in the bathroom mirror. She couldn't exactly see her beloved brother being the one to do it, not Derek: to Maureen's way of thinking, her brother, now and from an early age, was a wimp. Lorraine has a headache, isn't feeling too grand, getting her period, whatever—don't worry, love, you rest, lie down, go back to bed, I'll take care of the kids, do the shopping, run the car to the garage, mow the lawn.

What was that game they used to play as kids? O'Grady Says? Well, their marriage, Lorraine's and Derek's, that's what it was like. O'Grady says clap your hands, all clap your hands. O'Grady says sleep downstairs on the sofa, Derek sleeps downstairs on the sofa.

Maureen stretched her lips back from her teeth to make sure there were no telltale bits of last night's spinach lasagna, this morning's wholewheat toast. The last thing one of her customers wanted to see was a résumé of what she'd been eating the last twelve hours.

Lorraine's brother, though, Maureen was thinking, Michael, that was a whole different ball game. Him and Derek, chalk and cheese. She couldn't see Michael running around at some woman's beck and call, any woman, wife or no wife, it didn't matter how upset she was. And it wasn't as though she didn't understand what Lorraine had been going through, her mother dying like that, all the memories it must have brought flooding back. But Michael, he was different. Well, he'd proved it, hadn't he? She couldn't see Michael being any other way than what he was: hard.

Stepping back, she cupped both hands beneath her breasts and looked at their reflection admiringly. Okay, so they might not pass the pencil test, but at forty, well, what could you expect? At least, for the time being, they were all hers: nothing beyond the occasional dab of hormone cream, no silicone, no nips and tucks. Three mornings down at the gym and a couple of spells in the pool, that was what it was. Facials. The occasional sauna. Sensible diet—all right, more sensible than some. Elizabeth Arden Eight-Hour Cream and multivitamins. It was the only body she was going to get, so she might as well look after it.

Back in the bedroom, she pulled open several drawers, lifting things out and either discarding them immediately, or holding them up in front of herself before the full-length mirror. Saturday. Work day. So much to convey: good sense, practicality, style. Finally, she opted for a blue silk-chiffon strapless body and a black, calf-length pencil skirt. How many women her age could wear that and get away with it? She slipped a long cotton jacket, also black, from its hanger.

The watch on her wrist told her she should have left five minutes ago. On Saturdays she employed two girls to help in the shop and she always liked to be there well before them; promptness, the right attitude, so important. She hadn't got where she was by loafing around half the day, missing appointments, being late. From the plastic container inside the wardrobe door, she took a pair of ankle-strap shoes with a two-inch heel. The Nikes she used when she drove were on the back seat of the car.

Bridlesmith Gate and the narrow streets leading off it were the Fashion District of the city. Birdcage, Limey's, Ted Baker, the first ever Paul Smith. Maureen's shop was midway along King John's Arcade, between Bottle Lane and Token House Yard. By Design. The arcade had been revamped in recent years, a tiled floor and covered roof leading past the café where Maureen frequently went for morning coffee, along to the decorated steps leading up to King John's Chambers and the Fletcher Gate car park where she normally left her car.

Maureen had gained experience in just about every clothing

store of note in the region, spending eighteen months as manager of the local branch of Warehouse before setting up on her own. She'd picked up the shop lease cheaply enough when a shoe store went into liquidation. A year to prove herself, convince the city's shoppers of the virtues of second-hand designer clothes, two at most. Now, with the shop's third birthday celebrations almost at the planning stage, she was beginning to relax. Just a little. If business carried on like this, she might even talk to the bank about expansion. Derby. Leicester. Even as far south as Milton Keynes.

The bulk of By Design's stock comprised Suits from Hobbs and Jigsaw, outfits for her more mature ladies from Alexon or Jaeger, spangly little dresses from Karen Millen. Shoppers who ventured as far afield as Manchester or London sold her their last season specialties from Armani or Agnes b, Anna Sui.

Today she was particularly excited because one of her regulars had promised her a silver size 8 dress from Miu Miu and another, a woman closer to Maureen's own size, was bringing in a pinstripe halterneck jumpsuit from DKNY. Maureen thought she might have to try that on herself.

Keys in hand, she tapped on the window of the café and waved as she went past. It was still only a quarter to nine and neither Kelly nor Samantha would put in an appearance until half past at the earliest. The shop itself didn't open till ten.

Inside, she switched on the lights and looked around. The interior was quite long and narrow. Coats and suits hung in the dark wood unit she had had built along the rear wall, finishing at the door to her small office. Two changing cubicles took up the right-hand wall, boxed shelves of shoes and accessories filled the left. Dresses and skirts were on free-standing rails; knitwear, arranged by color, on a mahogany table. Catching a glimpse of herself in one of the mirrors, Maureen smiled. Everything was perfect.

She went back outside to unlock and remove the grille from the front window. Checked her watch. Plenty of time to nip back along the arcade for a coffee and a croissant, fetch them back to the shop.

Minutes later, she was back. As she was straightening a sweater sleeve she'd brushed on the way past, she noticed that one of the suit jackets seemed to have slipped a fraction lopsidedly from its hanger. Set it right now while you can. When she reached inside, a hand caught hold of her wrist. She screamed, but no sound came out because the other hand was tight across her mouth. She struggled and her assailant pushed her back, then flung her round, hard against the wall beside the office door. Old clothes that didn't fit and stank with sweat, sour breath, a smile that played around the corners of his tightly drawn mouth; a warning, unmistakable, in the flecked gray of Michael Preston's eyes.

They sat in the office, so small that from any point you could touch all four walls. Michael had pushed aside a pile of loose papers and was perching on the desk, catalogs and ring binders on the shelf close by his head. Maureen sat on the only chair. Michael had been sleeping rough, his hair was matted and his face unshaven; he could have been dossing down on the benches in the bus station or along the canal and no one would have looked twice. It was a quarter past nine. Their legs were touching. Both office and shop doors were locked.

"You're not supposed ..." Maureen stopped and began again. "It said you'd left the country, the news, it ..."

"Good."

"But why ... ?"

He was shaking his head. No questions other than his own. "You alone here today, or what?"

"No." Instinctively, she glanced round toward the door. "My two girls, they'll be here any minute."

"When?"

"Half past nine."

Michael nodded. "Send them home."

"I can't."

"I thought you were the boss?"

"Why would I? There's no reason. I don't know what I'd tell them and anyway, they'd just hang around. All their friends, they work nearby, the other shops."

"Then tell them you're leaving 'em to it. Not feeling too great. Hangover, whatever."

"I can't. It's my busiest day, I ..."

139

He leaned in toward her, not much, just a little, the smile back at the edges of his mouth. "Is that what you think this is about? Whether you're going to have a busy day? Sell a lot of poncey frocks?"

"No."

His leg was pressing hard against her knees.

"Right, here's what you do. Give me the keys to your car."

"I ..."

"Where is it? Up the top?"

Maureen nodded.

"Good. I'll wait for you there. Go buy me some clothes, nothing fancy, nothing that'll stand out. Shoes, size ten. You got a razor at home? A proper one, I mean?"

Again, she shook her head.

"Okay, get that sorted, too. And food. If you haven't got much in, pick something up. I haven't eaten a decent meal in days."

"There's that croissant ..."

"I said *food.*"

For a moment, Maureen closed her eyes. Then, because Preston had got to his feet she did the same. When she moved, she could feel the dampness of her body, the dry hollow inside her mouth. As well as Preston, she could smell herself, rancid through her perfume. It was like a room in which they had just made love, a sweated bed.

"You know better," he said, "than to try and tell anyone about this? The police. Anyone."

"Yes."

He could scarcely hear the word. "What?"

"Yes. I said, yes. I ..."

His hand was at her throat, the pressure from the bone at the base of his forefinger just enough to stop her breath. "If you do, I'll kill you."

Maureen's legs went beneath her and to stop herself falling she pushed out both arms sideways against opposite walls.

"Why?" she asked, recovering, catching her breath. "Why me?"

Slowly, Michael ran his hand down her neck and across the thin covering of her chest until it touched her breast.

Hurrying out of Blazer with a cotton sweater and chambray shirt, Maureen nearly bumped into a young policewoman turning the corner on to the Poultry. Two of the several bags she was carrying were jolted from her hand. "I'm sorry," she said hastily.

"No problem."

"I just wasn't looking ..."

"You're all right, don't worry."

The officer was half a head shorter than Maureen, ten, fifteen years younger; a roundish face, ends of dark hair poking out from beneath her uniform cap.

"Here." She retrieved the sweater, gray marl, safe in its plastic wrapper. "Nice," she said. "For you?"

Maureen shook her head. "A friend." She slid the package down into its bag.

"Not always easy, is it?"

"Sorry?"

"Buying for other people." The officer laughed. "Men, especially. Know what they want, at least they like to think they do; only problem, they can never get it into words."

"Most of them, yes, I know what you mean."

"Well, if you've got one as can, hang on to him, that's my advice. And watch out when you're stepping out on to the pavement."

How easy, Maureen thought, to say it now, tell her about Michael waiting up there in Fletcher Gate car park, hunched down in the back seat of her car. An escaped prisoner; a convicted murderer. *I'll kill you.* "Thanks," she said, moving toward the curb.

"Right," the officer smiled, turning to walk away. "Take care."

Ahead of Maureen, the corner bookstore, the fly-posted wall of Bottle Lane, splintered in a jagged blur.

"I thought maybe you weren't coming," Michael said, minutes later, when she got into the front seat of the car. "Thought you'd run off to the police instead."

And he laughed.

I'll kill you. She believed him utterly.

Twenty-five

Saturdays, for Resnick, especially once the soccer season had ground to a close, tended toward limbo. Though, truth to tell, even the prospect of watching his once-beloved County, perched for ninety minutes on a plastic seat designed for lesser backsides than his own, no longer filled him with the anticipations of pleasure it once had. Indeed, it was the seats, he thought, that were the problem, more so than the decline of the team. To watch those toilers in black and white plying their decidedly average skills among the trappings of a newly renovated all-seater stadium simply wasn't right. This was neither Old Trafford nor the San Siro, not even nearby Derby's optimistically named Pride Park. This was the wrong side of the Trent, nestling close against the old cattle market, the abattoir, and Incinerator Road.

What he wanted was the jostle and caustic wit of the terraces; Bovril on sale at the kiosks, Wagon Wheels and sausage rolls; urinals where you stood elbow to elbow in the wash of everyone else's piss.

Romanticizing, Resnick knew, and as dangerous as the efforts to dress up the past and sell it sanitized that drew tourists to the Lace Museum and Tales of Robin Hood and even the Galleries of Justice, where for a few pounds you could inspect the old police cells and the tunnel along which deported prisoners were shepherded into canal boats on the first part of their plague-ridden journey to the colonies.

From where he was leaning on the railing overlooking the Emmett clock, he spotted Hannah, with a bag from the new Tesco Metro in each hand, and called her name.

For a while, they wandered around the upstairs market, Hannah, having deposited her first batch of shopping in her car, buying fillets of trout, scallops, and squid, Resnick half a pound of pale herring roe tinged with pink and two thick slabs of cod, which he would share, inevitably, with the cats. Hannah bought green vegetables, fruit; Resnick, Polish sausage, bacon, smoked ham, gherkins pickled in spiced vinegar and dill. They both bought cheese.

"Coffee?" Hannah said.

Her own choice, Resnick knew, would have meant a brief walk to the Dome or Café Rouge, one of those other places where, within moments of entering, he felt too fat, too old, too entirely in the wrong clothes. But today Hannah led him back to the Italian coffee stall, where, she guessed correctly, he had been less than an hour before.

"This band young Ben Fowles plays in," Resnick said, "they're playing in one of the pubs this Sunday lunchtime. He's been doling out free tickets. If you're interested."

"You and me?"

"Why not?"

Hannah smiled with her eyes. "Thought your Sundays were spent listening to jazz at the Bell."

"Maybe a change'd do me good."

"That's my line," Hannah said. "Used to be. Anyway, I've plans for Sunday, I'm sorry."

Resnick nodded, unsure if he were disappointed or not.

"You go. You might enjoy it."

Resnick nodded; they both knew he wouldn't venture within a mile. He spotted a couple leaving around the other side of the stall and hurried to claim the seats.

"I think they will have soon to arm you," Aldo said, serving them their coffee. "These shootings."

"Do you think they will?" Hannah asked, moments later.

"What?"

"Arm you, the police?"

He shook his head. "No. No more than we are now."

"Something's going to happen, surely?"

He looked at her questioningly.

"Almost every time you open the paper …"

143

Resnick's laugh stopped her in her stride.

"What?"

"Not the kind of thing I expect a *Guardian* reader to come out with."

"Oh, don't worry, Charlie, the *Guardian*'s full of it, too. Shootings in London, a whole spate of them, drug-related. Some kind of gang war." She looked at him steadily. "Is that what's happening here?"

"Not exactly."

"But it might?"

Resnick tried his espresso, slightly sharp. "I was listening to someone on the Force the other day suggesting we should stand back and let them kill one another off."

"Them?"

"The dealers."

"Because they're black."

"Because they're criminals. Because they make vast amounts of money from keeping people who can least afford it hooked on drugs."

Hannah shot him a wry smile. "You almost sound as if you think it's a good idea."

"That's not what I said." He brought his cup down on to its saucer so hard it was a wonder one of them didn't crack.

"Charlie, come on." Hannah touched his arm and he shook her away. "I'm interested. It concerns me. Kids I'm teaching; fourteen, fifteen, younger ..."

"Like Sheena Snape."

"Yes, like Sheena. They're the ones likely to end up in the middle of all this. And suffer because of it."

"If their parents kept a proper eye on them, who they were with, made sure they were home at a reasonable time ..."

It was Hannah's turn to laugh. "For God's sake, Charlie, just listen to yourself. How old d'you think you sound?"

"As old as I am."

"Older. Those things you're saying, for huge numbers of the families round here, they're not relevant. They don't mean a thing any more."

"Well, they should."

"And you think your sitting there saying so will make it happen?" There was no humor in her laugh. "Sometimes I think you are living in the past, Charlie, I really do. Or else you wish you were."

Espresso unfinished, Resnick was down from his stool. "I'd best be off."

"Not like you to run away."

"Maybe there's things I'd sooner fight about."

"People you'd rather talk to."

"You said that, Hannah, I didn't." But all the same, he didn't once turn back as he walked away.

At the police's request, Jason Johnson had been moved into a quiet side room which closed off from the rest of the ward and there was a uniformed officer, bored, leafing through the pages of the *Sun*, on duty outside. As a precaution it made simple sense, but though there were no reports of anyone aside from authorized personnel entering or leaving, someone had got to Johnson somehow.

Lying there among the usual panoply of charts and pillows, head shaved and half-covered with bandages, Johnson looked young, younger than his years, and the eyes that flickered toward Resnick and away again, were pale and scared.

No, he hadn't been on the Forest to meet anybody; no special reason at all, just him and his girlfriend, looking to chill out, okay, maybe smoke a little dope, perhaps fool around. His sister? She was just there with them, in the car, that was all. Maybe he'd seen another vehicle, he wasn't sure. Suddenly there was this crazy bastard hammering on the window, aiming a gun at him, right at his head. No, he didn't know who it was. Or why. Couldn't say. Too dark, too fast, too much in his face. Pow! You know what I'm sayin'? He sticks the gun in the car and pow! No time to see a thing. And the knife? Yeh, maybe there was a knife. Self-defense, man. No, what? Valentine? Later, maybe later. It was hazy, man. He wasn't sure. Drew Valentine? He couldn't say it was or wasn't Valentine who shot him 'cause he didn't know. Okay, okay, he'd cop for the knife. But, hey, he'd just been shot, he was bleeding, could hardly think, never mind see. Self-defense, what I'm saying. What else was he supposed to do?

Resnick leaned forward across the bed. "Okay, Jason, I don't know who you've been listening to, though I could guess, but now listen to me. You're just off the critical list. Lucky to be alive. There's still a fragment of that bullet left near your brain. What that's going to mean in time to come, I don't know. But what seems clear is someone tried to kill you. Right?"

Johnson's eyes flickered and closed; he didn't want to hear any more.

Resnick touched him on the shoulder, only lightly; waited a count of three. "I can only guess the reason. Maybe it was something you did or didn't do. Teach you a lesson. Something that would serve as an example to others. But what you've got to think about, whoever did this, maybe now they've got more call for wanting you out of the way than ever. So if you have been talking to someone, striking some kind of deal, who's to say the minute you're out of here all bets are off and they're not going to try and kill you again?"

Resnick leaned even closer, his voice lower, more insistent. "Of course, if you know who it was that put that gun to your head, and I think you do, all you have to do is tell us and we can take him off the street right now. You identify him, agree to testify, and we'll forget any charges against you. More than that, we'll look after you, protect you, put you into a witness protection program if need be. Whatever it is, you need to feel safe. Understood? Jason, understood?"

Johnson didn't respond. Resnick stretched out a hand and rested the tip of his extended finger against the youth's bandaged head. "Think about what I said. Only not for too long. There's an officer outside, tell him you want to speak to me. And, Jason ... do it while you still can."

Resnick ignored the lift in favor of the stairs. Whatever threats or promises he'd made, stack them up against what he knew Valentine to be capable of, he had little doubt whom Johnson found the more persuasive.

Anthony Drew Valentine had visitors. A young woman wearing an electric-blue catsuit was lounging across the bed, while another, twin rings shining from her navel as she stretched back in a

146

hospital chair, legs splayed, was tearing away the gold paper from a bottle of champagne. A bullet-headed black man with muscles to spare was leaning against the bedside cabinet on which he had placed his packet of Rizla papers, meticulously skinning up.

"What the fuck …?" Valentine began and then stopped.

"All right," Resnick announced, "party's over. Out. Now."

"Who's he think he is?" asked the woman in blue.

"Yeh, this is a private room," her friend said. "Didn't anybody teach you to knock?"

"Easy now," Valentine said. "He the one I told you 'bout. Mean an' nasty." He laughed and the others laughed with him.

"Well," the bullet-headed man said, pausing to give his spliff a final lick before sliding it between his forefinger and thumb, "if he's so mean, he can suck my dick."

The girls were still giggling when Resnick swung his fist and hit the man hard to the side of the head. It was a lucky punch with weight behind it and it caught him off guard as well as off balance and, rocked sideways, his other cheek went smack against the cabinet's edge.

With a faint groan, he sank to his knees.

"Man," Valentine said, impressed despite himself, "you know who that is? He's a sparring partner for some of the best light-heavies in the business."

"Sure," Resnick said, picking up the joint from where it had rolled across the floor. "And quaint and old-fashioned as it is for me to say so, possession of this is still a criminal offense. So tell your friends I want them off the premises now, and this one, if I see him again, ever, I'm likely to put him under arrest and press charges. Understood?"

In less than two minutes, Resnick and Drew Valentine were alone.

"So," Resnick said, sitting down, "why the celebration?"

"Day after tomorrow. Monday. Out of here first thing. Released to enjoy me a long convalescence."

"Just as long as you're not thinking of taking it outside the city."

"My travel agent, he's recommending Bali."

"Save your money. There's still a little matter of attempted murder to attend to."

"I guess you i'n't talked to Jason yet? Smart kid. Knows which side his bread buttered."

The smile still on his face, Resnick brought his hand down onto the covers and squeezed Valentine's leg. Valentine gasped with pain.

"Jesus, man! That's my bad leg."

"Mean and nasty, remember," Resnick said and squeezed harder. Valentine screamed.

A nurse appeared in the doorway, looking concerned. "Nothing to worry about," Resnick said pleasantly. "It seems I rested my hand on the wrong part of the bed. No cause for alarm."

The nurse looked over at Valentine and remembered what he had called her earlier. "Very well," she said and let the door swing closed behind her.

Resnick relaxed the pressure of his hand, but not too much. "I'm here to tell you something. One way or another, and I don't know how, not yet, you've been able to steer clear of the law and carry on dealing right across the city."

"I ain't ..."

Changing the angle of his arm, Resnick applied pressure steadily downwards. "Car, clothes, jewelry: you walk around this town with more money on your back than most ordinary folk earn in a year. Up to now, you've got away with it. Not any more."

He gave Valentine's leg a parting, friendly pat and rose to his feet. "Oh, one other thing," he said at the door. "That gun you used on Jason, then tossed on to the Forest. We're going to do better than find your prints on it; we're going to trace it back to the supplier. Prince, Gary. Ring a bell?"

It was only there for an instant, but the jolt of alarm in Valentine's eyes was vivid, unmistakable.

Back outside, walking away from the hospital toward Old Lenton, Resnick's step was springier, lighter. He couldn't remember the last time he'd struck a blow outside of self-defense; couldn't recall when he'd last used force of any kind. And although he knew that later his conscience would be giving him gyp, right now he felt one hundred percent better, as if he'd cleared a lot of dead weight from his soul.

Twenty-six

One of the first things Preston had done after they'd arrived at Maureen's had been to down two large cups of tea laced with brandy; the other was to strip to his skin right there in the kitchen: twelve years of prison slop-outs and prison showers didn't leave much room for embarrassment. "Burn them," he said, indicating the pile of soiled clothing.

Maureen looked at him helplessly. "What?"

"I said, burn them."

"There's only a gas fire, natural effect."

"What about the dustbin?"

"Plastic."

Preston cursed. "Bin bags. You can take them to the dump later."

Reluctantly, Maureen bent down to pick up the clothes, her head level with his crotch; Preston watching her, a smile playing round the corners of his mouth.

"Well?" he said.

Maureen stood up, blushing, unable to look him in the eye.

Preston laughed and turned away, knowing that she was looking at him as he climbed the stairs, the long curve of his back, his balls just visible between his legs, that tight arse.

The first thing Maureen had done when she moved into her thirties house in Bramcote Hills was to have several acres of moss-green carpet cleared from the floors and the original boards sanded and varnished, polished till they shone with a deep hue that her cleaning lady worked hard to maintain. Layers of flowery paper were stripped from the walls and the whole of the downstairs painted creamy white. Aside from the kitchen, which resembled the stretched interior of a spaceship capsule, Maureen had been keen to mix old and new, the contemporary with items which brought out that original thirties feel. In the living room, a brown leather settee shared the space with a pair of upright Waring and Gillow armchairs; a trio of hand-thrown prewar vases sat on a molded plastic coffee table from IKEA.

It was a beautiful—to Maureen—stylish home. And now she was trapped in it with a man who had killed and could kill again.

While she was waiting for him to be done with his bath, she put food on the table—cold roast chicken, tomatoes, potato salad, cheese, two sticks of French bread. There was ice cream in the freezer, Ben and Jerry's, three flavors; she kept it there as a lesson in temptation. She thought for the hundredth time about making a run for it; she thought about opening wine. Maureen laughed nervously. Was that what you did when you were kidnapped by your brother-in-law who'd just escaped from prison? Get out the best silver and a bottle of Chilean Cabernet?

She was thinking about him, up there in that oval tub, feet up on the edge most probably, knees spread wide. How easy it would have been for her to slip her mobile from her bag and dial 999; lock the front door from the outside, jump into the car, and drive away. Anywhere. Surely that's what she should do?

Kill you. Since that first warning, he hadn't wasted words on another.

Hearing a movement upstairs, she slipped the clear plastic corkscrew over the head of the bottle and began to twist.

Shaved, a comb pulled through thick, short hair, Michael Preston stood in the doorway, barefoot. The clothes Maureen had chosen, the pre-faded denim shirt, the dark olive chinos, fitted perfectly. As they should. It was her job.

"Feeling better for that?" God, listen to her!

"Yeah." Looking at the food on the table, he grinned. "Been busy, I see." He pulled out one of the pale, high-backed dining chairs and sat down and poured himself a full glass of wine; as an afterthought, he poured a second for her.

Maureen sat opposite him and unfolded the napkin from beside her fork.

"Your idea, the bath? That shape?"

"Yes."

"Nice. Lets you spread out." He reached toward the chicken and, ignoring the carving knife, took hold of the bird with both hands and broke off a leg. "Fit two in, I dare say. At a squeeze."

Maureen cut the tomato on her plate in half and half again.

"Bit of a luxury for me, lazing about in all that hot water. Bath foam. Body lotion. Not needing eyes in the back of your head. Some bastard who's signed on queer for the duration; bar of soap in one hand and his scabby dick in the other." A piece of dark meat threatened to fall from his mouth and he caught it with his tongue.

Amused at her discomfort, he tipped potato salad on to his plate. "Make all this yourself, did you?"

"No, I ..."

Preston jabbed the air with his chicken bone. "You know, Maureen, there's one thing you're going to have to learn: when I'm serious and when I'm not."

He lay fully stretched out on the brown settee, eyes closed, enjoying the strangely warm softness of the creased leather, his wineglass on the floor alongside. It was at least ten minutes since he had spoken and, less than comfortable on one of her prize chairs, Maureen wondered if he had fallen asleep. How long was he going to keep her there, a prisoner? Tomorrow, Sunday, the shop was closed. Monday, too. And after ...? She looked down at him, so seemingly sure of himself, sleeping. How long did he intend to stay?

She was bracing herself to move when he said, not bothering to open his eyes, "The police, they been round?"

She hesitated. "To the shop, yes. They contacted everyone, I suppose. Everyone who'd been at the funeral."

"What kind of police? CID? Plainclothes?"

"Uniform, two young men in uniform. Why? Does it matter?"

"Sometimes."

"They just asked me if I'd seen you since the time at Derek's house and of course I said no. If I'd noticed anything unusual, that kind of thing. Nothing, well, specific, you know?"

"Not suspicious, then, you didn't reckon?"

151

"No. No. I mean, why would they be?"

He startled her by sitting up suddenly and swinging his feet round to the floor. "They haven't been watching the house?"

"Here? No, of course not."

"How 'bout Lorraine's?"

She blinked. "I don't know. I don't think so."

He leaned back against the settee. "Bound to have been. A while, at least. They're not stupid, you know. Not altogether."

He leaned back against the settee.

"You'll be wanting to see her, I suppose?" Maureen said. "Lorraine. You'll be wanting to get in touch?"

"Yes," he said. "Most likely."

It was silent for some moments, neither of them moving.

"Michael?"

"Yeah?"

"What ... what are you going to do?"

Slowly he smiled. "You'll see. Soon enough."

It was dark outside. The last she had seen of Preston, he was watching TV. Only now he wasn't; he was there in the kitchen, leaning against the door frame, staring. Maureen felt her skin go cold.

"That day," he said, "the funeral. Back at Lo's place. You were coming on to me."

Maureen blinked. "I don't think so. Was I?"

"You know bloody well you was."

She half turned away. "I'm sorry, I ..."

"What? Didn't mean it?"

"No."

"Talk like that to all the boys?"

She tried to swallow but her tongue, marooned, refused to move.

"The way you was leaning across me, touching me, every now and again, just a little. Here." He stroked the inside of his forearm with the knuckles of his free hand. "You remember?" Staring at her all the while, staring.

"Yes."

"Making sure I could get a good view of your tits."

Maureen wanted to go to the bathroom; she needed to pee. Now his hand was back in the pocket of his chinos and she could see the movement, slow and rhythmic, beneath the slightly shiny fabric.

"Fancied me, didn't you."

"Look, Michael, I'm sorry ..." She moved several quick paces toward him and then stopped.

"All an act, then, was it?"

"No, that's not what I'm saying. I ... I suppose ... Well, yes, I was ... attracted to you. I ..."

He was smiling with his eyes, gray eyes. "Not just a prick teaser, then?"

She shook her head.

"One of those tarts get turned on by someone doing serious time?" He took the slightest step toward her.

"No," she said, trying to stop herself shaking. "No, honestly."

He touched her. "Kiss me then. On the mouth. Now. Yes, now."

She felt his tongue push past her teeth inside her and the movement of his hand accelerating, clear and hard against her side. His teeth bit down into her lower lip, not deep; she felt a shudder travel through his body and then his hand was still, his tongue withdrew.

Maureen didn't know if she should stay where she was or move away.

After a few moments, he said, "I'm going upstairs, take a nap. I need to catch up on some sleep. Wake me in a couple of hours, right? Don't forget. There's a call I've got to make."

Maureen nodded, barely able to move her head.

She needed to feel clean. While he slept, she stood in the shower for a long time, temperature racked up high, and when she stepped out the bathroom was rich with steam. A towel round her body, another round her head, she sat on the toilet seat and sobbed.

The door to the main bedroom was ajar and she could see him spread diagonally along the surface of the bed, naked; hear the faint hiss and whistle of his breath.

She thought she could fetch a hammer and bring it down with

all her strength against his head; she thought that she could slip out of her robe and rest her face against the swelling of his chest.

She went downstairs and poured herself a drink, and didn't go back up until it was time for him to be called, and when she walked across the floor toward him he blinked instantly awake.

Twenty-seven

The first time Lynn woke and rolled over on to her side, reaching for the radio alarm, the face read 4:17. She tugged at the quilt and turned away again, pulling her knees up toward her chest: 4:43, 5:07, 5:29. Beneath the occasional whistle and call of birds, she could hear the hum of traffic, faint yet constant, as it wound its way along the inner ring road, from the old Boots building round by the ice rink and the bowling alley toward Ritzy's and the Victoria market. Living where she did, in a small block of modern flats near the center of the city, there was never any forgetting where she was or what she did, the choices she had made.

"Oh, Lynnie, pet, why?" Concern deepening the lines on her mother's already lined face. "Why there of all places? When you'd be so much better closer to home."

"Let the girl be, woman," her father had said, one of his rare interjections. "She's got her own life to live, hasn't she? Let her be getting on with it."

So Lynn had applied for her first ever post after finishing training, been measured for her uniform, finally climbed in the battered old Vauxhall, back seat jammed with bags and boxes, one of her dad's best chickens, double-wrapped in plastic from the freezer, sandwiches and a thermos tucked in by her mum at the last moment, just in case she felt peckish on the journey. Four hours at most, west to east across country.

She could still see her mother lifting her apron to trap the tears; her father squeezing two ten-pound notes into her hand as she raised her face to kiss him, the scrape of his bristles against her lips and cheek.

"You'll come back and see us, Lynnie. You won't forget us now. Come back soon."

And, of course, she did drive back across that familiar landscape skirting the edge of the fens, a slow dual-carriage road bordered by farm shops and market gardens, carrying her to a home from which she felt increasingly remote. Her mother, with round face and fleshy, freckled arms, baking something in the kitchen, making huge jugs of tea, helping out in the packing shed, hosing down the yard; her father wandering with less and less purpose between the long lines of hen houses, weight falling off his bones a little more each time, the skin around his Adam's apple wrinkled and loose till it resembled that of the birds he raised.

Without even realizing at first, Lynn would make excuses—not this weekend, Mum, I'm sorry; no, not that—a friend's party, a dinner invitation, overtime. And when she had lived with the cyclist, so much of her time had been wasted, standing hunched in her parka by the side of some arterial road, stop-watch in gloved hand, stamping her feet to keep away the cold.

Almost, she would dread her mother's weekly call, the painstaking recounting of events so unimportant and small, the pressure to return, the love and need. And when she did—one Sunday a month now at most—the long silences which neither of them could fill, until she would walk out to find her father, who seemed to spend more and more of his time outside now, and sit with him in a silence that was somehow less strained, broken only by the clack and ragged cry of birds with nothing else to do but peck and shit and die.

"Look after your mother, Lynnie. I don't know what might happen to her, else."

The nobbled coldness of his hand, dry scrape of his cough, yellow film that spread slowly from the corners of his eyes.

At the Norfolk and Norwich hospital, the registrar had been all smiles behind his rimless glasses, an accent buffed by years of breeding and expensive education. "The one thing I don't want you to do is worry. Not unduly. This little problem of your father's, the kind of thing we deal with every day. Run of the mill. Ten a penny."

Lynn turned the knob round to full and stepped into the shower. Eyes closed, she soaped her body, rubbed shampoo into her hair, the steady stream of water bouncing off her shoulders, coursing down her back, between her legs, splashing across her face. Driving back from the hospital after that first consultation with the doctor, vision obscured by heavy rain and the spray of water from the road, eyes stung by sudden tears, she had swerved from the slipstream of a lorry into the side of the road and cannoned against the verge, thankful for the seat belt which held her fast. She had still been sitting there, shaking, minutes later, when Michael Best had tapped against the window, anxious, smiling, wanting to know if there was anything he could do to help.

Lynn could never forgive herself for the foolishness of what happened next, how she had allowed herself to be charmed by this all too plausible stranger, tricked into believing his soft-spoken half-truths and promises, lured by his smile and his easy lies.

It had ended in an open field, helpless inside a caravan, a prisoner, a metal bucket and a chain. A man who had killed and would likely kill again. For the first time since she was a young child, Lynn had prayed. And over Best's insinuating voice, she had heard it, the rattle of the helicopter; the run, then, forced, across the rutted field. And Resnick, running toward them, arms flailing as he struggled for balance, the helicopter overhead sucking at his clothes and hair. And then he had held her, lifted her into his arms and held her, like her father and so utterly unlike her father, safe against his body.

One day, Lynn thought, she would be able to think of one without the other.

Climbing from the shower, she toweled herself briskly and then, tying another towel around her hair, went into the kitchen to make tea. Unless she got stuck behind a tractor or a caravan heading for the coast, she should have a clear run. A bacon sandwich with her mother and then the hospital well before noon. She finished off her hair under the drier, put on jeans and a T-shirt, grabbed a sweater at the last moment just in case. When she crossed the Trent over Lady Bay Bridge less than five minutes later, the sky behind her was eggshell white.

157

Lynn's mother was sitting just inside the back door, coat on, hands resting on the bag in her lap; she looked as if she'd been sitting there for hours. When Lynn bent to kiss her cheek, the skin felt heavy, like dough. Her fingers were bloodless and cold.

"Mum, don't you want a cup of tea?"

"I was sure you'd want to go straight off, see your dad."

Lynn touched her lightly on the shoulder. "I think we should have a cup of tea first, don't you?"

She found half a loaf of Sunblest, several days old, and made toast, which her mother made little attempt to eat.

"Mum, you've got to have something. You can't just starve."

"I've not fancied anything since your dad's been away."

"If you're not careful, you'll end up in there with him. Here, have some more of this."

Her mother took a bite, then pushed the plate away.

There were two drips attached to her father's arms, one at either side of the bed. He was lying with his head to one side, mouth slightly open, a stain where his face met the pillow. His lips were cracked and dry, pulling away in brittle patches. The whites of his eyes were covered by a milky yellow film; the skin that hung loose about his neck, stretched tight along his arms, a darker, murkier yellow. Lynn caught the sob that rose to her throat, but could do nothing about the tears.

Her mother busied herself with the bedside table, putting the fruit she'd brought into a bowl.

Lynn sat close and held the fingers of her father's hand. Between the knuckles, the flesh seemed to have fallen away; the nails, unclipped, were long and hard.

"Dad? Daddy?"

His eyes moved a little, a slow blink, and she could just feel the pressure as he squeezed her hand.

It was a different registrar, a woman not much older than Lynn herself, three pens of various colors side by side in the pocket of her white coat. She spoke slowly, not unpleasantly, the way an aunt might talk to her small niece, the one who wasn't very bright. "Your father was quite weak when he came in, really rather poorly. That's why we didn't operate straightaway. Let him rest, regain a little strength."

"He looks terrible. My mother's convinced he's going to die."

The registrar smiled, something almost violet in her eyes. "In your father's state, anything invasive … well, it will take him time to recover." She looked at the watch that was pinned to the front of her coat. "I'm sorry, I really should be getting on." She held out her hand.

"There isn't anything else?" Lynn asked at the door.

"How do you mean?"

Lynn didn't know.

The registrar's touch on her shoulder was surprisingly firm. "One thing at a time. Let's get this cleared up, get him home. All right? If there's anything else, anything worrying you, well, you know where I am."

While her mother sat in front of the small black-and-white television in the front room, watching a program about migrating birds, Lynn opened a tin of tomato soup, warmed shop-bought apple pie. The top of the cooker and all around the grill pan were rich with grease; tea-leaves and potato peelings clogged the sink. How long had it been like this, Lynn wondered? Since her father had gone back into hospital or before? *Look after your mother, Lynnie. I don't know what might happen to her, else.* They ate with a pair of metal trays balanced across their laps, free gifts with the coupons from however many packets of Huntley and Palmer biscuits. Conversation was sparse and bleak. Over the sound of the television, they could hear the whistling of the lad paid to come by and feed the hens, make sure they were all battened down safely at night. On the small curve of screen, a flock of young birds, like moving particles across the pink and purple of an equatorial sky, following their magnetic compass to a home they'd never seen.

159

Twenty-eight

The pub was smoky and full, and reverberating with noise. Ben Fowles was bobbing and weaving in front of the microphone, more like a man five rounds into a middleweight bout than Resnick's idea of a singer. He was wearing white gym shoes, combat trousers, and a white T-shirt torn at one shoulder. His voice was pitched somewhere between a yelp and a scream, and his delivery had all the subtlety of a fast-approaching train. There were lyrics, Resnick was sure, but he couldn't distinguish what they were.

In contrast to Ben Fowles's exertions, the rest of the band looked vaguely bored. A tall man with thick-rimmed glasses stood stage left, staring down at the floor, playing bass guitar, while opposite, also standing, a young woman in a black silk shirt, her hair in a ponytail, played a small electronic keyboard. Behind them, a drummer wearing Forest colors and a baseball cap swatted around a minimal kit, while a squat figure wearing headphones, eyes closed, released a weird array of noises from some computer-driven gizmo, at the same time as manipulating records on a twin-turntable to make rhythmic scratching sounds.

"So what d'you reckon?" Carl Vincent asked, leaning close.

Resnick didn't know.

The next number was altogether different: an instrumental, a sort of soul sound, but with a different beat; Ben Fowles alternating between rudimentary electric guitar and a toy saxophone, the kind found in the children's section at Woolworths around Christmas time.

Resnick bought a round of drinks and exchanged a few words with Vincent's friend, Peter, a computer engineer from Loughborough. The band were thrusting their way toward an interval,

Ben Fowles running on the spot and repeating over and over a line from which he could only decipher the word "murder." The bass player walked off the stage; a snare drum went crashing to the floor; a continuous, keening note came from the deserted keyboard; of the band, only one remained, hands a blur of movement over the turntables as the scratching intensified. Suddenly, Fowles threw up his hand and everything stopped. There was a moment's silence, a few shouts, applause, and a scramble for the bar.

Resnick waited long enough to say well done and shake Fowles's hand, then he was back out on the street and on his way to the center of town.

In the back room of the Bell, the usual musicians were into their final set. "King Porter Stomp," "Clarinet Marmalade," "Way Down Yonder In New Orleans." Resnick nodded to a few familiar faces, bought a pint of Guinness, and leaned against the corner of the bar.

When the band launched into "Dippermouth Blues," and the trumpeter played, note for note, the same three muted choruses that Joe "King" Oliver had first played in 1923, Resnick knew, if he wasn't exactly in heaven, at least, for those moments, all was right with the world.

"What the hell are *you* doin' here?" Norma Snape asked, back from her normal Sunday lunchtime session at the pub.

Her daughter Sheena was stretched out on the sofa, watching the *EastEnders* omnibus on TV. "I live here, don't I?" she replied, not lifting her eyes from the set.

"Not so's I've noticed," Norma said, glancing at the screen a moment before heading for the kitchen.

"Mum ..."

"What?"

"Make us a cup of tea."

Out in the back garden, the dog was digging a large hole, with the apparent intent of burying the axle and rear wheel of an old pram someone had tossed over the back wall. Norma fished two mugs from the cold, scummy water in the sink and wiped them with a tea towel. She wished she'd splashed out on the half-ounce of

161

Skunk she'd been offered an hour before, Teddy Eyles making it all too plain he was prepared to take payment in kind. And now the scuttering dog had realized she was back and was barking at the door. Jesus H. Christ! A nice fat joint was what she needed to get her through the rest of the afternoon.

Grudgingly, Sheena swung her legs round to let her mum sit down.

"I've had the police round again," Norma said.

"So?"

"So they were asking about you."

"What about me?"

"You and that mate of yours ..."

"Diane?"

"I don't know what she's called. Both of you mixed up in some business out on the Forest, some bloke getting shot."

"That weren't nothin' to do with us."

"You were there, weren't you? You telling me they're lying? Telling me you weren't?"

Sheena tossed her head.

"You want to be careful, my girl, hanging out with people like that."

"Like what?"

"You know."

"Christ," Sheena exclaimed, "you wonder I never come home? Nag, nag, nag. You're on to me the minute I walk in the fuckin' door."

"And mind your language."

"Yeh, fuckin' right." Sheena reached for her tea and cursed again as she spilt some of it down her leg. If only her mother'd stop moaning on and let her watch telly. Not that she knew much about what was going on. Same old faces saying the same old things. What was exercising Sheena's mind was what was wrapped in a couple of soiled towels underneath Diane's sink, the souvenir the pair of them had smuggled back from that night on the Forest, the gun with which Drew Valentine had shot Diane's brother in the head.

162

Resnick had pottered his way through the afternoon: mowed what he half jokingly referred to as the lawn; chatted to his friend Marian Witczak on the phone; made tea; taken a nap; glanced through the glossy booklet advertising jazz CDs. He knew that Hannah had driven over to her mother's for lunch, dreading a meal that would inevitably be soured by the news of her father's imminent remarriage.

So when the doorbell rang in the early evening he assumed it would be Hannah, back from performing her unwanted duty and in need of a little rest and relaxation.

But it was Lynn Kellogg smiling at him weakly from the doorstep, hoping that she wasn't disturbing him, but if there was any chance of a cup of coffee.

Lynn picked up Bud and cradled the small cat in her arms, stroking him while he purred and pushed his head against her neck, the underside of her chin. Resnick ground coffee beans and made an offer of a sandwich that was gratefully accepted.

They sat in easy chairs that had been old and in need of replacement when Resnick and his ex-wife Elaine had sat in them sixteen years before.

"No music?" Lynn said with a smile.

Resnick pulled something calming from the shelves, Bud Shank and Laurindo Almeida playing bossa novas, used and worn and comforting. Midway through the first side, Lynn set her plate aside and began to talk about the hospital, her father's illness, her mother's state of mind. When she broke off to sniff back tears, Resnick waited, silent, for her to regain control; and when the tears came again, unstoppable this time, he crossed the room and held her, Lynn's face tight against his shoulder.

Neither of them heard Hannah's VW approach as far as the curve in the road, Lynn's car clearly visible beneath the street light. Hannah switched off her headlights, opened the car door, but didn't get out. Minutes later, she reversed back toward the main road, turned, and headed for home.

Twenty-nine

The morning was beautiful: the sky was a flat, bright blue, cloudless and seemingly pure, and the sun, when he stepped out through the back door, was instantly warm on Resnick's face. Here and there, the shrubs that bordered three sides of the garden were showing pink and white and shiny red, and the cherry tree was still clinging to much of its bloom. Only the shed in which he kept the aging mower, tins of crusted paint, and his small array of garden tools was an eyesore. Past the stage of easy repair, what it needed was demolishing and burning, a new one purchased in its place. Bonfire night, perhaps, Resnick thought, he'd drag the planks off and add them to some communal blaze.

Away to the south, he could see the two sets of floodlights at either side of the Trent, Forest and County, and then, closer at hand, the tip of the clock tower marking the old Victoria railway station, the dome of the Council House catching the light at one end of the Old Market Square.

Standing there on the back step, he caught himself thinking about Lynn Kellogg, the sadness, the slow anticipation of grief that had hovered behind her eyes. He remembered his own father's passing, lingering and slow, the richly sweet smell of dying that had permeated the room. Skin like graying paper, nails like horn. The priest's words. The sacrament. His mother's prayers. The rest of his father's family had been Jews, practicing, devout. He had never properly understood the circumstances that had led to his father's Catholic upbringing, a catalog of changing homes, of largely faceless uncles and forbidding aunts.

Turning back into the house, he thought about ringing Hannah. By the time he had poured himself a second cup of coffee, he had thought better of it; if she'd wanted to talk to him about the visit to her mother's, she would have called.

There was an uneven slice of pepper salami lurking near the back of the fridge and he folded it around a chunk of ripe Blue Stilton, dipping them both into a jar of mayonnaise before popping them into his mouth and washing them down with apple juice from a carton whose best before date had long gone. He would walk to work: the exercise would do him good.

Lynn was in the CID room when Resnick arrived and his first impulse was that something had happened at home in Norfolk, but she stood chatting easily enough with Kevin Naylor, laughing even, and he realized it was probably something to do with the ongoing investigation. "Checking a few leads on Finney," she said. "These links with Cassady. I thought I might call round on Cassady, come at it sideways, see if I can weasel anything out of him." She gave him a quick smile. "I thought you should know."

"Yes, thanks."

"Anil, he's on to Finney himself. Likely report to you direct."

"After Siddons."

Lynn grinned. "Of course."

"Any news about your dad?" Resnick asked.

Lynn shook her head. "Not really, no."

"Okay. You'll let me know? If anything …"

"Yes. Yes, of course." And she was on her way, out through the door.

As she turned into the landing, Sheena fought to hold her breath against the usual stink of stale piss and vomit, and even worse. Though there hadn't been as much as a breeze down on the street, a wind cut along the eighth floor and she pulled the zip of her leather jacket up to the collar as she sidestepped the sheets of old newspaper and broken polystyrene food containers, hurrying on past three boarded-up flats, another with the door kicked in and hanging from a single hinge, fresh graffiti up and down the hall. When finally she got to Diane's, the top half of the door was reinforced with hardboard, a sheet of which had also been nailed to the wall alongside. The time before last the place had been burgled, unable to break through the actual door, whoever it was had simply smashed a hole in the wall and crawled through. Though, as Diane said, what the fuck they thought there was left to steal after they cleared her out five times this side of Christmas already, fuck only knows.

Sheena hammered and yelled, and after an eternity Diane, bleary-eyed, opened the door to let her in.

"What the hell d'you look like?" Sheena said.

"Fuck you, too."

Sheena followed her through into the living room, a single light bulb burning bare from the ceiling, old sheets tacked across the window. Butt ends and beer cans cluttered the stained carpet; piles of old magazines and free newspapers littered the corners. Aside from a sagging two-seater settee, the only items of furniture were a green plastic milk crate topped with a cushion and a television set Diane had bartered from one of the blokes who lived on the floor above, who'd almost certainly nicked it from the old lady on the floor below.

Diane's little boy, Melvin, was wobbling around precariously, face smeared with jam, dummy sticking from his mouth, nappy hanging low.

"Who's in there?" Sheena asked, nodding toward the kitchen.

"Just Lesley," Diane said. "Shooting up."

Sheena reached for her cigarettes, lit up, then wandered into the other room. Lesley was just lifting the heated spoon away from the gas ring.

"Here, fuckin' hold this."

Sheena steadied the spoon while Lesley, eyes narrowing in concentration, bit down into her bottom lip and drew the contents up into the syringe. With her free hand, she lifted up her skirt and, still squinting, slid the needle into a vein high in her bruised inner thigh.

"Oh, Jesus," she cried, eyes closing. "Oh, Jesus. Oh, yes. Oh, oh, Jesus. Oh, fuck! Oh, sweet fuck!"

She pulled the needle out and tossed it in the sink, a thin ribbon of blood running down her leg.

Great, thought Sheena, now that's over perhaps we can get round to sorting out what we're going to do about this fucking gun.

It had been chaos: bloody chaos. Blood down the side of her skirt and top, smeared across her face—and Diane freckled with it, gobs of it tangled in her hair. Jason and Valentine cursing and moaning.

Valentine had dropped the gun when Jason stabbed him and it had fallen inside the car; Sheena, not thinking, not thinking clearly, scrabbling on the floor to pick it up. Pushing the door open, one foot on the ground, she had been about to fling it out into the dark when she realized her prints were now plastered all over it. The toilet block was less than fifty meters away. Running hard, almost losing her footing not once but twice, she barged open the outer door and lunged into the dark. Whenever the council replaced the overhead bulbs, they were smashed within the hour.

Sheena kicked off her shoes and tugged down her tights, wrapping them around the gun before jamming it behind the cistern in the last cubicle, where it had remained, undiscovered, until Lesley, alerted by a phone call, had slipped in to collect it.

Now all Sheena wanted to do was get rid of it—but at a price.

Sheena knew Raymond Cooke through her younger brother, Nicky, who had used Raymond as a fence for much of the stuff he burgled round the neighborhood, Raymond ever eager to replenish the stock of his shop at knock-down prices. The shop, a single-story place in Bobber's Mill, with a storeroom up above and a flat over that where Raymond lived, had belonged to Terry. But in the terms of Terry's will, both shop and flat were Raymond's for as long as he wanted. And Raymond, whose only previous work experience had been hauling great tubs of offal and bone around an abattoir, had very much wanted to stay where he was.

So on that Monday afternoon, when Sheena pushed open the shop door and went in, it was Raymond who glanced up from behind his copy of the *Mirror* and wondered if he didn't recognize her from somewhere.

"Look around," he said, ever the smooth businessman, "take your time. Any questions, be only too happy to oblige."

167

Sheena surveyed the array of electrical goods piled high, every-thing available for a small down payment, easy terms, generous discounts for cash. There were car radios, mobile phones, microwave cookers, binoculars, cameras, laptop computers; CDs arranged alphabetically from Abba and Aphex Twin, by way of Oasis to The Verve and Warren Zevon.

Sheena fidgeted with the hem of her halter top, several inches of bare flesh between it and the belt that ran round her little black skirt. What she'd do, next chance she got, have her belly-button pierced like Diane. "You don't recognize me, do you?" she said.

Raymond set down his paper and smiled. "Should I?"

"Ray-o, that's what Nicky used to call you. Used to be dead skinny, didn't you? You've filled out; grown up, I suppose. Handsome."

Sheena was standing close to the chair, almost within reach, but not quite. Raymond, with his check shirt loose outside his jeans, a thin band of sweat darkening the faint mustache along his upper lip.

"Sheena, right? Sheena Snape?"

Sheena nodded and smiled.

"How is Nicky?" Raymond began, then realized. "Oh, no, look, I'm sorry. I forgot, I …"

"S'all right."

"Shane, then. Is he …?"

"Still inside, yeah."

Raymond looking at her, starting to weigh up his chances, no bra beneath that top, he was sure of that. Eighteen'd she be now? Maybe not that. A year or so younger than he was himself. "So," he said, "you just happen to pop in by accident, like, or was there something, you know, you wanted?"

Not looking at her now, staring; the end of his tongue like a bit of lamb's liver flopping between his lips. If one of us has got to fuck him, Sheena was thinking, I'm buggered if it's going to be me. Besides, she remembered, if what Nicky had said was true, Raymond only fancied them really young; rumor was he'd knocked up his cousin when she was not long out of junior school.

"I might have something," Sheena said, "you'd be interested in."

"Yeah?"

"Something to sell."

"Oh, yeh?"

"Only, you know, I'd have to be certain."

"How's that, then?"

"You could handle it, of course." She gave him one of those smiles and thought poor Raymond was going to wet himself there and then.

"Try me," he said. If Sheena came any closer, she'd be sitting in his lap.

"Okay." She slipped the bag off her shoulder and snapped it open before holding it toward him.

"Fuckin' hell!"

"Exactly."

The pistol lay among lipstick-smeared tissues, a foil-wrapped condom, sticks of sugar-free chewing gum, a strip of instant photos of Sheena and Jason they'd had taken in a booth down by the bus station. A chromed Beretta; most likely, Raymond thought, a .38. He reached his hand toward it and Sheena swung the bag away.

"So? You interested or what?"

"I might be, yeh."

"Might's not good enough."

"Okay, then, say I am."

"How much?"

"That depends."

"On what?"

Raymond shrugged. "Where it's come from, how hot it is."

"I don't know nothin' 'bout that."

"Say it's been used, right? Some blag? Shooting, even. Got to be worth a lot less'n if it's clean, nothin' the law can tie it into. See what I mean?"

"So?"

"So where'd you get it?"

"It ain't mine. Belongs to a friend."

"Where'd they get it?"

"I don't know."

"Let's have a look at it again."

This time when she stood next to him, Sheena let her hip brush against his upper arm.

"Seventy-five," Raymond said.

"Bollocks!"

"Hundred, then. Here y'are." Leaning forward, he slid a roll of notes from his back pocket and peeled off five twenties, holding them toward her. "Take 'em, go on."

"Two hundred," Sheena said and Raymond laughed and shook his head. "It's gotta be worth at least that much."

"Not to me."

"How much, then?"

"I told you, a hundred. Tops."

"Ray-o." She gave him a tight-lipped smile and touched his shoulder with her hand. Through the thin material of his shirt, his skin was slippery and damp.

"Okay," Raymond said, shifting less than easily, "I tell you what I'll do. You give me till tomorrow, let me ask around." He broke off, reading the expression on Sheena's face. "Don't worry, I won't use no names, nothin' like that. But if I can come up with a buyer, anything over the hundred I'll split it with you, fifty-fifty. How's that sound?"

Sheena wasn't sure how it would sound to Diane or Lesley. But the last thing she wanted to do was go traipsing around all over town with a bloody gun in her bag, chatting up every crooked bastard in the city.

"Let us have the hundred now," she said, "and it's a deal."

Grinning, Raymond put down two twenties, one on each knee. "There. Forty. Gesture of faith. For now. Less maybe you want to figure out some other way of earning the rest?"

Sheena snatched the notes and stuffed them down into her bag. "Tomorrow, right?" she said, opening the door. "You better have somethin' sorted."

Raymond was on his feet now, staring at her, not bothering to hide the bulge in his jeans. As Sheena told Diane and Lesley over Bacardi and Coke in the pub, she'd as soon go down on the Alsatian dog next door as give Raymond Cooke a blow job.

Raymond, back from the bathroom and still giving himself a good scratch, weighing up the implications of what he'd just seen: Jason

170

Johnson's picture, all snuggled up, lovey-dovey, with Sheena Snape, a strip of them, there in her bag; Jason, who everyone knew was stuck up in Queen's, after nearly getting his brains blown all over the Forest by some shooter who was rumored to be Drew Valentine; and, nestled up next to the photos, this gun that somehow Sheena had laid her hands on; Sheena, who'd been sitting there in the car, knickers round her neck the story went, when the gun went off against her boyfriend's head.

Raymond chewed on the fleshy inside of his mouth and wondered what the odds were on the gun in Sheena Snape's bag and the one that'd nearly killed her boyfriend being one and the same?

Like his Uncle Terry would have said, whatever the situation, Ray-o, what you have to do, think careful, figure out how you can make things work out best for you. Least risk, most profit. Most times that's the way. Once in a while, though, what it pays to do, up the ante, risk a little more, capitalize on what you've got. Nothing ventured, Ray-o, nothing gained.

Standing there, Raymond could feel the damp gathering in the palms of his hands.

Thirty

Lorraine had been going through the motions at work, going through the motions at home. She would catch Sandra looking at her curiously every once in a while, but that aside, the children seemed to have settled back into their argumentative selves. And Derek was taken up in a flurry of paperwork as the firm's owners prepared to launch a new range of colored papers in the coming autumn. Fifty classic and contemporary shades, each one available in a range of finishes, including several stunning new embossings.

In the kitchen, she scraped away the remains of the evening's ready-to-eat lasagna and slotted the last of the plates into the dishwasher. The kids were upstairs pretending to do homework. Derek had taken his coffee back into the dining-room with his charts, closing the partition door behind him. Lorraine's coffee remained near the sink, barely touched. She tipped it away and reached inside the fridge for the opened bottle of wine. Maybe later there'd be something she could watch on TV. Wind down. Something that would make her laugh.

She glanced up suddenly and saw him. Standing at the end of the drive, just beyond the far edge of the lawn, staring in. The glass fell through her fingers and she screamed.

Derek came running from the other room. "What? Whatever is it? What's the matter?"

Her skin had frozen and now her eyes were closed.

"Lorraine? What ...?"

When she opened her eyes again, there was no one there.

Somehow the glass had broken against the sink and blood was spooling from the fingers of Lorraine's right hand.

"Lorraine ..."

"It's nothing. I saw … I thought I saw …" Sandra stood in the kitchen doorway, Sean pressed close against her side.

"Saw what?"

"There was somebody … someone …"

There was only her own face, reflected in the glass. Derek seized a hammer from the drawer beside the sink and went outside.

"Mum, what is it? What's happening?" Sandra asked, frightened.

"It's all right, sweetheart, it's just your mum being silly."

"You're bleeding," Sean said.

"Am I? Yes."

Derek was on the pavement, looking first toward the field, then back along the street.

"What's Dad doing?" Sean asked.

Despite herself, Lorraine smiled. "Being brave."

After he'd come back in, she let Sandra pull the tiny slivers of glass from her hand with the tweezers and stood, patient, while Derek dabbed on Savlon with a ball of cotton wool, then smoothed three small plasters across the breaks in the skin.

It wasn't until later, upstairs in bed, that Derek said: "It was Michael, wasn't it? That's who you thought you saw?"

"Don't be daft, how could I? He's miles away."

"I know, but that's who you thought it was, right?"

She rested her head against the fleshy warmth of his upper arm. "No, Derek, no. I swear."

He didn't believe her, of course. Lorraine's imagination working overtime. With a small sigh, he leaned over and kissed her head. And Lorraine, she was certain whom she had seen and Michael it was not: it had been that prison officer, Evan, hands in the pockets of his blue zip-up jacket, anxiously staring in.

Raymond had been sniffing his way, rodent-like, from one dark corner to another. He finally tracked Tommy DiReggio to the drinking club on Bottle Lane. Tommy was sitting at a corner table behind a three-card straight, king high, and he wasn't about to shift for anyone, so Raymond ordered a lager and black, and perched on a stool as patiently as he could.

When Tommy had pocketed his winnings and promised in twenty

minutes he'd give them all a chance to get even, he went with Raymond into the back room and listened to his proposition. A Beretta, was that what Raymond had said? Well, Raymond nodded, just, say, for instance. Yeh, of course, Tommy laughed, for instance. Understood. And sure it was possible, a couple of hundred for a clean shooter, no history; without that guarantee the price dipped a lot, but still not below three figures. When Raymond pushed him a little, Tommy agreed he could maybe find a buyer himself for only a twenty per cent commission.

So Raymond downed his lager and scuttled out into the darkness, other agendas pressing on his mind, and Tommy DiReggio filed away the information, something to be passed on for a price, a promise of advancement, a debt needing to be squared.

On the corner of Thurland Street and Pelham Street, Raymond paused outside the entrance to a small cellar club he knew was frequented by Anthony Drew Valentine. And word was that Valentine was back on the street.

Raymond shuffled into the doorway of a shop selling discount jeans and suddenly he was remembering when he had stood outside that club before. A night—what?—a little over three years ago.

Four of them there'd been, coming for him out of the dark: white shirts, loud voices, threats and curses. At first, it had been punches thrown, the toe of a shiny shoe driving in. Then the glint and flash of a blade. The pain that jarred along Raymond's arm, sharp, when he drove his Stanley knife hard into one youth's face and met bone. And then this other guy, older, well-dressed, some Paki poking his nose where it wasn't wanted, out to impress his girl. "All right, put a stop to this." Unbelievable, the feller trying to grab hold of them, pull them apart. The whole gang had turned on him then, Raymond included, beating him to the ground and then the boots flying, going in hard. To this day, Raymond could never be certain whether he'd heard the man shout out he was a police officer before he'd slashed the Stanley knife at his head and caught his throat, severing the carotid artery with a single swing.

Bastard! Once in a while, still, Raymond woke in a muck sweat remembering. Wasn't as if the copper'd even been on duty. Why couldn't he mind his own business like everybody else? Stupid Paki bastard, no more than he deserved.

He tugged at his collar and crossed the street toward the club entrance, joining a small line slowly shuffling forward, waiting for admission. On the door, two bouncers, one black, one white, both wearing shiny black blouson jackets bearing the insignia Gold Standard Security, vetting everyone carefully, patting them down before letting them past.

There was no need, he reasoned, to speak to Valentine himself, not now. If one or two of his cohorts were around, maybe Raymond could plant a seed in the right ear. After all, if the weapon Sheena Snape was offering him was indeed the one that had almost terminated Jason Johnson, then Valentine might be willing to pay a lot more than it was worth on the open market. Double, at least. Nothing ventured, Ray-o, nothing gained.

Thirty-one

The only thing, Preston thought, that had changed about motorway services all the time he'd been inside had been the prices. Otherwise, especially at four in the morning, they were the same sad, scruffy places, smelling of grease and disinfectant.

He'd parked Maureen's car close to the entrance and glanced around for any sign of Cassady; no idea, of course, what kind of motor he drove now, but sensing that the Irishman had still to arrive. Maureen, snug in the bedroom where he'd left her; hopefully the rope wouldn't be biting too deep into her wrists and ankles. No matter how much you trusted people, you could only ever trust them so far.

He took a leak, then stood in line in the cafeteria behind a long-distance haulage driver from South Shields, making his way back from carrying a load of copper wiring to Germany. In no hurry, Preston waited while the man ordered his plate piled high with everything from chips to black pudding. He ordered two slices of toast for himself and a large tea to wash them down. Someone had left the previous day's paper on one of the tables, and Preston picked it up and dropped it on his tray, heading for the elevated area off to one side. The tea was weak, the toast thin but fresh; he was surprised at how many names in the paper he recognized, how many he did not. Although he made a point of watching the TV news once in a while in prison, you were so removed from what was happening nothing you watched seemed real: a shock, almost, then, to realize those stories about fat cats in business, soap stars and royals, millionaire Lottery winners were true.

He spotted Cassady before Cassady saw him. Shorter than he remembered, his features, even at that distance, decidedly older, his gaze uncertain as he paused and looked around.

Then he was heading straight for Preston, a grin brightening his face as they shook hands, Cassady punching him playfully on the shoulder, once and once more again for luck. "Jesus, Michael, you're looking good. You really are."

"Just as well one of us is; you look like shit."

Cassady laughed and stepped away. "What can I get you? Another—what?—tea, is it?"

"Tea, yeh, thanks." Watching him, then, as he crossed between the largely empty tables, circling jauntily around a tall Asian slowly mopping the same area of floor, a different man already from the one who had walked in.

A few minutes later, Cassady took a quarter bottle of scotch from his side pocket and tipped a generous shot into his cup. He offered the bottle across to Preston, who shook his head.

"So," Preston said, "I hear you've gone legit."

"Not so's you'd notice," Cassady replied with a sly grin.

"Security, isn't it?"

"Clubs for the most part, pubs. Couple of shopping centers, out of town. Nothing grand."

"Money in it, though?"

"Oh, yes. Especially with a little—what is it?—creative accounting."

Preston looked at him over the top of his cup. "Money enough?"

"Ah, never that, is it? And, besides, sitting in that poxy office every hour of the day, having to be polite to people down the telephone—sure, that's not me."

Preston still looking at him, staring now.

"Oh, I see, Michael. Yes, I get your drift. It's a loan you're wanting. Well, of course, I'll do what I can. I …"

But it wasn't a loan. Preston's hand was quick, gripping Cassady's fingers till the knuckles were white. "Miss it, don't you? The buzz. Going out on a big job, tooled up."

"Course I do."

"Well …?"

"Ah, Michael, things change. All that cash, used to be running around, there for the taking, it's not the same. Big firms, these days, they're as likely to transfer wages electronically, one account to another. I don't know. It's as if money, your actual money, never sees the light of day."

Preston lowered his voice even farther. "I need one big score, maybe two. And soon. You in?"

Cassady leaned back and, for a few moments, closed his eyes. He'd seen it coming, of course he had. What else would Preston have wanted with him? You take risks like this just to reminisce? And Cassady had been thinking for some little time now, things were ripe for moving on. A little overripe maybe, overextended, that policewoman coming round earlier, for instance, questions she was asking never quite the ones she meant. Yes, pastures new. Jacky would jump at that now, sure she would.

"Yeh. Yeh, of course I'm in, but where? I mean …"

"You've been outside, eyes open. That's what you're supposed to be telling me."

Cassady lifted his cup with both hands. Through a wall of plate glass, lights blistered and flickered along the length of motorway. "Drugs, then," he said. "Got to be."

Preston sat back and shook his head. "I don't want to be messing with all that shit. Buying, selling, it's not what I know. I don't have the time."

"No." Cassady leaning closer now, the whole thing coming to him, seeing it, even then, playing out before him. Working Planer and Valentine, one against the other, while they slipped away through the middle. "It don't have to be that way. The money, that's what we want, right? The cash. You know how much some of these monkeys have, making unsightly bulges in their shiny new suits? Do you?" The old grin was back on his face, wider than before. "And one thing they're not doing, keeping it all in the Midland at five point nothing per cent, rest assured of that. All we have to do, find out where they've got their stash, hit 'em at the right time. Bob's your uncle." He laughed at the simple joy of it. "What're they going to do? Go runnin' to the police, is it?"

"But finding out, it can't be that simple, right?"

Cassady was smiling fit to bust.

"What?" Preston said. "What's with that stupid grin? You can do that, is that what you're saying? Set it up, what?"

Cassady tipped a little more scotch into his tea. "My boys, Michael, working the clubs, they get to know a lot. Well, that's where a lot of this stuff is sold, moved on. Where a lot of these deals are made. Sometimes they're paid to turn a blind eye, that's fine. Some of them, the smarter ones, they've got these little deals going for themselves. Likely think I don't know, but of course, I do. No skin off my nose. But I watch what's going on, well, you know me, always have done. Ask me who the big movers are, the ones making the serious money, I know. Liam Cassady knows. One of them especially …" He held up his hand, one finger hooked over another. "Like that."

"And you reckon you can set something up? Fast? Couple of days?"

"Well, now, Michael, I don't know, I was thinking more like a week. You know, to be certain, get everything into place …"

But Preston had hold of his hand again, squeezing tight. "Two days, Liam. Three at most. That's what it's got to be."

"Plans, then, have you, Michael?" Cassady trying not to grimace, acknowledge the pain. "Spot of traveling, I expect that's on your mind. Now that the heat's died down a little, what? Get away. God! I wouldn't mind getting away myself."

Preston looked round at where the sky was beginning to lighten. "One last thing, I'll be needing a fresh place to stay. Just till this is through."

Cassady nodded. "No problem. Is there anything else?"

Preston punched Cassady's arm twice, not hard. "You won't let me down, Liam, I know that."

"Sure, sure. That's right, that's right."

Thirty-two

Sean was playing some kind of private game with his cereal, carefully pushing as many pieces toward the sides of the bowl as he could, then placing his spoon in the center and twirling it fast to send the cereal spinning. Milk, not surprisingly, covered his end of the table in a fine spray. Sandra, doing her best to ignore him, was tucking into toast and peanut butter while concentrating on the problem page in *Smash Hits*. Derek, standing, white shirt, tie as yet unfastened, second-best suit trousers, cup of tea in hand, was listening to the traffic reports on local radio; one of the new reps was making his first call on a major customer in West Bromwich and Derek was going along to smooth the way.

"That was weird," Lorraine said, coming in from the hall.

"What's that?"

"Your sister, Maureen. That was her on the phone."

"This hour of the morning?"

"I was just about to shout you, but she said she wanted to speak to me."

Derek gave the tea a swirl round inside the pot and freshened his cup. "What about?"

"Some stuff she's got, clothes, you know, for the shop. A dress and ... oh, I don't know, things she's taken on part-exchange, she reckons they'd be great for me, just my size ..."

"Sean," Derek said sharply, "just stop doing that."

"Anyway, she wants me to go round there, this evening. Try them on. Says she could let me have them really cheap."

"So go. What's the problem? I'll be back round six-thirty, seven. I can look after the ... Sean, I thought I just told you ..."

"Yes, I will. I said I would. Just strikes me as a bit funny, that's all."

180

"How come?"

"Well, in all the time she's had that shop ..."

Sean overdid his exploration of centrifugal force. The bowl skidded away from under his spoon, careening across the table and splashing milk and soggy cereal over Sandra's magazine and down the front of her school blouse. Sandra jumped back and yelled, and her last piece of toast landed face down on the floor. Derek clipped Sean round the back of the head and then, once again, harder, for good measure.

"Derek, don't ..."

"I warned him."

Sean was cowering behind his chair, wondering whether or not to cry. When she thought no one was looking, Sandra gave him a quick kick in the back of his calf and went up to her room to change.

"Mum, she ..."

"Shut it!" Derek said, thrusting a warning finger toward his face. "Just shut it, once and for all."

Sean stood there, rubbing his leg and staring at the floor.

"Derek, you'd better be going," Lorraine said, glancing at the clock. "You know what the traffic's like on the ring road."

Derek fumbled with his tie. "If it looks like I'm going to be late, I'll give you a call."

Lorraine nodded, collecting up the breakfast things and carrying them toward the sink.

Derek's jacket and briefcase were out in the hall. "I'm off, then."

"Hope it goes well."

"Thanks." She half turned her face toward him and he kissed her on the cheek.

Lorraine refilled the kettle and switched it on. Just time for ten minutes by herself with the paper before taking the kids.

Standing there at the window, waiting for the water to boil, she watched the milkman bustling from his float to houses right and left, the man on the opposite corner wave to his wife before driving off, a pale trail of smoke rising from his exhaust. Two teenage boys clambered over the fence into the field, rucksacks slung over their shoulders, taking a short cut to school. Had she really seen what she'd thought she'd seen, or had it been her imagination playing tricks?

She spooned instant coffee into her mug and tried not to notice the racket Sandra and Sean were making in the other room.

Anil Khan had walked the short distance from Major Crimes to Canning Circus and now sat in the detective inspector's office, watching Resnick demolish the last of a Leicester ham and Jarlsberg sandwich on rye.

Khan was in his late twenties and had been in the Force for close to seven years; after a somewhat hesitant start on the beat, he had developed into a good community policeman, applying for a transfer to CID when he judged, correctly, the time was right. Eighteen months working as a detective in Central Division had proved his mettle; he had served diligently, studied hard, kept his head down when discretion was what he thought was needed. Remember, lad, you don't have to fight every battle, every time.

He had first worked with Resnick closely on the investigation into Nicky Snape's apparent suicide while in Local Authority care and they had complemented one another well: Resnick's instincts, hewn from experience, Khan's meticulous preparation, his logical eye. It had been no surprise when Helen Siddons had snapped him up for her Major Crime Squad, nor that Khan had been pleased to go.

"Right," Resnick said, screwing up the paper the sandwich had been wrapped in and tossing it in the bin. "Paul Finney—what's new?"

Though Khan was sitting upright already, he made a move as if to straighten his back before speaking. He was wearing a four-button suit, nicely cut, a pale-blue shirt and muted tie. His hair was perfectly in place. "What I've been checking into, sir, concentrating on, is the greyhound racing. At one point, Finney owned three. Co-owned with a man named Newlands. Perry Newlands. He's in catering—hot dogs, pies, that kind of thing. He's got a number of vans, they seem to go from place to place. Race meetings, in the main. Colwick, of course. Lincoln. Farther afield. Fakenham. York."

Resnick nodded. "The dogs. Not his any more?"

"No, sir. Sold his interest to a Jack Dainty ..."

"Ex-Vice?"

"Yes, sir. Sergeant in the Vice Squad for six years. Resigned eighteen months ago on grounds of ill health."

"Under suspension at the time, wasn't he?" Resnick asked.

"Allegations of taking backhanders, asking another officer to tamper with evidence. Nothing was proved."

"It rarely is."

Khan coughed discreetly into the back of his hand.

"Finney and Jack Dainty, this suggests they're pals."

"I'm not sure, sir. Not yet."

Resnick got to his feet. "Keep digging. If Finney's still spending time hanging around dog tracks and the like, chances are he fancies a flutter, and if he's into gambling, I'd not be surprised to find he's into debt."

"Right, sir."

Khan was almost out of the door when Resnick called him back. "You've thought of this yourself, I don't doubt, but the officer Dainty was involved with, those allegations of fixing evidence—shouldn't be difficult to find out who it was."

What Lorraine liked to do, some days, was take her lunch hour early and drive into the city; leave the car in that new car park outside the Victoria Centre, the one where the bus station used to be, and wander round inside window shopping. Occasionally, she'd make an impulse buy, often not. But it pleased her to think she could do so if she wished.

Today, she thought hard about a pair of shoes in Dolcis, plain black with a low heel, quite stylish in their way, useful certainly; just inside the entrance to the new House of Fraser, there on the ground floor, she toyed with the idea of some nicely packaged soaps, all scented with fruits and herbs, something to brighten up the bathroom.

She was turning away, empty-handed, when she saw him, Evan, no disputing it, watching her from less than a dozen meters away. Evan, wearing a short leather jacket, blue jeans, hands in his pockets beside a display of men's cologne. Watching her and smiling uncertainly.

Lorraine didn't know what to do.

She turned away and began to walk, not hurrying, not wanting to run, out into the broad aisle that led to the rest of the center. And by the time she needed to make a decision, left or right, he was there at her elbow, something of a smile still on his face, uncertain.

"Mrs. Jacobs, it's Evan. From the ..."

"I know who you are."

They stood there, not quite facing, while people spilled around them.

"What do you want?"

"To talk."

"What about?"

"Your brother Michael." But she knew the answer, had read it in his eyes before he spoke.

They went back inside the department store and up several short escalators to a shiny cafeteria where they sat among ladies with hats, Lorraine with hot chocolate, Evan with a pot of Yorkshire tea and a slice of lemon cake that stuck to the ends of his fingers.

"What it is," Evan stumbled, "all this stuff about him, you know, going off to some Greek island, somewhere in Portugal, Spain, something like that. Well, I don't know, I mean, I don't think that's right. Don't, you know, believe it. Not really. No. I don't think that's what he's done."

Lorraine sitting there, staring at him until Evan had to look away. "Why?" she said, surprised at the steadiness of her voice. "Why should you think that? What did Michael say?"

"Nothing."

"It must've been something, or else ..."

"No, really. It's just—I don't know—a feeling."

Lorraine laughed. "What are you? Psychic?"

"No. No. I ... I can't explain. I'm sorry, I know it must sound pretty stupid. I ..." He stirred sugar into his tea and lifted the cup to his mouth with both hands.

Lorraine eased her head a little closer. "If you're right—just suppose—what concern is it of yours?"

Evan looked at her as if she had said something absurd. "It's my responsibility, that's why. You can see that, plain as me. He was in my charge. What happened, it was down to me."

Lorraine was wide-eyed, slowly shaking her head. "And now—what?—you've come to look for him, I suppose? Take him back."

"Yes."

"And how the hell d'you propose to do that?"

"I don't know. I thought, you know, talk to some people first, people Michael would have spoken to at the funeral, yourself and so on ..."

"What about the police? Don't you think they've done all that?"

"Yes, but they didn't find him, did they?"

"And you will?"

"I have to."

There was a certainty in his voice that was absurd and chilling.

Lorraine spooned away the skin that had formed over the top of her chocolate and watched as Evan ate a section of his cake and washed it down with tea before licking his fingers clean.

Lorraine looked at her watch. "Look, Evan, I'm only on my break from work." She pushed back her chair. "I've got to be getting back."

"I thought ..." he said quickly, half out of his seat. "I thought you might help."

"No," she said. "I'm sorry. There's nothing to help you with."

He pulled a sheet of lined paper from his pocket and thrust it toward her. When she glanced at it, she recognized the name of a small hotel on the Mansfield Road.

"That's where I'm staying," Evan said.

Lorraine tore the paper in half and half again and let it fall through her hands.

"Please," Evan said.

She turned and walked away.

Sharon Garnett was drinking instant coffee at her desk, a half-eaten Mars bar resting on a pile of blank incident report forms. "This time of the afternoon," she said, "I always need some kind of sugar rush, you know."

Resnick pulled over a chair. "Jack Dainty. Was he still in Vice when you were there?"

185

Sharon gave it a moment's thought. "Only just. I think we over-lapped by—oh, I don't know—a couple of months. Three at the most."

"You remember anything about him? This charge of interfering with evidence?"

"He was overweight, I remember that. Bit of a fat bastard." She laughed. "Too many Mars bars." Her face grew serious. "Other things, too. Only rumors, mind, but word was he turned a blind eye to some of the girls if they, you know, let him have a free ride. This evidence thing, I'm less sure. Something to do with pornographic videos. One minute, they were showing them in the back room for the lads, standing room only; the next, they'd disappeared. Dainty'd been the arresting officer."

Sharon went thoughtful for a moment, drank some more of her coffee. "There was something else, only a whisper. Something involving drugs." She thought a while longer, then shook her head. "No. It's gone. If I ever knew the details at all."

"You could find out, ask around? You've got friends still in Vice."

She made a face. "Get the idea I'm turning against one of their own, even someone like Dainty, they'll not be friends much longer."

Resnick held her gaze for a long moment before rising slowly to his feet. "If you think it's too difficult, of course, I'll understand."

Sharon laughed; snorted rather than laughed. "No, you're all right. I'll do what I can."

Thirty-three

Derek had called her on his car phone, stuck behind a brace of lorries delivering fuel to the power station at Ratcliffe-on-Soar. Sandra was doing her homework at the kitchen table, writing up an experiment she had performed on a frog, and Sean was round at a friend's, getting up to God knows what. Lorraine's afternoon had been highlighted by two queries over missing deliveries and another concerning an invoice that seemed to have been paid twice; so many faxes and aggravated phone calls, she scarcely had time to think about Evan—poor, dumb Evan, sitting opposite her, open-faced, truly believing that he could find Michael where all others had failed. Find him and—what was it?—take him back. For a moment, Lorraine felt pity. Michael would tear him in two without breaking sweat or shedding a tear.

Except that Michael was, whatever crazy Evan thought, relaxing on Paxos or Zante, stretching back on the beach in his trunks and soaking up the sun. That car he'd stolen to get to Birmingham airport, what else? She pictured him, dark glasses shielding his eyes, getting up whenever it got too hot and cooling off in the water, drinking an ice-cold beer, then later, around ten or so, wearing an open shirt and shorts, wandering along to this taverna for dinner, sitting there on the balcony and looking out over the sea.

Lorraine drank down the last of her gin and tonic and thought about the advisability of a second. The drive to Maureen's in mind, she made herself a weak one, Sandra's eyes flicking toward her at the hiss of the tonic bottle opening. Lorraine poured her a splash into a clean glass and added ice cubes and a wedge of lemon, setting it beside Sandra's science book and kissing her briefly on top of her head, the fading smell of shampoo and young skin.

"Mum?"

"Mm?"

"You know when you go round Auntie Maureen's, later?"

"Yes?"

"Can I come with you?"

No reason not to, except what Lorraine wanted was to nip straight in and out, no hanging about, and the way Maureen made a fuss of the kids sometimes it was likely they'd end up staying there half the evening.

"Best not, love. Stay here and finish that. Besides, you'll be company for your dad."

"Oh, Mum," Sandra complained, but she didn't really care; all she'd wanted was an excuse to stop what she was doing.

"You'll not be long?" Derek said. Lorraine was waiting in the hallway when he came through the door, the keys already in her hand.

"Sooner I go, sooner I'll be back." She kissed him quickly on the cheek. "An hour, tops."

"Should I wait dinner or what?"

"Chicken and ham pie; it's in the freezer. Pop yours and Sandra's in the microwave, I'll sort myself out when I get back."

"I'd rather wait."

"Suit yourself."

She closed the door with a crisp click and hurried toward the car, low heels tapping down the path.

So typical of Maureen, Lorraine thought, turning off the main road, to have read some article somewhere in the poncey color supplements about how these drab thirties places were becoming trendy and move out here where the only people you saw after seven were patrolling on behalf of the local neighborhood watch. Or lost. It wasn't even like living in the city; it wasn't like living anywhere. She shivered as she rang the bell.

Rang again.

Maureen's face was strained and pinched when she opened the door, and Lorraine thought she had to be coming down with something, a summer cold; either that or she'd been fretting about the shop. Maybe it wasn't doing as well as she'd thought.

They chatted briefly about the kids and Maureen offered her a drink.

"I don't know if I really should."

"There's a bottle of white wine open in the fridge."

"All right, then. That'll be fine. But, Maureen, listen, I don't want to be rude, but I can't stay long. These clothes you were talking about …"

Maureen left her in the living room, copies of *Vogue* and *Marie Claire* on the coffee table, new cushions at neat intervals along the leather settee, bright colors, black, yellow, and orange, each with a pattern of large red roses.

Lorraine glanced at her watch: how long did it take to pour a couple of glasses of white wine?

When Michael came through the door, she let out a gasp and clutched at her throat. If he hadn't caught hold of her she would have fallen, legs buckling, all the way to the floor.

Lorraine sat on the edge of the settee, head down toward her knees, clinging on to Michael's hand. From somewhere, he'd fetched a small brandy, which when she sniffed at it had nearly made her heave, and now it sat on the table, untouched. Michael content to sit there, waiting for her to pull round, get a hold of herself. After a few minutes more of this, he put his other arm tight around her and held her close, and the words he said she either didn't hear or didn't want to understand.

"Michael. Don't, don't."

He was kissing the back of her neck, pushing his face up into her hair.

"Don't. I don't like it."

Pulling away, he took hold of her face and turned it toward him, fingers hard against her jaw; she shook her head vigorously and he allowed her to push his arms away.

"What's the matter?" It was there in his voice, the flat gray of his eyes, something that frightened her more than the touch of his hands, his lips on her skin.

189

Lorraine's gaze shifted toward the door. "Maureen, she might come in."

"No."

She looked back at him.

"S'okay. I told her not to." He smiled, that slow wrinkling of the skin around the eyes, the creases that spread from the corners of his mouth, and she saw him then as she had all those years before. Hopeful. Sexy. Sure.

"What's the matter?"

"Nothing." Her breath had caught in her throat.

He laughed. "You look as if you'd seen a ghost."

She freed herself from his hand and got unsteadily to her feet. She crossed the room, Michael watching her every move. The way he used to do, all those years when they were young. Bedroom. Bathroom. Beach. Then not so young. Remembering his eyes staring at her teenage breasts, Lorraine's nipples ached.

"Why, Michael?"

"What?"

"Why are you here?"

He glanced around. "Why not? It's perfect. Perfect place for us to meet." He laughed softly. "You don't have to worry about Maureen, I can handle her."

Does that mean you're sleeping with her? Lorraine wanted to know. Fucking her? She was angry at the thought. Surprised at her own jealousy.

"I haven't laid a hand on her," Michael said, reading her mind.

"Haven't you?"

He stared back at her, daring contradiction. Lorraine retrieved the brandy, but one swallow was enough to burn the back of her throat and make her cough.

He took the glass from her hand and stood close, their bodies almost touching, actually touching when they both breathed out.

"Why didn't you go? Like everyone thought. Why didn't you get away while you had the chance?"

"Come on, Lo, I couldn't go without you. What'd be the point?"

"What d'you mean? You're not making any sense."

"Sense? 'Course I'm making bloody sense. If it wasn't for you, I might as well've stayed in jail. Done my time."

"But you can't think …"

"What?"

"Michael, you can't … You can't think we can just …"

"Can't what? Can't nothing. We can do anything."

He believed it; she could see it in his face. "Oh, God!" She moved away and he caught her by the wrist, and she looked back at him through tears. "Michael, it's just not … it's crazy, that's what it is. Insane."

He kissed her eyes and then her mouth, the slow fleshy warmth inside his lips and then the thrust of his tongue, forcing her. His hands moving her back against the wall, clumsy on her breasts, not the way she remembered them, pushing too hard, kneading. Needy. Edging her legs apart with his knee, a hand between her legs.

"No-o!" She bit down on the thickness of his tongue and when he pulled away she tasted blood. Her eyes suddenly fiery, threatening.

"All right. Okay." Michael, one hand out, backing away. "I know we can't … just like that … it's my fault, I shouldn't have rushed." He wiped his hand across the corner of his mouth. "I know it's gonna … it's going to take time. It's just, you know, thinking about you all this time. Banged up. Inside. Thinking about you so long." He was moving slowly back toward her. "Lo, believe me. I understand. I do."

She covered her face with her hands.

"Lo?"

"Oh, Michael, you don't understand anything."

"I can't hear you, what you're saying."

"You don't understand anything. At all."

Silence, the room, the whole house wrapped in cotton wool.

Michael standing there, waiting for her to look at him again. "Derek," he said. "You don't love him. I doubt you ever did. You told me. And you do love me. You know you do. You always have."

"Michael, that's not …"

"Not what?"

"That's not the point."

191

"Of course it's the fucking point!"

She stumbled back, frightened by the anger, the intensity of his voice.

"What else d'you think it's all about. What else has it always been about? What I did, then. What I'm doing now. It's for you. Us. That's all that matters. All that counts."

Tears running down her face, she leaned toward him and he held her in his arms, allowing himself to cry now, laugh a little, yes, that too, but crying most of all. The two of them like great kids, grinning through their tears.

"Come over here," he said. "Come on over here and sit down while I tell you. I've got it all worked out, all planned. Passport, everything, it's all fixed. Turkey, that's where we're going first. Travel separate, of course. No way round that. After, we can go anywhere. Anywhere we want. Just about. Send for the kids. You see, they'll love it. Sandra, specially. She's lovely, isn't she? A sweetheart."

"Michael …"

"Just a couple of things I've got to take care of first, couple more days and then we're away. Out of here." His face so serious, naive. "All you have to do, be ready, you know, ready to move. I'll let you know, as much notice as I can. Okay? Okay, Lo, okay?"

She let him kiss her then, her face, neck, tips of her fingers, palms of her hands. Lorraine unable to look at him, afraid she'd be blinded by the joy on his face, the light in his eyes.

As soon as she felt she could, she pulled away. "Michael, listen. I've got to go, get back. The kids. And Derek. I said I'd not be long. They'll worry. Come round. You don't know Derek. He'll have Sandra and Sean in the back of the car and be round here, double quick."

Pushing herself to her feet, she brushed her hands down the front of her clothes, straightening herself out as best she could. Her hair would need a comb through it and then some. Her cheeks felt as if they were on fire.

"Lo, you're okay, right?"

"Yes. Yes, of course. I'm fine." She smiled and he smiled back, doing that thing with his eyes.

Lorraine turned toward the door.

192

"A couple of days, Lo. Three at most."

"Yes, yes, all right."

He followed her out into the hall, but when he went to kiss her again she moved her head aside. "You'd best stay away from the front door," she said. "No point in risking being seen."

"Round here?" Michael grinned. "That's a laugh."

But he stood well back, and when Lorraine turned the catch he said, "I do love you, you know."

"I know."

Her hands were shaking so much it was all she could do to fit the car key into the lock, switch on the ignition.

Thirty-four

Carefully, methodically, Millington and Naylor had been questioning Gary Prince, Ben Fowles sitting in, listening and learning. And as they went through incident after incident, one set of stolen goods after another, Prince had talked himself into corners from which it was more and more difficult to escape. The one thing he hadn't admitted, nor even come close to, was selling a weapon to Valentine.

"Look on the bright side, Graham," Resnick said. "There's a dozen burglaries, more, some of them going back years—all those files marked closed. Do wonders for the crime figures."

"Aye, happen you're right."

They were stealing twenty minutes' sunshine, sitting on a bench in the tiny rectangle of public gardens at the end of Newcastle Drive.

"Besides, most likely thing," Resnick said, "'less the gun's at the bottom of the Trent, it's been sold on a couple of times by now."

Millington shook his head. "We've had feelers out and plenty, no word."

"Not to worry, Graham. Be thankful for what we've got."

Millington considered a cigarette, then thought better of it. "Raymond Cooke," he said. "Took over that place Bobbers Mill way when his Uncle Terry killed himself."

Resnick nodded. "What about him?"

"Name's come up a couple of times. Jobs we thought Prince might've had a hand in. One in particular—break-in out at the Science Park. Computer stuff up the wazoo."

"And he's suggesting Ray-o was involved?"

Millington shook his head. "Not directly. Fenced the stuff, that's all. Think there might be something to it?"

"Possible, Graham. Depends how closely he's following in Terry Cooke's footsteps."

Millington snapped the spent match in half. "Often thought about that, you know. That whole business. Cookie topping himself the way he did. That girlfriend of his ..."

"Eileen."

"Yeah, right next to him in the bed." He decided to light up after all. "Stripper, wasn't she? What? Twenty-three, twenty-four? No dog, either." Millington held in the smoke, then exhaled slowly. "You'd have thought, something nice like that alongside you, last thing you'd want to do, put your brains all over the pillow."

Resnick stood and stretched. "I might take a walk down there, Graham. Haven't had a word with young Ray-o in a while."

Millington grinned. "One of your waifs and strays, isn't he? Along of the Snapes."

"Time to be getting back, Graham," Resnick said.

"That social worker you went out with a while," Millington said, smiling broadly. "Five or so years back. Rachel, was it? Left her mark on you and no mistake."

But Resnick, striding away, was no longer listening.

At lunchtime, Lorraine left work and was crossing toward her car when she saw Evan, smoking a cigarette, over by the dividing wall. For just a moment, she stopped in her tracks and Evan dropped the cigarette and ground it out with the underside of his shoe. Lorraine put her keys back in her bag and headed straight for him. "What the hell d'you think you're doing?"

"I told you yesterday ..."

"And I told you. If you don't keep away from me, stop following me ..."

"Tell me what I need to know."

"You need to know nothing."

Evan shook his head. "I thought I'd explained all that."

"Listen," Lorraine said, not wanting to make a scene, conscious that someone else from her work could come out at any moment. "Listen, there's this law. Stalking." She jabbed a finger against Evan's chest. "You keep this up and I'm going to the police."

Evan looked hurt. "But that's not what ..."

"Not what?"

"What I'm doing."

"What else would you call it?" She rounded on her heel and strode toward her car. Before getting there, she turned again and headed back to Evan. "Which is yours?"

"Huh?"

"Which is yours?" Her head was half turned toward the line of other vehicles.

Evan didn't answer, but she could see where he was looking: a Vauxhall Carlton, dark blue, a hire car with last year's registration.

She took a pen and a slip of paper from her bag and made a show of writing down the number. "Okay, Evan, I'm telling you this. If I see either you or that car, anywhere near me, here or at home, I am going to call the law." And she stared at him till he lowered his head and scuffed his feet on the floor.

When she caught sight of him in her rearview mirror, he was still standing there like some overgrown kid in the playground, stubborn and close to tears.

Raymond hadn't been back in the shop much more than half an hour when Sheena Snape waltzed in. Sheena with her hair tied back, one of those skimpy sweaters that buttoned up the front and stopped several inches above the navel, black jeans that clung to her like a second skin. When she spoke, a smear of red lipstick shone bright on her front teeth.

"Ray-o, listen, I've been thinkin'."

"Yeh?"

"What we was talkin' about yes'day, you know."

"Yeh, what about it?"

"I was thinkin' maybe I should never've come here, right? Maybe I should've gone to someone else all along."

"Why? What ...? What you on about? What ...?"

Sheena looking around at the second-hand tumble-driers, third-hand fridge-freezers. "I mean, you know, I don't want to be rude, Ray-o. Insulting. But, you know, somethin' like this, it's a bit out of your class, know what I mean?"

"Bollocks!"

"Charming."

"I can handle it," Raymond said, puffing himself out. "No problem, you see."

Sheena stood looking at him squarely: the watery eyes that never seemed quite true, the pallid skin that was always damp with sweat. "You got a buyer, then? That what you're saying?"

"Yeh."

"Yeah?"

"Almost." Raymond held up finger and thumb to illustrate how close he had come. "I was talking, just now, just before you come in. This bloke, dead interested. Exactly what you've got. Exactly."

"Yeah?"

"Yeh."

"Two hundred."

"At least."

"So when you seeing him?"

"Couple of days, tops. Relax."

Sheena sucked at her bottom lip; she didn't know whether to believe him or not. But when she'd tried talking to the others about it, Diane had been preoccupied with Melvin, who was throwing up all over everywhere, and Lesley—Lesley was so far out of it, she didn't even know who Sheena was. Which left Sheena herself walking round town with a handgun that could, in all probability, be tied into a shooting, even attempted murder.

"Sure I can trust you, Ray-o? You're not winding me up, stringin' us along?"

"Course not."

"Here. You'll be needing this, then."

She had unsnapped her bag and lifted out the Beretta and was passing it across into Raymond's willing hand, when Raymond saw, in the corner of his eye, Resnick briskly crossing the street toward them.

"Fuck!"

"What? What's up? What?"

Raymond barely had time enough to tuck the weapon underneath the loose flap of his shirt, down inside the back of his jeans, before the bell above the door rang and Resnick walked in.

197

Seeing him, Sheena's face set like sour milk.

"Sheena. Ray-o." Resnick smiled, sniffing the air between them.

"Mr. Resnick," Raymond stumbled, balance shifting from one foot to the other.

Sullen, Sheena said nothing.

"Didn't know you two knew one another," Resnick said pleasantly. "Though if I'd thought about it, I suppose I should."

"Sheena was just looking for something for her mum," Raymond said. "For the kitchen, like."

Sheena's look cut him off at the knees.

"How is Norma?" Resnick asked.

"Fine," Sheena managed. "Better wi'out seein' you."

"I dare say."

"You reckon the microwave, then?" Raymond said. "This one over 'ere."

"Sod off, Ray-o," Sheena said, turning toward the door. And, with a parting look at Resnick, "I don't know what he's on about. I was passin', that's all."

The shop door closed with a slam and left Resnick and Raymond staring at one another, Raymond aware of nothing as much as the cold metal hard against his spine.

"Nice lass," Resnick said.

Raymond carried on staring, open-mouthed; he had to be taking the piss.

"Seeing one another, are you?"

"Am I buggery!"

Resnick shrugged easily. "Just a thought."

"Slag like that."

"She wasn't in here for the microwave, then, not like you said?"

Raymond could feel himself beginning to blush. "She were, yeh. 'Course she were. What she said, just, you know, showin' off."

Resnick smiled benevolently.

"Girls." Raymond laughed. "Who can fathom 'em, eh?"

"You wouldn't have anything in the way of computer software?" Resnick asked. "Fresh in. Top-of-the-range stuff, mostly. Adobe Photoshop. QuarkXPress."

Raymond blinked, backpedaling. "Not my thing, Mr. Resnick.

Dixons, Curry's, that's where you want to try. That place along Castle Boulevard, never can remember the name."

"You're sure of that, Raymond? You've got nothing?"

"Yeh, dead sure." He was beginning to breathe more easily now, the color in his cheeks starting to fade. That break-in out by the University, the Science Park, that's what this was about. He'd been offered the gear, sure enough, but had turned it down.

Resnick wandered over toward the boxes of CDs. He'd picked up a few things here before, some Charlie Parker, a Chet Baker set recorded in Milan, Baker singing as if he were wearing somebody else's teeth. Now all that tempted him was a Mills Brothers compilation with Ella on one track, Louis on another.

"Third off to you, Mr. Resnick," Raymond said encouragingly. "Fair close to givin' it away."

"Okay, Ray-o, you've got a deal." He handed over a five-pound note and told him to keep the change.

"You know pretty much what's going on, Raymond," Resnick said, stuffing the package down into his pocket. "Keep your ear to the ground."

"Don't know 'bout that." Raymond said hesitantly. Was that what this was all about? Resnick trying to turn him into one of his snouts?

"You've not heard of anyone trying to sell a pistol, a Berretta, last few days?"

The barrel was burning a hole into Raymond's back.

"Raymond? Ray-o?"

"No, no. Nothin' like' that, I swear."

"But if you did, you'd give me a call?"

Raymond wiped his palms down the sides of his jeans and nodded. "Okay, yeh. Yes, sure."

Resnick took a card from his top pocket and placed it alongside the till. He could have as easily reached round behind Raymond and lifted the Beretta out from underneath the tail of his shirt.

"Any complaints with the disc," Raymond said, "full refund, right? No questions asked."

Resnick pulled the door open and, with a final glance back at Raymond through the glass, began to walk toward the bridge.

Thirty-five

The first thing Resnick did, after bending to scoop up the post, was sneeze. And sneeze again. It could have been the beginning of an unseasonable cold, far more likely a reaction to cat hairs and dust. He'd tried paying a woman to come in and keep the place under control, clean and tidy; had tried several times, in fact, without avail. If they'd been any good they'd soon moved on to more profitable things, less than good and he would swear when he looked around the house was in more of a state than it had been before. And they lost things, moved things, broke a cup that had belonged to his grandfather and which had survived the journey from Poland, snapped an arm from a statue of Duke Ellington his favorite uncle had given him for his twenty-first.

So Resnick kept the dirt at bay as best he could; his favored method being to wait until the dust had collected itself into wispy balls in the room corners and along the skirting boards, then reach down and snag them as he passed.

On the way home, he'd stopped off at the deli and bought a small container of sun-dried tomatoes, a larger one of marinaded aubergine. He dipped a finger into the oil at the bottom of the latter and brought it to his mouth—coriander, garlic, and something else he couldn't immediately identify.

A swig of beer and he cut two slices of rye bread and covered each lightly with mayonnaise; scorning a fork, he laid the slippery flesh of the aubergine across one of the slices and several of the skinny strips of tomato here and there over that. Licking his fingers clean, he ferreted around for what else he could find. There was a thickish piece of smoked ham, from which he stripped away the fatty edge; the fat he shared with Bud, the smallest of the cats, the

200

rest of the meat he smeared with mustard before placing it on the second slice of bread. From various and sundry chunks of cheese, he selected a soft Taleggio, cutting away the orange rind before setting the cheese on top of the ham. The rind he dropped on to the floor, where it was argued over by the cats.

All Resnick's sandwich needed now was something crunchy at its center and he cut a dill pickle in two, eating one piece there and then before placing the other on top of the cheese and swiftly pressing the whole thing together. Holding it together with one hand, he cut the sandwich in half with the serrated edge of the bread knife and carried it on a plate into the front room.

Among the stacks of black and brittle 78s Resnick's uncle had allowed his young nephew to browse through whenever he had visited the house, along with others by Dinah Washington, Billie Holiday, the Ink Spots, and Ella Fitzgerald, there had been several records by the Mills Brothers. "Dinah," "Swing it, Sister," "You Always Hurt the One You Love." Resnick had liked the smooth sweep of their voices, had been intrigued by the way they mimicked the sounds of instruments with their mouths.

He set the CD he'd bought from Raymond to play and was biting into the second half of the sandwich and listening to "Paper Doll," when the phone started to ring. Twisting in his chair, he could just reach the receiver.

It was Hannah. She was going to the eight-thirty performance at Broadway and wondered if he'd like to join her. A film some friends from school had seen and said was a lot of fun. *Big Night*, that's what it was called. Two brothers trying to keep their Italian restaurant going despite the competition. You'll love it, Charlie, great food scenes, apparently. Music, too. If he hadn't already eaten, they could go across to Mama Mia's afterwards for a little supper.

Resnick couldn't think of a reason for saying no.

There was time for a drink in the Café Bar before taking their seats. The movie was warm, funny, an unalloyed delight. Sandwich or no, the constant shots of food made Resnick's mouth water, his stomach rumble. And the music—the music was by Louis Prima, another who'd featured in his uncle's collection. Louis Prima and

Keely Smith with Sam Butera and the Witnesses. "Just a Gigolo," "Buona Sera," "Come Back to Sorrento."

When it was over, they crossed the street to Mama Mia's and Resnick, thinking he would drink espresso while he watched Hannah eating, ordered lasagna and finished every mouthful. On the pavement outside, Hannah kissed him and he kissed her back and without questioning he drove with her back to her house in Lenton, where they divested themselves of most of their clothes before reaching the upper floor and bed.

How is it, Resnick remembered thinking just before falling asleep, life can sometimes be as easy, as joyous as this?

Lorraine had gone out into the kitchen to stack the dishes midway through the evening and seen the hire car parked across the street, Evan's shape behind the wheel. Derek and Sandra were laughing together at something on the television; Sean was upstairs, getting ready for bed.

Evan wasn't going to listen to reason; and sooner or later he might stumble on the truth.

She thought about carrying out her threat and contacting the police. Remembered Resnick, his bulk as he stood against the French doors looking out into the garden; tried to imagine herself telling him and failed. Suppose he talked to Evan, took him seriously—she didn't want to be responsible for getting Michael captured again. Returned to prison.

Out in the hall, voice hushed, she called Maureen and asked to speak to Michael. Listen, she said, and gave him the address of Evan's hotel, the number of the car. Her hands were shaking when she hung up the phone.

Resnick was suddenly awake and for that instant uncertain where he was. Then he heard Hannah's breathing, low and even beside him, and he settled down again against her warmth, her hand opening in sleep to take his as his arm curled round her body. "Charlie," she said, not waking, and he fell back to sleep at the sound of his name, the smile still on his face.

✦✦✦

Drew Valentine was sitting in the Caribbean restaurant run by one of his aunties and her ex-wrestler boyfriend, his back angled toward the wall. The doors were locked, the blind pulled down, the kitchen still open. Two of his acolytes sat across the narrow aisle, drinking rum cocktails and sharing a spliff. Valentine had already polished off a plate of salt cod and ackee, and now he was tucking into jerk chicken and festival dumplings with okra on the side. A little Red Stripe to wash it down. After, he wouldn't mind another smoke himself. Get properly relaxed.

A tall blonde, not so many pounds this side of anorexic, came through the curtains at the rear and clicked toward him on brittle heels. She was wearing a shiny blue dress that shimmered as she walked. Valentine could have closed one of his hands around her thigh and touched finger to thumb. When she sat opposite him and smiled, there was white powder frosted across her gums.

"Eat," he said, pushing the plate of chicken toward her, but she shuddered and reached for her pack of Marlboro Lights.

Sooner or later, Valentine was thinking, he would have to get around to facing down Anthony Planer and he needed to be sure he'd figured all the angles right. Too many stories of other dealers getting ripped off after doing business with Planer; smiles and handshakes in the upstairs room of that fancy gaming club he fronted, champagne cocktails and cigars, and back out on the street it was cars and guns, and someone else making off with both drugs and money.

"Tell you what, Anthony," Valentine had said. "You an' me, we been doin' business all this time, how come you never invited me out to that place of yours? Southwell, i'n't it? Near the Minster. What you say? Meet the wife and kids. Catch a glimpse, you know, how the other half live."

Planer smiling as he shook his head, smiling with his lips, eyes hard and staring, understanding what it was Valentine was saying, the threat that he was making. Anything happens, we know where to reach you, how to hurt you, and we will. And Planer not caring, throwing it back at him, "How would you like it, Drew, eh? Me coming waltzing into hearth and home. No. Not right, is it? Not on." Planer, the smile on his face like a cheap shirt from the market.

"Just 'cause we're forced to do some of our business in the gutter, doesn't mean we want to open our doors to it, watch it ruining the Wilton."

Valentine bit into a piece of chicken, wiping the juice from around his mouth. He wasn't afraid of Planer; Planer would learn to be afraid of him. Delicately, he spat a piece of chicken bone down into his hand before depositing it on his plate. If only things had gone right out on the Forest, if that uppity nigger Jason hadn't stuck him just as he was pulling the trigger, then Jason Johnson would be good and dead, and a clear message to Planer and anyone like him. And now there was this kid, Raymond Cooke, Ray-o he believed they called him, sneaking round whispering in corners, sending messages, something he'd got that Valentine wanted, worth paying good money for. Okay, so he'd send a message back, an invitation, you want to do business, fine, bring the merchandise, let's see what it's worth. The kid had the balls to walk in there, face to face, maybe they could do a deal.

Valentine checked the clock on the wall against his Rolex: not like Paul Finney to be late for an appointment.

Neither of them had bothered with the blinds, and when Resnick woke again a low level of light illuminated the room. The green digits on Hannah's clock radio read 5:47. Above the even sound of her breathing, he could hear birds, busy between the trees bordering the recreation ground. He would have to go back to his own house before reporting for work. The level of Hannah's breathing changed and he realized that she was stirring awake, peering at him through partly opened eyes. His hand moved across to rest on her thigh and with a small smile Hannah lowered her face down on to his chest.

"Charlie ..."

"Mmm?"

"It's good that you're here."

He thought they might make love again, but the moment passed, as these moments do. Before the hour, Hannah was slipping out of bed to use the bathroom and Resnick, in boxer shorts and barefoot, was padding down to the kitchen to make coffee.

They sat in Hannah's small back room eating toast and some of Hannah's mother's homemade marmalade, runny and sweet.

"How was she?" Resnick asked. "When you told her about your dad. Marrying again."

Hannah shook her head. "At first, I didn't think she'd heard. Or understood. But then, when I mentioned it again later, she almost bit off my head: I know, you've already told me once—do you think I'm totally stupid or merely deaf? I found her later in the garden, pretending to deadhead some flowers. She was crying. She said it made her feel old, dried-up. I hated to leave her there, drive back."

"I had half a thought you might have called round."

"I did."

Resnick looked at her.

"There was another car, parked outside. I didn't want to interrupt."

Resnick smiled. "It was only Lynn."

"Only?"

"Her father, there's been some kind of relapse. She'd just heard."

Hannah cut the last piece of toast in two. "I thought the treatment had been successful. I thought he was all right."

"Yes, so did she."

"I'm sorry."

"Yes." He didn't know where he'd left his watch. Jacket pocket? Upstairs beside the bed? "Look, it's probably time I was going."

There was no more than a hint of resignation in Hannah's smile. "I know. The cats."

"And other things."

At the door she said, "Maybe next time you'll call me?"

"Yes. Okay. I will." He kissed her on the cheek, close alongside her mouth.

"Charlie ..."

"Yes?"

"Nothing. Take care. Have a good day."

"You too."

She didn't watch him walk to the end of the narrow strip of path, turning where it broadened out and met the road. Back inside the house, she busied herself with clearing away.

Resnick all the way home thinking about two men, two fathers, Lynn's and Hannah's, close in age; the one seriously ill, possibly dying; the other rejuvenated, living a new life in a new country, about to remarry. By the time Resnick arrived back at his own house, the cats were clamoring to be fed and the telephone was ringing insistently. Some things didn't change.

Thirty-six

"Catch!"

Maureen spun round in time to see her keys come arching through the room; at the second attempt, she held them fast.

From the doorway, Michael Preston grinned. "It's time."

"What for?"

He winked. "Me to move on."

"Oh." She didn't know what else to say. Her mouth was dry and, as Preston began to come toward her, something caught hold of her stomach and twisted it hard.

Close to, he could read the pain, the fear in her eyes. With the knuckles of his right hand, he brushed her cheek. "If I thought …"

"Yes?

"If I thought for one moment you were going to open this gorgeous mouth …" His index finger pressed against her mouth. "You know what I'd do?"

"Yes."

"What I'd come back and do?"

"Yes."

"Even after I've gone. Really gone." The finger slid between her lips. "I've got friends. They'll know. If you talk, tell anyone. Anything. They'll know."

Maureen's eyes were wide; the sweat she could smell was her own.

"And you know what they'll do?"

She nodded; made what sound she could.

Smiling, Preston hooked his finger inside her mouth, then pulled it free with a pop. "Good girl," he said. "Good, good girl."

Even after the front door had opened and closed, she stood

there for a long time, not bothering to stem the tears that ran down her face.

Lynn's voice on the telephone had been scraped bare: her father's condition had worsened, she was driving over straightaway. Resnick had wished her the best, without knowing what that was.

Entering the CID room, he glanced at the clock. A little after ten; given clear roads, she would be there now, there or thereabouts.

Sharon Garnett intercepted him on his way to his office. "Jack Dainty, you wanted me to ask around. That allegation, tampering with evidence, the other officer involved, it was Finney right enough."

Resnick smiled.

"There's more. Just before Dainty resigned, there was another allegation; a case they were working on together, him and Finney. According to the rumors, Dainty went to question a prisoner in Lincoln, promised him a supply of dope if he gave them the answers they wanted. Grade A cannabis resin. Worth a small fortune inside."

"And Finney was involved? Directly?"

Sharon shrugged. "There's no proof. Dainty was on his way out anyway, let the blame fall on himself."

"Okay, Sharon, thanks."

Inside his office, he dialed Helen Siddons's number.

"You bloody psychic, Charlie, or what? I was just about to phone you. Anil was tailing Finney last night. Two o'clock, something after, must have been feeling peckish. Stopped off at a restaurant near Hyson Green. Cassava. Know it?"

Resnick didn't.

"According to Anil, looked like the place was closed. Finney knocked on the door and they let him in. Anil hung around and forty minutes later Finney comes out and who's he with?"

"I don't know," Resnick said, thinking she was going to say Dainty.

"Anthony Drew Valentine."

Resnick whistled. "Anil's certain?"

"Positive. Saw them talk together a few minutes on the pavement, then they shake hands, the pair of them, laughing away. Valentine pats Finney on the back and off they go."

"Together?"

"Separately."

"Anil followed him?"

"What do you think?"

"Where to?"

"Home. Semi-detached in Sherwood. Wife and three kids."

Resnick was trying to arrange his thoughts. "Are you going to have him in, question him?"

"Not yet."

He heard the sound of Siddons drawing on her cigarette.

"D'you want me to have a word with Norman Mann?" Resnick asked. "See if he can shed some light?"

"And risk Finney being warned off? No, thanks, Charlie. Not on your life. We'll watch Finney a while longer, see where he leads us. Lucky enough, just might be able to nab him and Valentine together, heads down at the same trough."

The address Cassady had given him was a nondescript house in Cinderhill, within easy reach of the motorway. Get there and wait. Preston waited.

The place was sparsely furnished, no pictures or photographs, nothing personal, only a two-year-old calendar tacked to one of the downstairs walls; it smelled of damp and when he first ran the water it came out a sludgy brown. In one of the rooms, there were a small television and a VCR, along with a pile of duff videos. In the kitchen, there were a radio cassette player and a few tapes, Queen, Van Morrison, the Chieftains. Preston had thought there might be Guinness, too, but there were only cans of cheap supermarket lager. There was bread in a paper bag, a carton of tea bags, frozen pizza, milk in the fridge.

Preston was watching a scratchy kung-fu movie when Cassady arrived bearing gifts—a bottle of Black Bush and two Melton Mowbray pork pies. "Tonight," he said, breaking the seal on the bottle.

"What about it?"

Cassady blew the dust out of two glasses and tipped in the whiskey. "We do it. What else, sure?"

"How about this other business?" Preston asked, a sip or two later.

"What business is that?"

"That bastard prison officer, sticking his nose in."

"Oh, that," Cassady said casually. "That's sorted."

The man standing in the doorway of Raymond Cooke's shop needed to stoop several inches to avoid banging his head on the lintel. His shoulders were so wide, Raymond thought he might have to lean, first to one side, then the other, so as not to collide with the frame as he came through. His name was Leo: it was stitched in crimson lettering, high on the right side of his cobalt-blue Tommy Hilfiger jacket; he was wearing loose gray warm-up pants and Converse basketball boots. There were two gold studs in his left ear, one in his right; a heavy gold chain around his neck. His hair had been shaved till he was completely bald.

"Ray-o? You the one they call Ray-o?"

And with a grin, he stepped into the shop. Raymond didn't think he was there to buy a reconditioned microwave oven.

"Ray, yeh, that's me. Ray or Ray-o, doesn't matter."

"This your business, huh?"

"Yeh, yeh." Raymond watched as Leo wandered between the piles of second-hand or stolen goods. He wiped the palms of his hands down his jeans; already he was patched with sweat.

"What can I …? I mean, was there anything special …? Maybe something you want to get shot of? Sell?"

Leo spun faster than Raymond could follow and a finger longer than any he'd ever seen poked hard against his chest. It was all Raymond could do not to stumble backward.

"That's a joke, yeh. You're jokin', right? Get shot of. Got to be a joke, yeh? Clever bastard." Each syllable of the last two words was accompanied by a jab of the same finger at his chest.

Raymond just looked back at him, open-mouthed; he hadn't realized what he'd said.

"You the one," Leo said, "been spreading the word, want to see Valentine? Got something special for him, that you?"

"Yes." Raymond blinked and blinked again. The sweat was running into his eyes. "Yeh, that's me."

"Fine." Leo's face was suddenly all smiles. "You know Cassava? That eatin' place?"

Raymond couldn't picture where it was and then he could. "Yeh. Least, I think so. Never been in, mind. But, yeh."

"Tonight. Two-thirty. Drew, he see you there. Bring what you got to sell. Okay?"

"Yes. Okay. Course. Half two."

Still smiling, Leo pointed his index finger at him, crouching in the doorway. "What you want to get shot of." And, aiming at Raymond's heart, he fired the finger like a gun, lifting it toward his mouth so that he could blow away the smoke before stepping back out into the street.

Thirty-seven

Valentine was high. Why wouldn't he be? The Dutchman had shown up as arranged half an hour before and was, right then and there, at the back of the room talking weights and training regimes with Leo. And the two cases he and his brother had brought with them, slightly battered and leather-bound, were right there under the table, close against Valentine's feet. Two kilos of cocaine, all handily separated out into clear bags with a resale price of five hundred each; which would be broken down farther by Valentine's crew; fifty-pound bags that the small-time scufflers like Jason Johnson would peddle on street corners, in pubs and clubs, on high-rise walkways and through the iron railings of schools.

Twenty thousand Valentine had paid over, throwing in another five as a sweetener, keep the Dutchman coming to him and not Planer. Twenty-five in all and nothing compared with the sixty the contents of those cases were worth to Valentine out on the street. Thirty-five thousand profit and all he'd done so far was cut open one of the bags and lift a taste of the powder to his tongue, rub a little across his gums.

Sure he was high. Wouldn't you be?

He was calling back toward the kitchen in search of chicken and dumplings, when the knock came at the door. The Dutchman's hand moved inside his jacket, fingers touching the grip of his Glock 9mm, the 17L, the kind that doesn't set off metal detectors at airports.

Leo shook his head and grinned. "Stay cool. It'll be the kid."

"Which kid?"

There were two others sitting with the Dutchman's brother, and one of them got up and checked through the blinds before unlocking the door.

Dressed up for the occasion in his best leather jacket, new Pepe jeans, Raymond gingerly walked in. Valentine had hoped the Dutchman would have been long gone by this time, but what did it matter? This youth already close to pissing himself, acne pits all over his sorry face.

"You Ray-o?"

Raymond nodded.

"Come on in. Get over here. Someone get our visitor something to drink."

One of the men threw Raymond a can of Red Stripe, which he fumbled and caught; another relocked the front door.

"Sit." Valentine said, pointing at the vacant chair opposite.

Raymond sat.

"You want something to eat?"

Raymond shook his head.

"Curried goat, all kinds." Valentine laughed. "Dog, if you lucky. You should give it a try."

Raymond thought he was being sent up, but wasn't sure. A woman, small and with her hair in a net, came out from the kitchen with a plate of food and set it down in front of Valentine. It smelled good. Valentine took the top from a bottle of red pepper sauce and sprinkled it liberally over his supper. Raymond was beginning to wish he hadn't said no.

He popped the can and drank some beer instead. One of the men passed a large spliff to Valentine, who drew on it deeply, holding the smoke in his mouth, before passing the joint across to Raymond. It was strong enough to make him cough and Valentine laughed again, but pleasantly. This was okay, Raymond thought, this was going to be all right.

"So, little brother," Valentine said, "you got something to trade."

"Yes."

"With you. You got it with you?"

"Yeh."

"Some kind of weapon, I understand."

"A Beretta. Chrome-handled. A .38."

Valentine raised an eyebrow high. "Nice." He held out a hand. "Best let me see."

213

Raymond hesitated, Valentine watching him closely to see what he would do.

"I want eight hundred for it, cash," Raymond said.

Laughter and whistles all round.

"Boy," Valentine said, leaning forward. "I say one thing for you, you may be one ugly little fucker, but you got some balls."

Raymond could hear the breath, squeezing out of his lungs. "Eight hundred," he said again.

"Six fifty, that's your price. Seven tops. You tell me why I should pay over the odds."

The words came tumbling out in a rush, not the way Raymond had practiced it at all. "It's the gun from the Forest, the one you used on Jason. It's worth eight hundred to you, make sure it don't fall into the wrong hands. Got to be. Gotta."

Valentine sat back and shook his head. "Ray-o, boy, your balls ain't just brass, they big as a house." And glancing over his shoulder toward Leo, he said, "Count me out eight hundred, why don't you?" Leo winked at Raymond as he set the notes, fifties, on the table between them, Raymond thinking he'd tell Sheena the price had been two fifty.

"Now," Valentine said, "time for you to show me yours."

Raymond's mouth was too dry for him to speak. Slowly, he reached round to the back of his jacket and pulled out the Beretta.

"Set it down."

Raymond placed it next to the money.

"That loaded?" Valentine asked.

Raymond shook his head.

"Leo." Without looking back, Valentine reached a hand over his shoulder and Leo slapped a full clip into it; before Raymond knew what was happening, Valentine had pushed the clip into the pistol and snicked the safety off with his thumb.

"Oh, Jesus," Raymond said and felt his insides start to melt.

The tip of the gun barrel was only inches from his face. "Thing about Jason Johnson," Valentine said. "I never did get quite close enough to that skinny bastard. Which must have been why I missed."

Raymond closed his eyes and started to jabber meaningless sounds. When the barrel end touched, cold, against his forehead,

214

immediately above the bridge of his nose, he shouted "No!" and in the middle of his shout he heard, or thought he heard, a double click.

Nothing happened.

Raymond forced himself to open his eyes.

Valentine was sitting there with the Beretta in one hand and the clip of ammunition in the other, a fat smile all over his happy face.

"Jesus," Raymond breathed. "Jesus, oh Jesus. Jesus fucking Christ."

"There," said Valentine, barely able to contain his laughter. "Didn't your daddy tell you it was good to pray?" And he reversed the pistol so the butt was toward Raymond. "Your turn. Maybe now you should take a shot at me." He tossed the clip high through the air toward Leo. "Long as we all know it ain't loaded."

By now, everyone was laughing and even Raymond, who had long since learned it was important to be able to take a joke, especially if you were on the wrong end of it, laughed along with the rest.

They were still laughing when the door to the restaurant came crashing in and two men followed through fast, both dressed in black from head to toe, black balaclavas covering their faces, narrow slits for the eyes. One was armed with a shotgun, the other with an Uzi submachine-gun.

"What the fuck …!"

Raymond half-rose, three-quarter turned, the Beretta still in his hand.

A burst from the Uzi hurled him back and across the table in a clumsy cartwheel. Five bullets threaded through him, neck to pelvis; he was probably dead before he hit the floor.

"What the …"

The man nearest to Valentine smacked the barrels of the shotgun hard across his head and Valentine cannoned off the wall and sank down to his knees, spitting blood.

At the back of the room, the Dutchman moved his hand carefully away from the handle of his semi-automatic and stood to attention.

"Okay," one of the men said, his voice strong but muffled. "The money. Who's holding?"

First the Dutchman and then Leo emptied their pockets: close to

215

thirty thousand between them. With the eight hundred Raymond had scattered across the floor and what the others were carrying, there was close to thirty-two all told.

"That's it," Leo said. "That's all there is."

"Is it fuck!" one of the men said and the other one lifted the suitcases, one at a time, up from the floor. They took one each and backed toward the door.

"Stick your head out too soon, you'll get it shot off."

Nobody moved, not till they'd heard the roar of a powerful engine, the squeal of tires. And all the while, Raymond's blood spread slowly across the stained and pitted floor.

Thirty-eight

They were in Helen Siddons's office, Resnick, Norman Mann, and Siddons herself. Despite the relative warmth outside, the windows were closed tight and the air was thickening with blue-gray smoke.

"So what we've got," Siddons said, "this sorry article, Raymond Cooke, shot to pieces for no reason anyone can think of. A penny-ante restaurant raided in the early hours of the morning by two heavily armed men who got away with a couple of hundred from the till, a couple of Rolexes, and small change. That's the cock-and-bull story they're offering us?"

Drew Valentine, Leo Warner, and two others had been questioned by teams of officers since first light and so far none of them had deviated from their prearranged story. The interior of the Cassava had been searched and photographed by Scene of Crime. Raymond Cooke's body had been shipped out in a heavy-duty plastic bag to the morgue.

Before the police had arrived, there had been time for Valentine and his crew to effect a minimum of salvage work, if not as much as they would have liked. First off, the Dutchman and his brother had been bustled into their car and clean away; by now, they were safely out of the country. Second, the Beretta had been stashed out back in a bin of vegetable peelings and old bones, from where it had been taken, wrapped and weighted, and thrown into the River Trent. If Valentine had had his way, and the time, that was where Raymond's body would have been, too. Less to explain away.

"You knew him, Charlie. This Cooke. His being there, that time of night, it make any sense to you?"

Resnick shook his head. "Not right now, no."

"Not dealing then, working for Valentine."

"Not as far as I know."

"Norman?"

"Cooke, I don't see as he matters a toss one way or another. No, this was serious, a rip-off. Some other gang's come in, taken Valentine for everything he's got." He shook his head, cleared his throat. "Christ knows what they got away with, thousands, probably, cash or kind."

Siddons picked up her coffee cup, but it was already empty. "Any idea who might have been responsible?"

Mann laughed. "Too many. Could be someone lightweight, chancing his arm, looking to move up. I might've reckoned Jason Johnson for it, if he'd not already been nursing a sore head. If it's not that, it's one of the big boys, out to keep Valentine in line, make a tidy profit on the side."

"Come on, Norman," Siddons said. "Get off the bloody fence. You're the one supposed to have your finger on the pulse. Or is that just so much bullshit?"

The look in Mann's eyes was smarting and dangerous. "Bullshit, nothing. You want to know what I think, the way this was planned, executed, I'd say this was a major player, confident, not afraid."

"Names?"

"Planer, that's where my money'd be. Not that he'd risk dirtying his hands himself. No one too close to him, either. He'd bring somebody in from outside. Manchester, London. Whoever it was, they'll be well home by now, late breakfast, celebration. Champagne. Bastards."

"And it's not worth picking him up? Planer?"

"Not unless you want him laughing in your face."

Siddons scraped back her chair and walked to the window, stared out. "Charlie, you go along with that?"

"Norman's area, not mine."

"Listen," Mann said. "Either Valentine knows who ripped him off, or he's got a pretty good idea. And he's not about to sit around and do nothing about it. We might not be able to lay a hand on Planer, but that's not to say Valentine won't find a way himself."

Siddons knotted her hands tight. "That's the one thing, the one thing I dreaded, the likes of Valentine taking the law into their own hands."

"Bread-and-butter stuff," Norman Mann said with a smile. "Slag-on-slag. Long as they stick to shooting themselves, why not keep our heads down, let 'em get on with it?"

"And if another Raymond Cooke gets in the way?" Resnick asked.

"Own up, Charlie," Mann sneered. "Who the fuck cares about an arsewipe like that?"

Resnick didn't recognize her at first, sitting close against the wall adjacent to his office door. Save for a few stray wisps, her red hair was hidden beneath a dark beret, the only makeup careful around the eyes. She was wearing a plain, button-through dress and flat shoes. Terry Cooke's former common-law wife.

"Eileen, come in. Come on inside." Holding the door, he let her precede him. "Can I get you anything? Tea? Coffee?"

She shook her head and he motioned toward a chair, sat down himself.

"I'm sorry about Raymond."

Eileen bit down into her lower lip. "I've just come from seeing the body."

Ray-o's mother had run off when he was four, his father had not been seen in years, his uncle dead by his own hand; Resnick supposed Eileen, in a manner of speaking, was his next of kin.

"They pulled back this sheet," Eileen said, not looking at Resnick, but at the floor. "They pulled it back and he was just laying there like … like meat. Something they'd hunted and shot down, that's what I kept thinking. Meat."

When Resnick had first run across Raymond, the lad had been working at the abattoir close by the County ground, up to his elbows in tubs of guts, intestines, blood, and bone. The stink of it had clung to his hair, his body, had followed him everywhere, rank, like a second skin.

"I'm sorry, Eileen. Sorry you had to see him like that."

"Whatever he'd done, whatever he was like, he never deserved that."

She fumbled for a tissue and Resnick waited, patient. Noisily Eileen blew her nose. "Nobody'll tell me, not really, tell me what happened."

Resnick leaned slowly forward. "There was an armed robbery at the restaurant. Some shooting. Raymond, as far as we can tell, just happened to be there at the wrong time. Unfortunately he got in the way, the line of fire. Of course, we're making inquiries, but for now that's all we know."

"It's not right."

"No."

"You're not going to bother, are you? Over Ray-o, I mean. You're not going to be pulling out all the stops because of him."

"Eileen, I assure you. We're taking it very seriously."

"Yeah? And so far you've got nothing, right? You go on about how he just happened to be there. I don't think Ray-o'd set foot in that place in his life. I know him. I don't think he would, not without a reason."

Resnick bent toward her. "There's nothing you can think of that would help, like you say, give us a reason for why he was there?"

"No."

"Maybe if you thought about it …"

"I told you, I don't know …"

"Okay." He sat back again. "I'm sorry there isn't any more I can tell you. Not now, anyway."

Pushing the tissue down into her bag, Eileen got to her feet. "Don't hold my breath, right?"

He waited till she was almost at the door. "Sheena, Sheena Snape, you know her a little, don't you?"

"A bit. Yes, why?"

"She and Raymond, were they, you know, friends? Anything like that?"

"Not as far as I know."

"Only I was in the shop not so many days back and she was there. Raymond seemed embarrassed at me seeing them together. I thought there might be something going on between them, that's all."

Eileen shook her head. "Ray-o, he might not have been God's

gift, bless him, but he knew better than to get involved with a slag like that."

"Business, then. I remember Raymond making out she was there to buy something, but she didn't back him up. Maybe she was the one with something to sell."

Now Eileen was looking at him hard. "And you think, whatever it was, it might have something to do with Ray-o getting shot?"

"I'll be honest, I don't know."

"Honest?"

He looked at her questioningly.

"You tried to get round me once before, remember? When Terry was still alive. All nice and understanding. Getting me to inform against him, that's what you were trying to do. Grass. Same as what you tryin' now. You want me to go round Sheena's, don't you? Do your dirty work for you. 'Cause you know, after what happened to her brothers, she wouldn't give you the time of day."

Resnick took a breath. "All I'm saying ..."

Eileen raised her head. "I know what you're saying. And I don't want to hear."

What Resnick heard was the quick closing of the door and footsteps, fast across the floor.

Maureen was serving a customer when Lorraine walked in, Maureen doing her level best to persuade a matronly body from Wollaton that gold chiffon was the very thing for her husband's firm's annual dinner. When she saw Lorraine, Maureen took a deep breath and carried on, Lorraine standing off to one side, feigning interest in a deep-green wool and silk mix jacket by Yohji Yamamoto, a snip at £499.99.

As soon as the customer had left the shop, Maureen went to Lorraine and held her tight. "Have you heard anything?" she asked, stepping away.

Lorraine shook her head. "That's what I came to ask you."

"I've not seen him since yesterday, yesterday early."

"You don't know where he is?"

"No." Maureen shook her head vehemently. "I don't know and I don't want to know. I don't ever want to see that bastard again."

Lorraine caught hold of Maureen's hand. "Did he ..." She was looking Maureen in the eye. "Did he hurt you?"

Maureen attempted a smile. "Not so's you'd notice."

"And you really don't know where he went?"

"No. I haven't a clue." She gave Lorraine's shoulder a sympathetic squeeze. "I wish there was something I could tell you. But I'm afraid I don't know anything." She paused. "Except I'm glad he's gone."

Lorraine half turned toward the door. "If you do see him ..."

"I won't, but ..."

"If you do, tell him to be careful, all right?"

When Lorraine walked up the brightly painted steps toward the car park, she could feel the unsteadiness vibrating in her legs.

The news on all channels carried extracts from the Chief Constable's press conference: serious points, seriously made. Society. Responsibility. The public good. A number of drug-related incidents. The unfortunate spread of firearms. Firm policing. Trust. Decisive action. With a slow and deliberate movement, the Chief Constable removed his rimless spectacles and delivered his final sentences straight to camera. "There will be no no-go areas, no yielding of the streets to lawlessness. You have my word—the situation is under control."

Somewhere between midnight and one, a maroon convertible slowed almost to a halt outside Planer's casino, bass speakers booming, and from the rear seat a young black man hurled a homemade firebomb into the foyer.

It had started with a vengeance.

Thirty-nine

Millington was waiting for him with a face most undertakers would have given their eyeteeth for. "That young prison officer," he said. "Evan."

"What about him?"

"Couple pulled into a lay-by, early hours. Wore out, wanting a rest. Loughborough road, not so far short of Keyworth. Bloke got out, wandered over t'field edge for a piddle. Found Evan face down in the ditch. Back of his head stove in. Been there a good twenty-four hours, far as we can tell, maybe longer."

Resnick cursed softly.

"What he was doing back in these parts, Lord alone knows."

"Follow it up, Graham. Talk to whoever's handling the investigation. Find out what you can. God knows how it fits in with all this, but if it does we want to know."

Resnick had scarcely had time to read the night's reports before Helen Siddons was on the line, her voice raw and tired.

"I've just sent Khan round to see you, Charlie, something else about our friend Finney. Just might be the lead we're looking for. You wouldn't have time to follow up on it yourself? That explosion last night, we're jumping round like blue-arsed flies as it is."

Khan had followed Finney up the Mansfield Road, assuming he was heading home. Instead, Finney had carried on driving, north out of the city. Some ten miles short of Newstead Abbey, he'd turned off on to a small single-carriage road, not much more than a track. Three-quarters of a mile along, Finney had parked close by a small house, a cottage. White walls, a garden, a small cobbled yard. Somebody's

223

home. Washing on the line and a child's bike, a red tricycle, on its side near the front door.

"You saw him go inside?" Resnick asked.

"No, sir," Khan answered carefully. "Not actually saw him. But there was no sign of him anywhere else, nowhere else he could go, so I assumed he'd gone in. Unfortunately, I didn't think I could hang around. Too risky. I drove back down to the main road and waited. A little under an hour later, Finney reappeared and this time he did drive home to Sherwood."

"This place," Resnick said, "can you show me on the map?"

"Definitely, sir. You think it's important?"

Small lines crinkled up the corners of Resnick's eyes. "I think it might be, yes."

Resnick drove north on the A60, the same road Anil Khan had followed the day before. The edges of the city soon left behind, he passed between gently sloping arable fields divided by low hedgerows, here and there a cluster of trees, a tractor standing deserted by an open gate. Lapwings. Crows.

The cottage was as Khan had described it, picture perfect. Resnick left the car a little way down, where the lane slightly broadened, and walked back, not hurrying. The warmth from the sun was such that he had no need of a coat.

As he passed through the gate, a small child, a toddler, came running through the open door and stopped, uncertain, at the sight of him. Resnick smiled and the child, a boy, turned and ran inside. Moments later, his mother appeared, holding his hand.

"Hello." Just slightly anxious. Wary. "Can I help?"

She was in her thirties, Resnick guessed, brown hair, an open face, quite tanned; wearing a loose floral-print dress, tennis shoes, unfastened, on her feet. Her pregnancy was far enough along for it to show.

"I was looking for Paul," he said. "Paul Finney."

"Oh," relaxing, "you've missed him by a good hour or so. Work, is it?"

Resnick nodded and she smiled.

"It's a wonder anyone can keep up with all his comings and

224

goings," she said, the child pulling at her hand, anxious to be away. "Sometimes I'm blessed if I can myself. But like Paul says, it's all part of the job. Adam, don't wriggle so. Be still." The boy succeeded in breaking free and stood a little way off, staring up at Resnick, thumb in mouth.

She smiled again. "Who'd marry a policeman, eh?"

Resnick smiled back.

"I'm sorry, I didn't mean to be rude, I never introduced myself. Laura. Laura Finney."

Resnick shook the proffered hand without offering a name in exchange.

"And that there is Adam." Adam frowned and turned his face away. "We don't get many visitors, living out here. You get out of the habit of being sociable, I'm afraid. It is lovely, though. Days like this, especially. Paul says he wouldn't change it for anything."

Resnick followed her gaze, down across the garden and the lane to the broad field opposite, a line of poplar trees breaking the low horizon.

"You work together, do you, you and Paul? I've not met so many of his colleagues. Likes to keep them separate where he can, you see, work and family."

Resnick assured her that he understood.

Laura pointed back toward the house. "I could make a cup of tea. It wouldn't take long to get the kettle boiling."

"No, it's okay. Thanks, but better not. Just passing, you know how it is."

She brushed at a strand of falling hair. "Maybe some other time."

"Maybe."

The boy was close against her now, thumb still in his mouth, hanging on to her skirt, and for a moment she smiled down at him indulgently. "Lord knows what he'll be like when this one comes along." Patting her belly. "Jealousy won't be in it.

"I'll tell Paul you called," she said when Resnick was at the gate.

"Yes, please. You do that."

For several minutes, Resnick sat in the car, windows wound

down, thinking. Once or twice, he heard the boy's voice, shrill and sweet on the air.

Finney's house was on the edge of Sherwood, not far from the City Hospital. A two-story semi in need of some paint, net curtains at the lower windows. A cat, orange and brown, lay asleep on top of a green wheelie-bin. Resnick rang the bell and, when it didn't seem to work, used the knocker. A woman's voice and then a child's. The woman opened the door just enough to show her face and little more.

"Mrs. Finney?"

"Yes. Who wants to know?" She pulled the door all the way back and came out on to the step. A small woman, maybe an inch or two over five foot, blue eyes, brittle hair. Forty, Resnick wondered? She was wearing a baggy top and jeans. "I thought you were Jehovah's Witnesses. Oxfam. One of those." She looked at him keenly. "You're on the Job, though, aren't you? You can always tell."

"Paul. I don't suppose he's here?"

"Is he ever?" She shook her head. "If we didn't need the over-time, I'd tell him to chuck it in tomorrow. Get something normal, nine to five. None of this working nights, weekends." She glanced up at him. "How does your wife cope?"

Resnick hesitated too long.

"Left you, did she? Had enough." From inside the house, there was a clatter and a fall, followed by a child's cry, boy or girl Resnick couldn't tell. "I'll be glad," the woman said, "when she goes off to school with the others. You have any kids?"

Resnick shook his head.

"Wise. Nobody thanks you for it." The cries got louder and she shouted back into the house, "All right, all right, I'm coming."

"Sorry to trouble you," Resnick said, backing away.

"No problem."

The door closed heavily behind him and, slowing his steps, Resnick stroked the cat as he passed.

When Finney walked out of the building and across the car park that afternoon, Helen Siddons and Anil Khan were waiting for him, two other Serious Crimes officers parked nearby in case of trouble.

"Paul Finney?"

"Yes?"

"Detective Chief Inspector Siddons."

"I know who you are."

"Then you won't have any objection to coming with us, answer a few questions."

"Questions?"

"See if we can't clear a few things up."

"Does this mean I'm under arrest?"

"Not at this stage, no."

"Good." He moved between her and Khan, heading toward his car. "Because I'm off duty and I was just making my way home."

"Really?" Siddons said. "And which home is that? Which of the two?"

Finney stopped in his tracks.

Finney was handsome in an indeterminate way, the sort of face you acknowledged and then forgot, perfect for his chosen line of work. He had quite a strong nose, brown eyes, dark hair which he wore without a parting and which hung down toward his collar a little more than was fashionable. Warm, in the room, he had removed his jacket and hung it across the back of his chair, unbuttoned the cuffs of his white shirt. Which wife, Helen Siddons wondered, had ironed that?

From time to time, Finney glanced, pointedly, at the watch on his wrist. "How much longer is this going to take?"

"That depends," Siddons said. She was sitting across the table from Finney, a buff-colored manila file in front of her; Anil Khan sat alongside, his notebook open, the pages so far blank. There was a tape-recorder with twin decks attached to the wall, so far not switched on.

"This is informal," Siddons had said at the beginning. "At this stage, at least. I assume you'd prefer it that way. Of course, it's up to you. How long it takes to get certain things established."

"Such as?"

Siddons smiled. "Drew Valentine, for starters."

227

Finney didn't miss a beat. "What about him?"

"You know him, what he does? How he—I hesitate to use the word 'earns'—how he makes a living?"

Finney not looking at her now, bored, staring idly at the cream-painted walls. This interview room like the others, like the whole two floors of the old General Hospital into which the Serious Crimes Squad had moved, had yet to lose its surface sheen.

"Paul?"

"Mm?"

"You know what he does, Valentine?"

"Of course, it's my job to know." Finney looking at Siddons again, Khan, like a pet beside her. If she thought this was a way to get under his skin, the same questions over and over again, she could forget it. He knew this game, this and all the others. It was his training, too; what he did best.

Displaying a certain degree of weariness, Siddons opened the file and read through the top sheet with exaggerated care. "Can you explain," she said eventually, "the circumstances in which Valentine, having been taken into custody on four separate occasions on suspicion of being in possession of significant quantities of a controlled substance, more than could reasonably be ascribed to his personal use, should have been set free without any charges having been filed?"

Finney shook his head.

"No?"

"No."

"You don't remember?"

"I don't remember those incidents clearly."

"Well, let me refresh your memory." Siddons lifted the page from the desk. "Twenty-seventh of October 1996. Fourteenth of February 1997. Fourth of June 1997. First of April 1998."

Finney shook his head.

"Are you telling me you don't recall anything about those occasions?"

"I'm afraid not."

"What about the most recent, April of this year?"

"Without my notebook, case notes, I'm afraid ..."

"Do you take me for a fool?"

Despite himself, Finney smiled.

Siddons got up from her chair and paced the room, four paces to the rear wall, four to the side, four more to the door. Khan kept looking at Finney, the confidence behind his eyes. When Siddons sat back down, she took out her cigarettes and offered one to Finney, another excuse for him to shake his head.

"When did you last see him, Valentine? And don't tell me you don't remember."

"I don't remember."

"It was three days ago, three nights."

Finney allowed himself mild surprise. "It was?"

"At a restaurant, Hyson Green. The Cassava."

"Red-pepper soup, they do a really good red pepper soup. Spicy."

"You were there with Valentine."

"I was?"

"Good buddies, bosom pals. You were seen on the pavement outside, back slapping, shaking hands. Best of friends."

Finney smiled. "It's my job."

"Palling up with drug dealers?"

"Letting them believe that to be the case. How else are you going to find out what's going down?"

"And that's what you were doing? What you do?"

"Of course."

"Getting on the inside track?"

"Yes."

"So why is it this inside track you've been cultivating so assiduously with Valentine hasn't resulted in a single arrest? A single case going to court? Being proved?"

Half smiling, Finney shrugged.

"Not, surely, because you are not very good at your job?"

"Not for me to say."

"And not because there was any advantage to you in Valentine staying free?"

"Maybe."

"Maybe?"

"Maybe he could give me information others couldn't." Finney

229

tapped the edge of the file. "You see how many arrests are down to me, cases which came to court, got a result. How many dealers off the street."

Siddons blew smoke off to one side. "Leaving the field clearer for Valentine."

"That's nature, isn't it?"

"What?"

"Abhorring a vacuum. Maybe sometimes it's a case of better the devil you know."

"What you're saying, there was a deliberate policy, on behalf of the Drugs Squad ..."

Finney held up a hand. "I didn't say that ..."

"On behalf of the Drug Squad ..."

"That wasn't what I said."

"On what? Your own behalf, then? Unilateral. Pick up a few crumbs from Valentine, bang up a few street corner dealers, strictly small time, let Valentine go free. Is that it? Paul, is that what happened, what's been happening?"

Finney shifted his weight, almost imperceptibly, from one buttock to the other.

"What else has been in it for you? Some other gain? I mean, I'm sure your friend Valentine must have felt inclined to show his gratitude in some way you both could understand? Or am I supposed to believe it was all in kind, I scratch your back if you scratch mine? That and the odd bowl of soup thrown in."

"I never," Finney said, "accepted a free meal. Not policy. Always paid my way. I expect I've got the receipts at home somewhere, if you're interested, filed away."

"Like the wives, the children, each in their own compartment, is that what you mean?"

Finney's eyes narrowed. "You stay away from that, you hear? Steer well away. That's nothing to do with what we're discussing here."

Siddons blew a lazy smoke ring. "Maybe you could tell me, Paul—I'm sure you're familiar—exactly what the law says about bigamy?"

Finney scraped back his chair, started to stand, but she caught his sleeve. "When you were with Valentine three nights back, did he tell you he was expecting some kind of delivery the next day? Is that how come somebody knew exactly where and when to go wading in there, waving guns? Whose back were you scratching that evening, Paul, other than your own?"

Slowly, Finney released a long breath, a smile. Yes, he thought, you nearly did it that time, didn't you? Almost got me going and no mistake. Carefully, he sat back down.

"I rather think the informal part of the proceedings is now over, don't you? Before we go any farther, I'm requesting the opportunity to speak to my immediate superior and my Police Federation representative. Any more questions, I'm afraid they'll have to be asked in the presence of a solicitor."

Forty

Resnick was standing up at the bar in the Borlace Warren with Millington and Vincent, Millington describing the welter of bruises to Evan's body, blows that had damaged him severely before those that had killed him. Officers from the Met had contacted his mother, but in her confusion she'd had no satisfactory explanation for why Evan was in the East Midlands.

Vincent was getting a round of drinks when Norman Mann pushed through the crowd and spun Resnick round by the shoulder. "If anyone had told me, you of all people, setting up one of my team behind my back. Not got the guts to tell me to my face."

Resnick stood his ground, kept his silence: there wasn't a great deal he could say.

"Well? What's the matter, Charlie? Run out of halftruths, lies?"

"DCI Siddons," Resnick said. "If there are questions you think need answering, maybe you'd be best off speaking to her."

"What? You what?" Mann's face contorted. "You shiftless bloody coward, hiding behind that tart's skirts. You ..." And he swung a fist.

Off balance, Resnick took the force of the blow high on his arm and it sent him stumbling back. Mann moved in for another punch, and Vincent and Millington grabbed him by the arms and held him fast.

"All right, all right. Okay. Let me go. Let me go."

Millington glanced toward Resnick, and Resnick, straightening himself, nodded.

Freed, breathing heavily, Mann stood there a moment longer before turning on his heel and stalking away.

"Ought to control that temper of his," Millington said. "Man of his age, overweight, drinks a bit, I dare say. Past forty."

Resnick grinned.

"You okay?" Millington asked.

"Yes. Yes, thanks, Graham. I'm fine."

"The way you took that shot, let him hit you, you know, sapping his strength. It was good to see."

"Yes, well. Maybe next time I'll try to duck."

"Maybe next time he'll punch straight."

Resnick accepted Carl Vincent's offer of a malt whisky and settled for a Laphroiag, more peaty than he was used to, but warm enough to burn away not the pain, more the embarrassment and the surprise. He tried to convince himself that Mann had been drinking too, an early belt from the bottle in his desk drawer. Something to explain a reaction so uncharacteristic, over the top. Resnick wanting to believe that rather than some more sinister implication: Norman blustering to cover up something he didn't want to admit to, something to which he'd turned a blind eye for too long.

When he arrived home, an hour or so later, Lynn Kellogg's car was parked in his drive, Lynn herself curled sideways across the driver's seat, asleep.

Resnick let himself into the house, did his duty by the cats, set the kettle on to boil, and went back outside. Looking down at Lynn through the dusty glass, Resnick remembered the first time he had set eyes on her, six, almost seven years before. Lynn, redder of face, stockier, her native Norfolk burr more evident in her voice. He remembered another night, later than this, she and Naylor had been called out to a house not so many yards from where Hannah now lived. A young mother, out for the evening with a man she scarcely knew, the children, two of them, left with their grandmother across town. It was Lynn who had found—almost stumbled across—the body, the moon sliding out from the cloud in time for her to see the woman, partly clothed, stretched out beside the garden path, drying blood for ribbons in her hair.

The first dead body Lynn had seen.

Talking to her in the victim's living room soon after the discovery, concerned to know how she was feeling, Resnick had caught her as she fell, a cup of sweet tea spilling from her hands. One side of her face had pressed, momentarily unconscious, against his chest, the fingers of one hand catching against one corner of his mouth.

A long time ago.

And now?

He realized she was stirring and took a pace away.

Rubbing her fists across her eyes, yawning, Lynn lowered the window. "I'm sorry, I didn't want to go back to the flat. I couldn't think of anywhere else to go."

Resnick nodded. "You'd best come on inside."

"Are you sure it's no bother?" But she was already getting out of the car.

They stood in the kitchen, Resnick between fridge and stove, Lynn close to the center of the room, one of the cats, curious, twisting in and out between her legs, occasionally nudging his head against her shins, the caps of her shoes. She was wearing a long cardigan, charcoal-gray, a pale-gray cotton top; navy-blue chinos, a pair of lace-up DMs that had once been bottle-green but had faded now to a chalky shade of black. Her hair was fudged up at one side where she had been sleeping.

"Do you want to talk?" Resnick said.

"No. Not yet."

"Coffee, then? Kettle's boiling. I can have it ready in a few minutes."

Wanly, she smiled. "You know what I'd really like?"

"Tell me."

"A bath. A nice, hot bath."

Resnick smiled back, more a grin than a smile. "Wait here. Well, not here. I mean you don't have to. Sit down. The front room. Over there. Anywhere. I'll run the water now."

Upstairs he checked the temperature from the taps, tipped in Radox and swirled it round, found a towel that was both dry and clean. Stepping out on to the landing, he heard music from below and, when he eased open the door to the living room, Lynn was sitting with her legs pulled up in one of the armchairs, Bud lying full length, belly up, along the crack between her chest and thigh, and the Mills Brothers were singing "Nevertheless." He had left the CD on the machine.

This time, she woke up almost at once.

"Your bath's running now. It won't take very long."

"Okay." Lynn stretched and Bud moaned, and she rubbed her fingers along the length of his tummy and tickled his neck. His bones seemed impossibly fragile, impossibly close to the skin. "I just pressed play on the stereo, I hope you don't mind?"

"Oh. No, of course not." He nodded in the direction of the speakers. "Nevertheless" had become "I'll Be Around." "Funny old sound. Old-fashioned."

"I like it." Depositing Bud back on the chair, she headed for the door.

"You know where it is? It's just along the first landing and ..."

"I'll find it, don't worry."

Resnick fidgeted around for a while, not knowing quite what to do. The Mills Brothers were starting to get on his nerves, too much of a good thing, and he replaced them with the Alex Welsh Band, changing them almost immediately—too bright and loud—for Spike Robinson playing Gershwin, nice melodic tenor sax.

He made coffee anyway, two cups, and carried one upstairs.

"Lynn?" He knocked softly on the bathroom door.

"Yes?"

She answered immediately. He'd thought the warm water might have lulled her back to sleep. "I've brought you up some coffee. I'll leave it outside the door."

"Okay. Thanks."

From the hall, he heard the door open and then close. In the kitchen, he peeled and chopped first an onion, then a potato, the latter into pieces no bigger than the tip of his little finger. Butter and a splash of olive oil hissed in the pan and he dumped in both potato and onion, gave them a stir, and turned up the heat. From the fridge, he took a piece of chorizo and sliced it into rounds the thickness of a ten-pence piece. Eggs he broke into a basin and whisked, adding salt and pepper and the last inch from a pot of cream. By now, the potatoes were starting to stick, so he gave the pan an energetic shake. The bits he didn't think the cats would eat from the floor, he shooed in the direction of the bin with last night's paper.

"Something smells good." Her hair was still wet and shone. Her gray top hung loose over her belt and her feet were bare.

"How was the bath?"

"Great. Perfect. If it hadn't been for the thought of the water getting cold, I could have stayed there for hours. Soaked."

"Then you'd have missed this."

He added the sausage to the potato and onion, and cut an edge of butter into a second, smaller pan.

"Can I do anything?"

"Watch."

When the surface was close to smoking, he gave the omelet mixture a final whisk, then poured it in. With a wooden spoon, he moved it around a little, let it settle, starting to pull it away from the edges when it threatened to set; a couple of good shakes and he added the contents of the first pan.

"You should be on television," Lynn said.

Resnick grinned. "Radio, more like."

She laughed. It was a good sound.

"There is something you can do," he said. "Knives and forks, in that drawer over there."

"Right. Plates?"

"That cupboard. About level with your head. You could put them just here."

He divided the omelet into two and served it out.

"There's bread," he said, "in that bin. I forgot."

"Butter?"

"On the side."

They sat at the kitchen table, facing one another, Resnick's face flushed from standing over the stove, Lynn's from her bath.

"We should have some wine," he said.

Lynn was already attacking her omelet with a fork. "Later. We don't want this to spoil."

"No, you're right."

There was a bottle of red in the cupboard, he thought, some-

236

thing Hannah had brought round and they'd never drunk. He didn't know what it was, but guessed it would be okay.

Rarely, there was no music in the room. The curtains were still pulled back and though the light was starting to go, it was far from dark. They sat in the same easy chairs that Resnick and Elaine had bought, second-hand, at the start of their marriage, too comfortable to replace. The wine, indeed, was fine, though neither of them had so far gone beyond the first glass.

"I think," Lynn said, "what I think now, although they never said, not outright, when they let him come home before, it was because there wasn't anything more they could do for him. The cancer, it had spread too far." She was sitting quite upright, legs tucked under her, running her fingers through the smallest cat's fur as she talked. "But then—I don't know—the pain got so much worse, suddenly, and they took him back in. His skin, it had become really yellow again, this kind of murky, bilious color; the thing they put in, inside him, to clear the obstruction to his liver, maybe it wasn't working. Not properly."

Reaching down, she took a sip of wine.

"When I got there, Mum was just sitting beside the bed, crying. Not making any sound, hardly, just crying. Dad was hooked up to all this stuff and he had a mask over his face. To help him breathe. One of those hard plastic masks.

"I don't know how much anyone had said to Mum, if they'd said anything at all. She was so upset, confused, I doubt if she would have taken it in if they had. After a while, I went off and found a nurse and she told me as well as his liver, he was suffering from kidney failure. They'd made him as comfortable as they could. She didn't think he was in too much pain. She said if I could stay a while longer the doctor would come and see me, explain."

The clock across the room seemed unnaturally loud. Resnick moved the wineglass around in his hand, but didn't drink.

"The doctor, when he came, he looked so young. Too young to be doing what he was doing. But he was nice, nice to Mum especially. There must be something you can do, she said, and he patted her hand. All we can do now, he said, is make sure he's comfortable,

237

not suffering any pain. I'm still not sure she understood what he was saying, what it meant. She kept on at him, you will do something, operate. He'd been sitting with her, on the edge of the bed, and got up and looked down at Dad, who'd been sleeping all the way through this. He's lived a good life, he said, let him go in peace. No heroic measures. It wouldn't be right, believe me. It wouldn't do any good."

"I'm sorry," Resnick said.

Lynn sighed and rubbed a hand across her eyes as if to brush away tears, but for now there were none there.

"I sat with him, holding his hand. Talked, just a little, but I don't know whether he heard. The sound of my voice, perhaps. Maybe he recognized that. Once or twice, he moved his head as if he wanted to try and say something and I leaned over and lifted away the mask, but all he could do was make these sounds, sort of low in his throat. His mouth, it was all dry; the skin flaking back from his lips.

"I do think he knew that we were there, Mum and me. The nurse said, why don't you go? Go home for a while, get some sleep. But I couldn't." She sniffed and fumbled a tissue from inside her pocket. "Just before the end, he squeezed my hand, tried to. He ..."

She stopped and looked, helpless, across the room. Resnick moved and, half-kneeling, held her till her face dropped forward on his shoulder and she cried. Sobbed.

And when the worst of it was over, her skin warm against him, his shirt wet from her tears, he kissed her on the neck and she twisted up her face and kissed him close alongside his mouth where her fingers had caught years before. "Lynn." He said her name and she kissed him again, lips moving over his, the first touch of her tongue. "Lynn." She wriggled her mouth away and he said, "I'm getting a cramp in my leg, I've got to move." And then she laughed and so did he, and they were sprawled, half on the chair, half on the floor, the cat clambering between them.

"My wine," she said, still laughing, though there were tears smudging the corners of her eyes. "I don't think I can reach it from here."

Resnick could, just, and he leaned across and handed it to her and they both drank, from the same glass, until it was empty. Then Lynn looked at him squarely and said, "I should go" and he said, "You don't have to, you know," and she said, "I know. Thank you. But I think I will," and she started to disentangle her legs from his until they were standing face to face, the dark around them, not quite touching.

At the door, he checked she was okay to drive and she assured him she'd be fine. He asked when was the funeral and she told him three days' time. He almost said, did she want him to come, but held his tongue.

"Thanks." She had the car keys in her hand.

"What for?"

She smiled. "Supper. The bath."

"Take care."

"You, too."

He stood there watching as the tail-lights of her car faded around the curve in the road, and longer than that, trying to recapture the feeling of her mouth on his, Dizzy watching him reproachfully from his perch on the stone wall beside the path.

Forty-one

Cassady had cleared out his safety deposit box at the bank, transferred five thousand from his personal account into the one he shared with his wife and withdrawn the rest. Walking back to where he'd parked the car, he punched a number on his mobile phone. "Jacky. Yes, it's me. On the way now. Right. Yes, love you too."

She arrived in Cinderhill first, fair putting the wind up Preston. Jacky breezing in with her own key, hold-all slung over one shoulder. "Hi, you must be Michael. I'm Jack. Jacky." Smiling as she held out her hand.

More than a touch of the tar brush about her, Preston thought, skin a sort of Milk Tray color, though she sounded north of the border. A looker, though—tight jeans tucked down into her boots, white top that could have been put on with paint.

"That the wife?" he asked, when Cassady arrived twenty minutes later.

"Don't," Cassady said, "be so fucking stupid!"

Jacky kissed Cassady on the mouth and lightly cupped his crotch.

"It's like Dodge City out there all of a sudden," Cassady announced. "Not that it'll do us any harm. But we'll make our move tonight, Michael, I'm thinking. Not tomorrow."

"Why the rush?" Preston asked.

"My inside man. A mite nervous all of a sudden, too many of his colleagues buzzing round, asking questions." He looked at Preston. "That'll not affect your plans? For after, like?"

Preston shook his head: now everything was so close, the sooner the better.

◆◆◆

Planer owned a *pied-à-terre* in west London and a villa in the Algarve; where he lived was a listed building in Southwell, the house set back from the road, a brick archway with an electronically operated wrought-iron gate barring access from the street.

It was a fine night, clear yet mild. Even this short distance from the city it was possible to see more stars in the sky. They would need, Cassady had said, no driver tonight, no extra risk. This not being a case of in and out, piston sharp. Preston was pleased with that. Pleased to be sitting there in the passenger seat of the BMW, the short barrel of the Uzi hard against his knee. Two thousand it had cost, Liam had been sure to tell him. Two grand and worth every penny.

"How much longer?" Preston asked.

Cassady looked at his watch, the details illuminated green in the dark of the car. "Two thirty," he said. "We go in at two thirty." He angled his wrist round toward Preston. "Four minutes from now."

"What's so special about two thirty?"

Cassady shrugged and smiled. "Sometimes he watches the late-night movie before turning in."

Finney had drawn for him the layout of the house. Shown him where to find the control box for the alarm, the whereabouts of the safe—not the obvious one in the second bedroom, the decoy with fifty quid inside and a copy of his will—no, the real McCoy. Of course, all this had cost him, the combination to the safe most of all, and Cassady had been glad to pay. Expenses to be recovered from Preston's end when it was done.

What had cost him more, though of a different kind, had been the code controlling both the gate and the front door. Planer's housekeeper, her son had a virulent crack habit in need of constant fueling. Pulling on his gloves, Cassady had a nasty thought the combination of numbers and letters he'd committed to memory might have been changed. The sort of precaution someone as security conscious as Planer might easily have taken. "Okay," he said, the minute hand flicking round to signal the half-hour. "Michael, let's go."

Getting out of the car, Cassady had a sudden vision of Jacky, waiting for him back at the house in Cinderhill, upstairs in the bedroom probably, sheet pulled up to her chin, eating cereal and watching one of her favorite videos, *Something Wild*, *The Fabulous Baker Boys*, *Married To The Mob*. Jacky, who would be Michelle Pfeiffer if she could.

The buttons on the gate control were small and shiny, chrome against matte black. A second, maybe two, in which the muscles of his stomach knotted tight, then Cassady heard the click of the mechanism and when he pushed against the curve of iron, the gate swung back.

He'd left the shotgun locked in the back of the car, no need. A canvas bag, loose over one shoulder. Michael had the Uzi, for God's sake, armament aplenty.

The same combination, in reverse, let them through the front door. The box controlling the alarm system was in the closet to the left of the paneled wall. Cassady knew that the first-floor landing, the windows, the door to Planer's bedroom and study were all alarmed. The last switch to the right. Cassady levered it carefully upward and the system went dead.

When he eased back the closet door, it squeaked and Preston, advancing down the hall, brushed against a low oak table as he turned, scraping the legs along the floor.

Both men froze.

Small sounds only, no more.

Nothing moved.

The housekeeper went home every evening between nine and nine-thirty; the gardener and odd-job man who slept in the base-ment was away visiting family in Glasgow. Planer's daughter was in her first year at Swansea, reading philosophy; his two sons were boarders at Oakham School. His recently ex-wife was in Santa Cruz de la Palma, living off the proceeds of the divorce. The blackjack dealer with whom he was having an affair had left at a quarter to one.

Planer aside, they had the place to themselves.

Cassady drew level with Preston and flicked on the pencil torch. The study was down three steps and to the left. The brass handle stuck and then turned.

Books were shelved floor to picture rail along two sides; an old-fashioned roll-top desk, big enough to hide a man inside, took up most of the third wall. There was another desk toward the center of the room. Two broad armchairs upholstered with studded leather, one with a green-shaded reading lamp close behind it, a Dick Francis on the table nearby, an empty whisky glass.

"Now," Cassady said quietly, "just give us a hand."

Working from either end, they maneuvered the rolltop far enough away from the wall to give them access to the safe. This was the series of numbers he'd not been able to commit to memory; the Gold Standard business card he'd written it on was in his back pocket.

"Here," he said, giving the card to Preston. "Read them out, why don't you?"

Cassady punched in the numbers and nothing happened, nothing budged.

"Read them again, careful. You must've got one wrong."

Again no reaction. Cassady snatched the card back and held it in one unsteady hand, while he used the other.

"It's not gonna fuckin' work," Preston shouted.

"Hush your mouth, can't I see that?"

"What the fuck we gonna do?"

"Keep your voice down, will you? Get Planer down here, that's what we're going to do."

Cassady snapped on the light in the hall. Planer was already midway down the stairs, a fleshy man in his late fifties with silver-gray hair. He had a silk Paisley dressing-gown on over his pajamas, a pistol, one of the ubiquitous Glock 17s, in one hand.

"Drop it!" Preston shouted. "Drop it fuckin' now!"

Carefully, Planer extended his arm until it was over the banister rail and dropped the pistol to the floor, where it bounced and skidded against the oak skirting board. Preston picked it up, ugly fucking gun, and stuck it into his belt.

"Come on along down here," Cassady said to Planer. "We're in a little need of your help."

Planer started to descend, but not quick enough for Preston, who ran toward him, two broad steps at a time, and jammed the Uzi in his ribs. "Get fuckin' down!"

In the study, Planer looked over at the safe and smiled.

"Open it," Cassady said.

Planer turned toward him. "Surely you've got the number?"

Cassady moved in very close. "I wouldn't advise it now, being clever. Foolin' around."

"There's an extra number," Planer explained. "It changes all the time. A bit like the Lottery, I suppose. That's why, when I thought Paul Finney had the rest of the combination, I wasn't overly worried."

Preston swung at him with the barrel of the Uzi and Planer fell heavily to his knees, a bloody line raked across his face.

"Never mind your fucking mouth, give us the fucking number. Now."

Wincing, Planer touched his cheek. Preston raised the gun.

"It's two numbers," Planer said. "Seven and one."

Cassady moved quickly to the safe.

"I called the police, you know," Planer said, pushing himself up on to one knee. "From the bedroom, before I came downstairs."

"You're lying."

Planer smiled his smug smile. "Do you really think so?"

Faint, not so very far off, the sound of sirens filtered through the heaviness of the room.

"Bastard!" Preston said and squeezed the trigger.

As if in the grip of a sudden fit, Planer's body flailed and shook along the floor.

"Jesus!" Cassady exclaimed. He fumbled with the numbers, all fingers and thumbs.

"Quick! Quick!"

The sirens were louder, closer.

"It's too late. Get out!"

They ran for the front door, flung it open, and raced across the courtyard, out through the gate. Cassady pulled the car keys from his pocket, dropped them on the road.

"What the fuck!"

At the second attempt, he retrieved them and unlocked the doors. The engine fired to life first time. The sound of police vehicles was almost upon them now, headlights visible on the road behind. Cassady floored the accelerator and took off with screaming tires.

"Lose 'em, fuckin' lose 'em!" Swiveling back in his seat, feeling Cassady accelerate again, Preston snapped his seat belt into place.

Swerving left and right, the car rode up on the curb, skidded, kept its balance: when they turned at the intersection leading back toward the city, another police car was heading directly toward them.

Cassady gripped the wheel tight and held both line and speed. At the last moment, the driver of the police car swung over hard, his off-side striking a low wall, before spinning broadside on to block the road. The BMW struck the other side of the police car as it passed and glanced off, careening on its way.

"Great!" Preston yelled. "Fuckin' great, man. You did fuckin' great."

"Didn't I, though," Cassady said. "Though I say so myself and shouldn't, didn't I just?"

At a fork in the road beyond Oxton, he took the turn too fast, went through a hedge and crashed, head on, into the trunk of an English oak.

For several moments, Preston couldn't breathe. He felt as if he'd been slammed against something invisible but strong. There was pain across his chest and down his spine, his neck. One of the head-lights was still shining, a spool of light spilling across a field of yellow rape. He released the seat belt and got, unsteadily, out of the car.

Cassady had been hurled through the windscreen and now lay wedged between the front of the BMW and the tree, his neck at an impossible angle, his face shredded by glass.

Preston could hear another vehicle, one at least, approaching from a distance. The Uzi he pushed under the driver's seat and seizing the keys, opened the trunk and lifted out the shotgun and as many shells as his pockets would carry. The Glock was still in his belt. Limping slightly, he ran off into the dark.

Forty-two

Resnick was awake when the phone rang: downstairs at the front of the house, listening in the near dark to Thelonious Monk warily threading his way through "Ghost of a Chance"; fingers testing the keys as if afraid what each cluster of notes might hide. It was close to three-thirty. Resnick had given up trying to sleep and was drinking coffee, strong and black. If he thought of Lynn, that thought led him, as often as not, to Hannah's sardonic, knowing face. When he began by thinking of Hannah, he finished up imagining himself in Lynn's arms. It was a relief to pick up the ringing telephone.

Helen Siddons's voice was loud and jagged. "More shit on the fan, Charlie. Big time. Planer, you know the ..."

"Yes, I know who he is."

"Seems as if he was woken by intruders in the house. Rang us. Then instead of staying low, waiting for the cavalry to arrive, he went downstairs to investigate. Either that, or they dragged him out of his bed."

"They?"

"Two men, we think only two. Liam Cassady and one other."

"Jesus."

"Trying to break into Planer's safe and didn't succeed. I think we got there too soon."

"This second person, Planer couldn't identify him, didn't know who he was?"

Resnick heard Siddons lighting a cigarette at the other end of the line. "Planer's not identifying anyone. Half a dozen bullets in him, more. And from close range. My guess the same weapon used on Raymond Cooke; same team probably, same shooter."

"Clean away?"

"Not exactly clean. Cassady wrapped himself round a tree. DOA on the way to hospital. Totaled the car. Looks as though whoever was with him got away on foot."

"No sign?"

"Not so far. There's a helicopter out waking all the sleeping farmers. Tracker dogs, the works. If he was injured in the crash, he'll be lying low. If not, my guess is he's hijacked another car somewhere."

"There's road blocks?"

"Where we can. Main roads, motorways. He'll be wanting to put as much distance between himself and the incident as he can."

"No."

"Sorry?"

"I said, no. He won't. Listen, where are you speaking from?"

"Headquarters. There didn't seem ..."

"Meet me at the corner of Woodborough Road and Mansfield Road. Four, five minutes. I think I know who he is and where he's going."

Preston had already arrived.

The owner of a Ford Mondeo, heading back late after the annual pharmacists' dinner-dance, had been left at the roadside in evening dress, lucky to be unharmed. Preston's neck hurt him as he drove, and as he crested the hill that would take him down to Lorraine's house he ground his teeth, sensing the relief. Since being back in the city, the only sounds of police activity he'd heard had been distant and sporadic, moving away.

He hurried, still limping slightly, across the front lawn and pressed his finger hard against the bell, hammered with the stock of the shotgun against the door. Come on, come on, come fucking on! Then it was Derek, calling from inside, wanting to know what was wrong. The kitchen blinds moving, Lorraine's face. Her voice raised in fear, anger. Both voices, arguing. Preston yelling, striking the door again. Harder. Back across the street, one bedroom light went on and then another. Someone, inside, unbolting the door, freeing the chain.

As soon as the door began to open, Preston pushed it wide.

Lorraine had pulled a cardigan over the shoulders of her night-dress; her face was ashen as she moved back against the wall. Farther along the hall, Derek, wearing pajamas, was standing by the telephone, receiver in his hand.

Preston slammed the front door shut behind him; three strides and he'd wrenched the phone from Derek's fingers, smashed the set from the wall with the gun, torn the wires free with his hand.

The children, Sandra and Sean, were clinging to one another on the stairs.

"Lock it," Preston said to Lorraine, pointing toward the front door. "And then get them back upstairs. And you …" He rounded on Derek, the end of the shotgun barrels hard against his neck, under his chin, forcing back his head. "Get in my way, anything, you're dead. Understand?"

Eyes wide, Derek nodded.

"Don't hurt him," Lorraine said. "There's no need to hurt him."

"I thought," Preston said, "I told you to get those kids out of the way." Sean was crying, Sandra trying to comfort him. "While you're there, get some clothes on, chuck a few things in a bag. Passport. We're leaving."

Lorraine's eyes widened in understanding. "Oh, Michael. Michael, Michael." She sighed and slowly shook her head, eyes closed.

"Do it," he said. "There isn't the time."

She looked at him, looked at her children. "The gun," she said. "You won't need it."

Preston nodded. "We'll see."

Sitting alongside Resnick in the back of the car, Helen Siddons was busily punching numbers into her mobile phone. "If you're wrong about this," she said.

Resnick shook his head. "I'm not wrong." The pieces were in place now: he knew. "Maybe I wish I was."

"What happened to your head," Lorraine asked. They were in the middle room, the dining room, partition doors closed across. She had sent Derek upstairs to be with the children. "It's swollen, there above the eyebrow. There's blood. A cut."

248

Preston touched it absentmindedly. "I don't know."

"What happened?"

"You don't want to know."

Lorraine had pulled on a T-shirt and cotton sweater, sneakers, jeans. There was a black travel bag near her feet. "Michael," she said, "you know this is stupid. Crazy."

"Get me an aspirin," he said. "Something. Then we're going."

Hearing her in the hallway, Derek called down in a loud whisper, asking if she were all right. She didn't answer. Back in the dining room she gave her brother two Neurofen and a glass of water.

"Michael, please ..." She touched the back of his hand, sliding her fingers between his. "Listen to me."

"Come on," he said, pulling away. "We're leaving."

They were almost at the front door when an amplified voice broke through from outside: "This is the police. We have the house surrounded. I repeat, this is the police ..."

There were four of them inside the command van: Siddons and Resnick, Bill Claydon, in charge of the Tactical Response Unit, and Myra James, a sergeant with special training in hostage negotiation. With the telephone in the house out of commission and Preston showing no disposition to engage in dialogue, negotiation was difficult.

Three monitors gave them grainy black and white pictures of the house; one camera by the fence at the far end of the garden, covering the rear; another, using a zoom lens, was focused on the front; the third was in the helicopter, turning noisily overhead.

Thirty officers from the Serious Crimes Squad and the Special Support Group were surrounding the house; of these, all were wearing body armor and half were armed. Six marksmen from the Tactical Response team were positioned at intervals around the building, each in continuous contact with Claydon through their headsets.

There were two ambulances waiting on standby, uniformed police holding back the television crews and cameramen. The houses close by had been evacuated.

It was now almost fully light.

Claydon pointed toward one of the screens. "We could be through those French windows in what? Five seconds, six. Set up a diversion at the front."

"He's got kids in there," Resnick said. "Two of them."

"We don't know if they're with him, if he could harm them. If he would."

"We don't know enough."

"We don't even know," Siddons said, "what he wants."

Claydon laughed. "What he wants, get out of there in one fucking piece, a plane to the other side of the earth, untold riches, happiness ever after, that's what he wants, poor sod."

They sat in virtual silence, save for the helicopter chattering overhead.

"Seven," Claydon said, suddenly clapping his hands. "Seven on the dot. If he's not given us something by then, I say we go in hard. What d'you say?"

"He's already killed twice," Resnick said.

"Three times," Siddons corrected him.

"Three times," Resnick said to Claydon. "Why are you in such a hurry to have him do it again?"

Inside the house, Preston had watched Derek and Lorraine, as under his instructions they moved furniture to barricade the front and rear doors. When the police made their move, and he was certain they would, he wanted what little time these precautions would earn him. One minute. Two. What he didn't yet know was how he would use it.

"Talk to them," Lorraine kept saying. "You have to talk to them."

Myra James knew the bulletproof vest she was wearing under her blue sweatshirt would protect her from anything but the highest velocity bullet fired at close range. Maybe. But the helmet? Ruefully, she smiled. So much of her unprotected. Her Gap jeans already had a small tear below the knee.

Using the megaphone, she announced her intention: to walk toward the front door and place the mobile phone she was carrying down on the step. All someone had to do was open the door a few

250

inches and take the phone inside. Then they could talk, find a way out of this situation before anyone was hurt.

After setting down the phone, Myra forced herself to stand there for several moments, staring at the door and waiting. But nothing happened, there was no immediate response. Slowly, she turned and walked away, willing herself not to lengthen her stride the closer she came to safety, not to run. The sweat was running freely down her back and legs and soon, she knew, unless she could change, it would be chafing her thighs.

Sandra came and stood just inside the dining-room door, working her lower lip between her teeth. She looked at the shotgun, which now lay diagonally across one end of the dining-room table. She felt Preston staring at her and, though she didn't want to, made herself look back at him. He seemed old, older than her mum and dad. Tired. She wondered what it was he'd done. There was a lump, a bruise, right over his eye. She tried to remember him, there at their house, in that room after the funeral; the way he'd looked at her when she'd handed him something to eat, smiling, but still sort of funny, and his voice, nice and soft, not like now.

"What is it, sweetheart?" Lorraine asked.

"It's Sean. He's in the toilet. I think he's being sick."

Lorraine started to move toward the door and Derek stopped her, a hand on her arm, a shake of the head. "Run back up," he said over his shoulder to Sandra. "Sit with him. Hold his hand. He'll be okay."

Sandra hesitated, looking past Derek at her mother, wanting to do the right thing.

"Go on," Derek said. "Do like I say."

When she'd left the room, Derek said to Preston. "Let them go. Let the kids go, why don't you? What harm have they ever done to you?"

"Derek ..." Lorraine began.

"What? You going to take his side about that as well?"

"Don't be so ridiculous, I'm not taking his side."

"Like hell you're not."

"You've not got the first idea what you're talking about," Lorraine said.

"No?" Derek looked at them, one to the other. "Don't I?"

Preston got to his feet. "Bring them down." He told Lorraine to fetch the mobile phone from the front door, waiting fast by her as she eased it open, ready if the police should try anything. But all that happened, as soon as they had it inside, the phone rang.

"Talk to them," Preston said. "Whoever it is. Tell them the kids are coming out. Tell them if they try anything, someone will get shot."

The children were at the foot of the stairs, on either side of Derek, listening.

"Come here," Preston said.

Hesitantly, Derek walking close behind them, they did as they were told. They had coats on, Sandra had her school bag on her shoulder.

"Come here," Preston said again and Sandra knew he was talking to her.

She went forward half a dozen paces, then stopped. He could reach out to touch her and he did. Touched his fingers to the side of her face, her cheek, and she flinched.

"You know who I am?" he said.

Sandra nodded, eyes downcast. "Yes."

For a moment, his hand rested on her shoulder. "Tell them," he said to Lorraine, "they're coming out now."

"Go with them," he said to Derek, who was bending down, adjusting Sean's laces.

"I can't." He was trying to see Lorraine's face, read her expression.

"Go," Preston said.

"I'll be all right, Derek," Lorraine said. "Go on."

Siddons leaned forward and jabbed a finger at the screen. "It's Preston, he's coming out."

Resnick shook his head. "It's the husband."

Siddons was already on her feet. "Myra, come with me. Let's talk to him, find out what's going on."

"Curiouser and curiouser," said Claydon ponderously. "And then there were two."

But Resnick was still staring at the front door, wondering what was going on in Michael Preston's mind, what was going on inside.

"Are you sure you don't want any?" Lorraine said, and when Preston shook his head, she poured gin into a tumbler, sipped at it, poured in a little more. Ten minutes since he'd spoken anything more than the occasional word. She carried her drink around the table to where he was sitting and stood close behind him, one hand resting high on his shoulder, fingers splayed. He leaned his head sideways against her arm. His breathing was ragged as cloth caught in the wind.

"It would never have worked, Michael. You know that, don't you?"

It was a while before she realized he was crying.

"You remember that time," Lorraine said, "we were on holiday with Mum, a caravan. Filey, I think it was. You were just sixteen."

"Bridlington. It was Bridlington."

"We made that kite, well, you did. Flew it along the beach, from the dunes." She paused. "That was the first time."

"Don't." He half turned, red-eyed.

"Why not? Isn't it what this is all about?"

"No."

"Isn't it?"

He turned away, reached up for her hand. "You said you loved me, Lo."

"I did."

"We'll always be together, that's what you said."

"We were kids."

"No. Your two, they're kids. We were older, knew what we were doing."

"Did we?"

Standing, he touched her arms, the nape of her neck, kissed her hair.

"Don't." She pushed away but he caught hold of her wrist and pulled her back; held her tight, tighter.

"You know I want you."

"No."

"All I've thought about …"

"Michael, no." She wrenched herself away and moved again till the corner of the table was between them, the shotgun still lying there, blunt and inviting. "It's not the same; I'm not the same. I know it's been different for you and I'm sorry, but you've got to see …"

"See what?"

"This … this person you've been, you've been dreaming about, fantasizing about, whatever—it isn't me. I've got all this, a home. Kids. Michael, I'm married now, don't you understand?"

He laughed, harsh and ugly. "That's not a fucking marriage, it's a sham."

Lorraine pushed a hand up through her hair, swallowed down some gin. "It's not a sham, Michael. It's what marriages are."

His fingers brushed the shiny stock of the gun. She was beautiful, beautiful to his eyes. "That night …"

"No."

"That night it happened …"

"Michael, please …"

"Listen, you got to listen."

"Michael …"

He lifted the shotgun and slammed it down, gouging the table. "Listen to me."

"All right," she breathed, "all right." So many years she had gone without exactly knowing; anxious to keep it that way. The evidence Michael had refused to give in the dock, the plea in mitigation; the expression in his eyes when they took him down, the last thing she saw.

"He caught me," Preston said. "Sneaking out of your room. Laughed. Slapped my face. Snatched hold of my hand. Pressed my fingers up against his nose, sniffing. "Lovely, isn't she? Choice. Ripe. I was wonderin' when you'd start getting yours." And he laughed again and winked. "Keeping it in the family."

Tears were running down Lorraine's face, unstopped.

"I hit him," Preston said. "Kept hitting him. Dragged him downstairs and into the shop. Kept hitting him till he was dead. Our fucking father!"

She held him then and kissed him and, not looking him in the eye, she said: "He'd come into my room, after I'd gone to bed; the way most dads, I suppose, do. Tuck me in, tell me a story. This little piggy went to market, this little piggy … It was just tickling at first and then he started, you know, down there, his fingers, down between my legs. Still tickling. Later on, when I was older, it would be when he came back from the pub, then it was more, he … When I got my first period, he stopped. Never came near me, not again. Not after that."

Michael's voice was far off, strange. "You didn't tell anyone?"

"Not till today, now."

He looked at her. "How could you? I mean, let him. Without saying?"

"Oh, Michael, I was a child."

"But later …"

"Later it was you came, oh so softly, to my room. I could hardly confess one without the other now, could I?"

He flinched. "That was different."

"A matter of degree."

"You loved me."

"I loved him."

"Even after …"

"He was my father."

"He fucking abused you."

"I know, I know. But it's not that simple, nothing is." She stepped away and said, "We have to finish this. We must."

After a long moment, he nodded and told her to dial the number taped to the phone. "I'm coming out," he said, when they had the connection. "We're both coming out."

"Throw the shotgun out first." Siddons's voice.

"Right." Preston looked at Lorraine and handed her back the phone.

"What d' you think?" Siddons asked, turning away from the screen toward Resnick.

"I think he's going to do as he says."

"We'll soon see," said Claydon, pointing.

Derek was sitting at the rear of the van, the children had been

255

driven off by one of the officers to be with Maureen. He leaned forward as the front door slowly opened, there was a quick glimpse of a face, an arm and then the shotgun spiraled through a curve and landed with a dent near the middle of the lawn.

"Good boy," Claydon breathed.

They stepped, Lorraine and Michael, through the front door together and the spotlight from the helicopter lit them up like stars. He took her hand and they began to walk along the path, Lorraine lifting an arm to shield her eyes from the light.

"Keep going," Preston said to her, several yards along.

"What?"

"Keep walking."

She hesitated, uncertain, took three more steps forward, stopped again. Preston took one pace, then another, back toward the door.

"What the hell's happening now?" Siddons asked.

Preston reached beneath his shirt.

"He's got another gun," Derek cried out. "A handgun."

"Why the fuck didn't you say?" Siddons yelled.

"Watch up, watch up," Claydon said into the harnessed mike. "He may still be armed."

The pistol in Michael's hand was aimed at everything, at nothing.

"No!" Lorraine screamed and began to run toward him.

"Take him," Claydon said into the mike, and three high-powered rifles opened fire.

For what seemed to Lorraine an eternity, but was only seconds, Michael seemed to be dancing from unseen strings: then the strings were cut and he folded at the center, fell to earth, blood pumping from his neck, one side of his face, the side where his face had been.

She crawled across the ground toward him, men running past her, shouting, reaching down. She had just touched his arm when they lifted him away to where the paramedics with the stretcher were waiting.

Resnick started to walk across the grass toward her, till Derek stumbled past him and sank down on his knees beside her, holding her against him, sobbing, both of them sobbing, Derek repeating her name over and over, "Lorraine, Lorraine, Lorraine …"

Forty-three

The media rubbed its hands. Special news bulletins, network specials, analysis, speculation. The Jacobs' house was besieged: Lorraine and Derek took the children out of school and went to stay with an aunt in Rochdale. Maureen sold her story to the *Sun*. Helen Siddons bought a new Donna Karan suit for her appearance on *Newsnight*, a round-table discussion with the Home Secretary and a former Chief Constable of Manchester. Jacky and Jean made the arrangements together for Liam Cassady's funeral.

In the middle of a slow afternoon, Resnick picked up the phone and it was Eileen Cooke. "Sheena," she said, "she was in the pub last night with her mates, pissed. I talked to her. About Ray-o. She'd given him this gun, to sell. Been used in a shooting, she reckoned. Out on the Forest. She thinks maybe that's why Ray-o had gone to see this Valentine." Eileen hung up.

Resnick talked it over with Millington and the rest of the team. Variously, they would interview Sheena Snape and her friends, Diane and Lesley; they would speak again to Drew Valentine and Leo Warner. They would do what they could. All the other information suggested that Planer's death had left a vacuum in the region's drug trade and Valentine was one of those working hard to fill it; if there was a perfect time to bring him down, this was it.

The Major Crime Unit, meantime, continued its investigation into the activities, personal and otherwise, of Paul Finney. Other officers from the Drug Squad, including Norman Mann himself, were called in.

For the best part of three days, Helen Siddons sat across a table from Finney, the tape deck softly whirring, question after question meeting the same response.

"What was your relationship with Roland Planer?"

"No comment."

"You were aware that, in addition to gambling, Roland Planer's other principal business activity was the distribution of illegal drugs?"

"No comment."

"How about Gold Standard Security? Liam Cassady? In what capacity did you receive payments from them totaling several thousands of pounds?"

Finney's Police Federation lawyer coughed and leaned forward: "Detective Chief Inspector," he said in the East London accent he found it useful to affect, "my client has made it clear it is not his intention to respond on these matters. As is his right."

"Jesus, Charlie!" Siddons said, when she bumped into him in the corridor. "Why the hell take the right to silence away from every other sod and leave it with the likes of Finney? You know what's going to happen as well as I do. The bastard'll drag the investigation out as long as he can, get signed off with stress. Couple of years from now, he'll get himself invalided out on a pension and there won't be a bloody thing we can do about it."

Resnick went to a dinner party with Hannah, some friends of hers from school, a couple with a house in West Bridgford, looking across open land toward the river. There was a psychotherapist there also, a graphic designer, a worker for the National Council for Single Parent Families. In between talking about their jobs and the wine and plays they'd read about but not actually seen, they discussed the apparent breakdown in law and order, the alarming rise in the use of guns.

"What's your view, Charlie," the therapist asked, forking up some asparagus. "This guy who was shot and killed. The police, your chaps, they didn't need to take such extreme measures, surely?" He looked across at Resnick earnestly. "I'd love to know what you think."

Resnick thought it was time he left. He touched Hannah's shoulder as he passed and did exactly that. Tense in the car, angry, he thought he was driving home, but that wasn't where he was heading.

Lynn opened the door to her flat, her hair pulled back, no make-up, a man's white shirt torn at the collar, baggy jeans. "Something's the matter," she said.

"No."

She closed the door behind him and he looked around the cluttered room; surfaces covered with boxes of old papers, photographs.

"The funeral?" he asked.

"Yesterday."

He nodded.

"I could put the kettle on, some tea …"

But he was already reaching for her and she could never remember, nor could he, the path by which they made their way, clumsily, from settee to floor and floor to bed.

"This was my dad's," she said later. The shirt had somehow wound between them and Lynn tugged it free and shook it out, bringing it to rest like a flag across the pale-blue patterned quilt.

When she leaned forward, Resnick kissed her back, her side where it dipped between hip and ribs, her breast.

"I think', she said brightly, "we could have that tea now, don't you?"

He looked at the clock: it was past one, nearer to two.

When she stood in the doorway minutes later, naked, posing almost, a large mug in each hand, he felt—what?—excited? Proud?

"The funeral," he said when she was back in bed, the pair of them sitting back against the pillows. "How was it?"

"Oh, strange. As if it wasn't happening somehow, not to me. My mum, she was in a right state. You know, carrying on. I was so busy fretting about her … It'll hit me in a few days, I expect." Dipping her head, she kissed Resnick's shoulder. "I was glad for him, I suppose. My dad. That he went when he did. Better than dragging on."

He thought she was going to cry, but she sniffed and squeezed his arm, and reached again for her tea.

When he noticed the clock again, it was a quarter to three.

"Do you want to go?" Lynn asked.

He shook his head. "No."

Waking again later, hunched up against him, Lynn said, "Charlie, why does this feel so comfortable?"

There was no reply: he was asleep.

When finally they woke, the pair of them, it was beginning to be light outside and Lynn was holding her father's white shirt close against her face.

The Crown Prosecution Service informed Resnick that on the strength of what they'd seen so far, in the matter of illegally purchasing, carrying, or discharging a firearm in a public place with the specific purpose of causing injury, there was insufficient evidence for proceeding against Drew Valentine.

For receiving stolen goods and dishonestly assisting in their disposal, Gary Prince was sentenced to two years' imprisonment, automatically reduced to eighteen months. Vanessa immediately took a job as hostess on a cruise ship to the Azores.

At the inquest into the death of Evan Donaghy, the coroner returned a verdict of murder by person or persons unknown.

Paul Finney rose early, for a Sunday; the questioning had been going on now, one way and another, for almost two weeks. Siddons niggling away, bringing in his colleagues, friends, on and on, always holding the charge of bigamy over his head.

He made himself a cup of tea and sat for a while in the kitchen, scanning the sports pages. Notts all out for a hundred and twenty. What sort of a performance was that? The kids were down now, two of them anyway, in watching TV, and he made a big pot of tea for everyone, took a cup up to his wife, along with bits and pieces of the papers.

"Just off out for a spell. Back in an hour."

Laura was painting the old cottage scullery, bright yellow daubed all over her hands and in her hair, and in Adam's hair, too. "Let me just finish this bit here," she said. "I'll put the kettle on."

"Why don't we go for a walk first?"

They wandered down the lane and back, taking their time, Adam riding on Finney's shoulders much of the way, kicking him with his heels, tugging at his hair.

He said no to a drink, said he had to be getting on.

"Tomorrow, then," Laura said.

"I hope so, love."

Finney drove south to Loughborough station, bought a KitKat in the little newsagent's kiosk, and crossed the bridge to the south-bound platform. "Please stand well back," said the announcer, "the next train is the Midland Main Line express to London, St. Pancras, not stopping at this station." Near the end of the short platform, Finney closed his eyes and stepped out into space.

He had posted letters to his wives and children; a letter, too, to Helen Siddons, a packet really, fat, registered. Like the good officer he had once been, Finney's documentation was thorough, cross-referenced. Times, dates, places. Within an hour of reading through the material, photocopying it for safety, Siddons sought, and was granted, a meeting with the Chief Constable. Less than an hour after that, three Drugs Squad officers were arrested on charges ranging from the illegal possession of controlled drugs to conspiracy to pervert the course of justice. Norman Mann was placed under suspension pending the results of these and other inquiries.

Resnick had not spoken to Hannah since he walked out of her friends' dinner party. He had phoned twice and left messages, but she had not returned his calls. Now he bumped into her, almost literally, crossing Upper Parliament Street, Hannah heading in the direction of the Theatre Royal, Resnick, hands in pockets, going the other way.

They hesitated, uncertain whether to carry on walking or what. Drivers sounded their horns. "This is stupid," said Hannah, as much to herself as anyone, and pointed back toward the curve of pavement outside what had once been a bank and was now an Irish pub.

"I rang," Resnick said, sounding defensive.

"I know."

He shuffled his feet. "That business … at dinner …"

"It doesn't matter."

"Well, I'm sorry. I shouldn't have just gone charging off like that. It was childish, silly."

"Charlie, it doesn't matter."

People brushed past them, hurrying, heads down.

"You haven't got time," Resnick said, "I don't know, for a drink or something?"

Hannah looked vaguely at her watch. "I haven't really."

Still neither of them could quite make a move. A double-decker bus, green and dirty cream, turned noisily left from Market Street, leaving a strong smell of diesel.

"I think I'm seeing someone," Resnick blurted. "Someone else."

"You think?"

"Well, I …"

"God, Charlie, one of these days, with any luck, you'll know."

He hung his head. "Yes, yes I suppose so."

"Who is it?" Hannah asked brightly. "Anyone I'm likely to know?"

"Lynn. It's Lynn."

"Your Lynn?" she said, amazed. "That Lynn?"

"Mine?" He almost laughed, chuckled at the thought. "Yes, I suppose. That Lynn."

That seemed to be that. Hannah smiled. Deftly, she kissed the air close by his cheek. "Look after yourself, Charlie. Take care."

"You, too."

With a wave, Hannah turned and crossed with the traffic. By the time she had reached the forecourt of the theater, Resnick was almost at the Old Market Square.

Skelton called him in two days later. A bright morning, but somehow promising rain. Everything on the superintendent's desk was at a perfect angle to everything else. The creases in his suit trousers were so true as to give credence to the rumor he had them sewn in. Resnick even thought there was probably some kind of mathematical formula that would give you the exact position of the knot of Skelton's tie; the length from one end to the other divided by the sum of the two adjacent sides, something like that.

"Well, Charlie, good news. She's packing her bags. Leaving."

Resnick was confused. Who was going and where?

"Siddons. She's been head-hunted, National Drugs Campaign. Second in command, apparently. Not be satisfied with that for long. Still, our loss, eh ..."

The super was looking bright this morning, Resnick thought, quite a gleam in his eye.

"What this does, of course," Skelton went on, "it leaves a gap. Major Crimes."

"They'll advertise."

"Did that last time, Charlie, look what happened."

"But they'll have to."

Skelton smoothed his fingers down the fine grain of his lapel. "Come on, Charlie, where there's a will."

Resnick's mind was racing in overdrive. Detective Chief Inspector. He'd passed up the chance once, and now ...

"Face facts, Charlie," Skelton said, "you're not getting any younger. Done what you can do, job you've got now. Done it pretty well. Not outstanding, maybe, but pretty well. How many more chances like this d'you think are going to come along? Unless you'd rather vegetate, of course. Grow old."

Resnick rose to his feet.

"It's a yes, then?"

"Twenty-four hours."

"Charlie ..."

"Just time to think it through. I'll give you my answer tomorrow. First thing."

Skelton made a gesture of mock-exasperation. "Suit yourself. But first thing, mind. No more shilly-shallying around."

Resnick set off down the hill from Canning Circus, walking briskly into town. He'd been right in his fears about the rain, it was starting to spot now, large drops, dark on the paving stones. What chance there'd be a fuss, he thought, himself and Lynn part of the same team? Again. Always assuming things carried on as they were. Only more so. He caught his reflection in the restaurant window as he passed, grinning like some great kid.

Well, nothing was definite yet, nothing settled.

DCI, though; he'd regretted not going through with the application before and Jack Skelton was right, if he didn't put himself up for it this time, then likely that was it.

Outside Yates's, he bought a *Post* and glanced at the headlines walking along the north side of the Square; up King Street past the Pizza Express—jazz every Wednesday evening, he'd have to give it a try. The usual congregation of elderly Poles in elderly suits was gathered outside the entrance to the market and those who knew him raised a hand in recognition. Aldo saw him coming and was making his espresso before Resnick had taken his seat.

"Good day, Inspector? You are doing well, yes?"

Resnick nodded. He thought he was. He thought he might be on the verge of doing better.

Coda

No reason he would know this, but my foremost thanks go to Elmore Leonard; it was reading him with so much unalloyed pleasure and admiration that got me thinking about writing crime fiction again. Thanks for inspiration, also, to all those oft-watched episodes of *Hill Street Blues*, to Harold Becker's marvelous film of Joseph Wambaugh's *The Black Marble* and to fond memories of reading early Ed McBain. Leonard aside, the masters I have come back to, again and again, are Chandler and Hammett—there's more than a little of *Red Harvest* in this particular book—Ross Thomas and George V. Higgins.

I would never have set Resnick walking, shabby and careworn, down from Canning Circus to Nottingham's Old Market Square, if it hadn't been for the advice and help of the late Dulan Barber, whose own crime fiction was written as David Fletcher. Tony Lacey bought the first book in the sequence, *Lonely Hearts*, for Viking Penguin when no other editor would touch it, and for that I'm eternally grateful; at Heinemann, I owe considerable thanks to Louise Moore and, after her, to Lynne Drew and Victoria Hipps. In America, I have been blessed since the beginning with Marian Wood, who has been my editor at Henry Holt from first to last— fierce in her writers' defense and, as I have had cause to learn, as quick to upbraid them for their shortcomings. Marian has been a sure source of strength and I'm proud to be numbered among her authors.

None of this, as Bogart might have said, would have amounted to a hill of beans without the efforts of my agent, Carole Blake, who has worked and, where necessary, fought tirelessly on my and Charlie's behalf.

Thanks to the great enthusiasm and skill of producer Colin Rogers, the first two novels in the sequence, *Lonely Hearts* and *Rough Treatment*, were adapted and filmed for Deco Films and Television, and originally transmitted on BBC1. The team that Colin assembled, led by directors Bruce MacDonald and Peter Smith, were responsible for giving the programs a very particular visual feel, and Tom Wilkinson's performance as Resnick was so right, so complete, that it's impossible for anyone who saw it—including myself—to visualize Charlie in any other way.

Two of the books, *Cutting Edge* and *Wasted Years*, have been adapted for BBC Radio 4, where, under the guiding hand of producer David Hunter, they have developed a quite distinctive and strongly musical style.

These novels are fiction: they make no pretense at being primers in modern-day police procedure; that they bear some resemblance to it at all is thanks to the cooperation of the Nottinghamshire Constabulary and, in particular, to the considerable assistance of Detective Superintendent Peter Coles (retired) and Detective Superintendent Geoff Willetts (retired). I have shamelessly pestered friends and acquaintances with expert knowledge in other fields and especial thanks are due to Graham Nicholls, Margaret Phelan, and Liz Simcock.

For adding to my understanding of life in the inner city, I am indebted to the writings of Beatrix Campbell, Nick Danziger, Nick Davies, and Andrew O'Hagan; also to Duncan Campbell of the *Guardian*, to that newspaper in general, to *Time Out*, and to the *Nottingham Evening Post*.

Advice has also come from readers, most often positive and tempered by enthusiasm, and from critics, who, by and large, have been generous in their praise and restrained when pointing out my failings. Specialist booksellers, especially in the US, have been strong in their support and for that I am truly thankful. Perhaps my greatest debt of gratitude, though, goes to those of my fellow writers—colleagues and friends—who have given constant encouragement.

The odd sandwich aside, I think it was jazz that kept Charlie sane, that provided him with both release and inspiration. Me, too.

In the writing of these books I have relied, again and again, on the music of Duke Ellington, Billie Holiday, Thelonious Monk, Spike Robinson, Ben Webster with Art Tatum, and Lester Young. Let it live on.

John Harvey
London, December 1997–April 1998

To learn more about John Harvey and Charlie Resnick, go to www. mellotone.co.uk

For more information about the USA editions of the Charlie Resnick mysteries, go to www.bloodybritspress.com

John Harvey

John Harvey was born in London in 1938. After studying at Goldsmiths' College, University of London, and at Hatfield Polytechnic, he took his Masters Degree in American Studies at the University of Nottingham.

Initially a teacher of English and Drama, Harvey began writing in 1975 and now has over 90 published books to his credit. After what he calls his apprentice years, writing paperback fiction both for adults and teenagers, he is now principally known as a writer of crime fiction, with the first of the Charlie Resnick novels, *Lonely Hearts*, being named by *The Times* [London] as one of the 100 most notable crime novels of the last century.

Flesh and Blood, the first of three novels featuring Frank Elder, was awarded both the British Crime Writers' Association Silver Dagger and the U.S. Barry Award in 2004. His books have won two major prizes in France, the Grand Prix du Roman Noir Étranger for *Cold Light* in 2000 and, in 2007, the Prix du Polar Européen for *Ash & Bone*. Also in 2007, he was the recipient of the CWA Cartier Diamond Dagger for Sustained Excellence in Crime Writing.

After a gap of ten years, Harvey has returned to the character of Charlie Resnick in his most recent novel, *Cold in Hand*.

Having lived in Nottingham for a good number of years, Harvey has recently returned to London, where he lives with his partner and their young daughter.

www.mellotone.co.uk

Bloody Brits Press

OFF MINOR
A Charlie Resnick Mystery

John Harvey

"*Suspects, cops, grieving relatives, alarmed teachers, creepy kids from the neighborhood—no one escapes the glare of the author's insights or the warmth of his compassion for the pathetic frailties of human nature*"
—The New York Times Book Review

"*This Nottingham vibrates with crooked and tender tensions, the dialogue snaps with wit and Harvey has surprises for the most jaded reader*" —The Times (London)

Little Gloria Summers' body has been found hidden inside two plastic bin bags in a disused warehouse. Somewhere in the city, a child killer is on the loose, free to strike again.

Then Emily Morrison vanishes on a Sunday afternoon. A week later, there are still no clues. Inspector Charlie Resnick is as appalled as the media. But years of patient police work have taught him a thing or two—including his conviction that those who jump to easy conclusions are often the last ones to solve a crime.

Off Minor is the fourth Charlie Resnick Mystery

ISBN 978-1-932859-47-8 $13.95

Bloody Brits Press

WASTED YEARS
A Charlie Resnick Mystery

John Harvey

"*From Resnick's bruised marriage to his flamboyant sand-wiches, from the precisely drawn characters to the surpris-ing (yet strangely inevitable) climax, from the wonderfully telling details ... to the desolation of a decaying city,* Wasted Years *is a novel without one false note*"
—The San Francisco Chronicle

A series of brutal robberies takes Detective Inspector Charlie Resnick back ten years. To a time when a rash of very sim-ilar incidents left him face to face with a frenzied sociopath who nearly brought his life to a premature end—and to a time when his wife ran off with her lover, putting paid to their marriage and leaving him with an emotional wound that still hasn't healed. Now with the lookalike robberies escalating in violence, Resnick fights to track the men down before they kill, just as he fights to stem the poignant mem-ories that threaten to overwhelm him.

Wasted Years is the fifth Charlie Resnick Mystery

ISBN 978-1-932859-55-3 $14.95

Available at your local bookstore
or call toll-free 866-390-7426
or order online at www.bloodybritspress.com

Bloody Brits Press

COLD LIGHT
A Charlie Resnick Mystery

John Harvey

"Cold Light *is just about flawless ... a tale that will long trouble your dreams*" —Washington Post Book World

When Nancy Phelan, a young woman who works at the Housing office, goes missing after an office Christmas party, suspicion falls on a young client who attacked her earlier that day. Little in Resnick's life is that simple, however, especially at Christmas, and as the mystery of Nancy's disappearance deepens, the most trusted of his team, Lynn Kellogg, unwittingly puts herself in the path of danger.

A cabbie's been beaten up, there's a drunk and disorderly in the interview room, and a possible child abuser is on his way in. Just a normal Christmas holiday for Resnick and his team. Then not long after Nancy is reported missing, comes proof that she was kidnapped. And when—as the New Year celebrations wind down—the first tape arrives, Resnick knows they're dealing with a dangerous psychopath.

Cold Light is the sixth Charlie Resnick Mystery

ISBN 978-1-932859-57-7 $14.95

Bloody Brits Press

LIVING PROOF
A Charlie Resnick Mystery

John Harvey

"*Harvey's seventh procedural is smartly paced, slyly humorous, unsentimental about police work, violence, and other alienations of affection—altogether one of his best. Just like his first six*" —Kirkus Reviews

When a man is found in the middle of Alfreton Road in the early hours of a Sunday morning, stark naked and bleeding heavily from a chest wound, he is the latest victim in a series of vicious attacks on men. But inquiries in the mean streets of Nottingham's red-light district have brought the investigations to a dead end.

Charlie Resnick is the man for this job. And as if he hasn't had enough to deal with, he now has to provide police protection for a celebrity at the annual crime convention—an author with some very unpleasant "fan" mail. Chronically short-staffed as he is, Resnick fears it's only a matter of time before his lack of manpower has fatal consequences …

Living Proof is the seventh Charlie Resnick Mystery

ISBN 978-1-932859-58-4 $14.95

Available at your local bookstore
or call toll-free 866-390-7426
or order online at www.bloodybritspress.com

Bloody Brits Press

EASY MEAT
A Charlie Resnick Mystery

John Harvey

"*At its best, the crime novel illuminates the society we live in, showing us the painful truths that lie just outside our peripheral vision. When he is on form, no one does the British police procedural better than John Harvey. In* Easy Meat, *he has hit a peak seldom achieved by any writer, inside the genre or out. If this doesn't win awards, there is no justice*" —Manchester Evening News

"*John Harvey is lights out one of the best*"
—Michael Connelly

Why would a fifteen-year-old boy commit suicide?

Mind you, who cares when he's a no-good kid on trial for bludgeoning an elderly couple to death? But when the senior investigating officer is found brutally murdered, Detective Inspector Charlie Resnick is put on the case, which leads to some sinister and startling revelations. It also brings Resnick into contact with Hannah Campbell, with whom he finds himself falling unexpectedly and awkwardly in love ...

Easy Meat is the eighth Charlie Resnick Mystery

ISBN 978-1-932859-59-1 $14.95

Bloody Brits Press

STILL WATER
A Charlie Resnick Mystery

John Harvey

"Still Water *goes beyond fiction to provide a deeper perspective on the complexities of lust and love*"
—San Francisco Chronicle

"*John Harvey is lights out one of the best*"
—Michael Connelly

The battered body of a young woman is found floating in the still water of a city canal. Police suspect a serial killer, which makes it a case for the newly formed Serious Crime Squad. Not Charlie's case, then; not his worry.

But soon another body is found, and this time Charlie has a personal interest. His lover, Hannah, knew the murdered woman, knew too her husband was fiercely jealous. And very free with his fists. Arguing that her friend was the victim of domestic abuse, not the target of some anonymous killer, Hannah persuades Charlie to take on the case.

Investigating the murder, Resnick runs head-on into deeply disturbing questions about the nature of love, about the relationship of abuser and abused, and about our complicity in our own destruction.

Still Water is the ninth Charlie Resnick Mystery

ISBN 978-1-932859-60-7 $14.95

Available at your local bookstore
or call toll-free 866-390-7426
or order online at www.bloodybritspress.com